Startling Moon

驚 月

Liu Hong was born in 1965 in Manchuria, China. She came to the UK in 1989, and now lives in Wessex, with her husband and daughter.

Startling Moon

Liu Hong

review

First published in 2001
by REVIEW

An imprint of Headline Book Publishing

10 9 8 7 6 5 4 3 2 1

British Library Cataloguing in Publication Data

Hong, Liu
    Startling moon
    1.XXX
    I.Title
    823.9'14[F]

    ISBN 0 7472 7087 2

Typeset by
Letterpart Limited, Reigate, Surrey

Printed and bound in Great Britain by
Clays Ltd, St Ives plc

Headline Book Publishing
A division of Hodder Headline
338 Euston Road
London NW1 3BH

www.reviewbooks.co.uk
www.hodderheadline.com

To Ma and Dade, with love and gratitude

ACKNOWLEDGEMENTS

I thank my agents: Toby Eady for taking me on, and Jessica Woollard for her inspiration and warmth. I thank my editor, Mary-Anne Harrington at Review, for her professionalism and enthusiasm. Between them, these three people have made my dream come true.

I thank Ni Zhen for her beautiful calligraphy.

I thank my family, especially my husband Jon, whose love and encouragement I have relied heavily upon.

I would also like to thank Robbie Barnett, Batdelger, Catriona Bass, Chimgee, Charmian Cannon, Jane Fleming, Susie Jolly, Simon Long, Tim Luard, Alison McEwan, Andy Roche, Madeleine Rubach, Claire Russell and Uli Schmetzer for their generosity, advice and comment.

ONE

'Not Knowing the True Face of Mount Lu because You Are in it'

Chapter 1:

No Pheasants

I smelt a familiar face cream, opened my eyes and saw my mother bending over me. Her cold hand touched my cheek. 'Taotao, wake up. You are going to sing today, at Mama's hospital, the songs I taught you.'

I moaned, turned, then remembered – no nursery today. I also realised it was my fifth birthday. I didn't expect a present – you didn't, in those days – but I had hoped for a treat. Perhaps Mama, Baba and I would all go to the park and play hide and seek. Then I would get some good things to eat, maybe a fried egg. What I really wanted was some meat; we had finished our meat ration and hadn't had any for days.

Mama tried to haul the quilts off me. For a brief moment I felt the cold air on my skin and shivered. I rubbed my eyes until they were watery, and through the blur I glimpsed the white-frosted window. Freezing. I shrank further into the bed, towards Baba's side. I wished I could stay there for ever.

Mama's songs. She had taught me many, some I liked and some I didn't. I enjoyed 'I Love Tiananmen Square in Beijing', but was not so keen on 'We Must Liberate Taiwan'. I loved 'We Wave to Our Comrades, the Koreans Across the River', but did not understand all the words. She had taught me many sad songs, which struck a chord in me, but she said I was not to sing these in front of others. I was to sing 'Tiananmen', 'Taiwan' and 'Korea'. If people wanted to hear more: 'Odes to the East Wind' and 'Without the Communist Party There Will Be No New China'.

'Come on, we're going to be late.' I could hear that she was getting impatient. Mama was short-tempered, unlike Baba, who was more indulgent – Mama said he spoiled me. Baba stirred then jumped up and began tickling me until I screamed, breathless with laughter. He had been pretending to be asleep, I realised, and threw the quilts off us.

While we were having breakfast, our neighbour Thunder appeared. He was carrying a gun. He scooped me up with his free hand and pressed our faces together, his beard against my chin. 'Ouch!' I squealed. He put me down and turned to Baba: 'Are you ready?'

Baba swallowed his last mouthful and put on his jacket. 'Yes.'

'Where are you going?' I asked suspiciously.

They exchanged a look I could not decipher. 'To work,' Uncle Thunder shouted, before Baba could reply: he had opened his mouth, but closed it again. 'And we'd better hurry, we're late,' said Uncle Thunder.

After they had gone, Mama explained to me that they were going to shoot pheasants for my birthday treat. I was angry with Baba for not telling me – I would have loved to go with them – but I dared not let Mama see this. She scrubbed my face especially hard that morning. The towel was as coarse as sand and it hurt. I compared the two of us in the mirror. Mama's lips were the colour of cherries, and made her skin look pale. She had long eyelashes like mine, which you noticed because she cast her eyes down so much. We both had black hair, though Mama's was curly and cut short. I thought she was prettier than anybody else I had met, but I wished she would not frown all the time. She dressed me in the red top my aunt had knitted, and which I had worn only once – it was still a little too big. Then she chose a large

Chairman Mao badge, one depicting him in an army hat with golden rays radiating from his face. I glanced at myself again in the mirror, and caught Mama's gaze. She smiled briefly as she looked me up and down. We put on our mittens, woolly hats, coats, boots and cotton face masks – I was so well wrapped up that I could hardly walk. Outside the snow hadn't melted yet, the wind was like little knives on my face and even with the face mask, it hurt.

My town was called You Lin, Friendly Forest, and was in the north-east of China – Baba had shown me on the map that hung on the wall facing our bed. He had marked Beijing and our town with big black dots. You could find Beijing easily anyway – it had a picture of Tiananmen Building with red rays radiating from it – but our town was less obvious, on the border of the Democratic People's Republic of Korea. It was where the Chinese People's Voluntary Army had crossed the river to help the Koreans fight the American imperialists. We should be proud of ourselves, Baba said.

On the bus we took off our face masks. Ice was already forming on mine where my mouth had been. One of Mama's colleagues recognised us. 'Doesn't Taotao look pretty?' she said, white vapour coming out of her mouth.

I smiled, but Mama held my hand tight and looked down at me. 'Oh, no, she's not. Her eyes are not as big as your daughter's.'

I bit my lips and pulled away my hand. I was upset. I thought I was perfect. With Baba I was perfect. He told me I was the prettiest girl in the whole world. With Mama there was always something wrong with me – somebody else's child was better-looking, or cleverer. It hurt that she could say such things about me to other people.

I sulked all the way to the hospital, where Mama worked. We got off at our stop, and as we crossed the road, Mama grabbed my hand. 'Taotao,' her voice softened, 'shall we practise the songs you are going to sing?' She launched into 'I

5

Stand on the Beach and Gaze Longingly at the Treasure Island of Taiwan', but I was still angry and did not utter a sound. When she had finished the first verse, she bent down to me. I smelt her face cream again. 'Taotao,' she slowed her pace, 'you are going to be very important today. You are going to sing in front of hundreds of people. You will make Mama very happy.' Her voice was even softer now. I wished she would talk to me like this all the time.

We stopped at the sign for Number 1 Hospital and went in. My Mama was a doctor. She wore a white doctor's gown and a white face mask when she worked. I hated white clothes. They reminded me of hospitals, of doctors who gave me injections. White clothes got dirty almost as soon as I put them on, and Mama would scold me. I liked colours, the brighter the better. I had no idea why Mama had chosen this red top for me today, though: she had dressed me as though we were going to see a relative she did not like.

We went past the front of the hospital, where sick people lined up in a row to be treated. I clutched Mama's hand. We had just enough time to go to her office so that she could put on her white gown. Then we heard a bell. 'Come on,' Mama said, and led me out. We followed others into the big hall on the second floor. It was like a large theatre: there was a stage in the centre at the front, and the seats were like concrete staircases, rising so that everybody could see the stage. Some serious-looking people were already there. We sat in the fifth row.

I fidgeted and glanced around. This was the biggest gathering of people I had ever seen. They looked anxious about something, and did not chat among themselves. The quiet made me uneasy.

A man in spectacles appeared and the hall became even quieter, so quiet that if I had dropped a pin I would have heard it hit the floor. He read from a piece of paper, something about movements, storms and situations. I remembered having heard some of these words over the radio, and wondered if he was talking about the weather. Towards the end of his speech he raised his fist and shouted, 'Long live Chairman Mao!' Everybody around me joined in – so loudly that I was frightened. Mama raised her fist and she picked mine up with the other hand. The man shouted again, but I could not understand what he said. 'Down with . . .'

'Down with what?' I turned to Mama for explanation. She ignored me.

The man returned to his seat. Another man sitting on the stage stood up and went through the same routine. At the end of his speech he, too, shouted and raised his fist. Another man stood, then another. I counted to seven, got bored and fell asleep in my Mama's lap. Angry voices woke me. When I looked up, at last I saw someone I recognised on the stage. It was a man who worked in the same office as Mama; I called him Old Uncle Beneficial. Mama said he was the best surgeon in their hospital. He always gave me sweets when she wasn't looking, and let me play with the strange tools in his drawer. He didn't talk about movements and situations, but about repentance, self-criticism and correction. While the others had stood erect, his back was hunched, and his voice no more than a whisper.

Now the first man appeared again but instead of calling out slogans, he shrieked at Uncle Beneficial. Each time he shouted, the people around me joined in and raised their fists at the old surgeon, who bent even lower. The first man pulled Uncle Beneficial roughly to the side of the stage. I was afraid for him – I was sure he had been hurt. 'Mama . . .' She shushed me and held me close.

Then, one by one, the people sitting in front of us went up to the stage, pointed their fingers at Uncle Beneficial and yelled at him. Returning to their seats, they breathed heavily and sat down. Mama's hands gripped me so tightly it hurt – I could feel her heartbeat fast against my back. When it was our turn, she pulled me up abruptly and we walked to the stage. Her hand was hot and sweaty and made mine wet and uncomfortable. We stood facing the crowds. I could see only people's heads and there were so many. They all wore white and looked solemn, as if they had been told off for doing something wrong. Mama coughed before she spoke and when she spoke I could hardly recognise her voice: it was broken as though she had been crying. 'Comrades,' she said, 'I am very stupid, I do not know how to make a speech in public, so I will ask my daughter to be my representative to express my revolutionary feelings, my love for Chairman Mao, and my hatred for all class enemies.' She nudged me to the centre of the stage and made her way down. I trailed after her, terrified of all these eyes on me. She turned and hissed at me, 'Stay and sing.' I dared not disobey her.

But I could not sing. I opened my mouth and my voice was not there. The silence was frightening. The stage felt huge, like the sea, and I feared I might drown in it. Almost instinctively, I stepped towards Uncle Beneficial, who still stood on the stage, now almost doubled up. We were the only people in this huge sea, and if I was to swim out of it I had to hold on to something. He was my friend and could save me, I was sure of it.

Before I reached him he raised his head, looked me in the eye, and smiled. I thought he would reach out his arms to hug me but then I saw that his hands were bound behind him. I returned his smile, then out of the corner of my eye saw the pleasure of the people sitting below. It was as if they had all been given their favourite treat. There was clapping, then somebody called out, 'Sing us a song! Sing us a song!'

My eyes found Mama's, and she nodded. My voice returned and I sang, 'Tiananmen', 'Taiwan' and 'Korea'. The audience clapped and began to chat to each other, their anger forgotten. When I had finished, they shouted for more, so I went on and sang my two extra songs. Still they wanted more and, carried away, I forgot Mama's warning and started one of the sad songs. I was just finishing the first line, 'Why is the flower so beautiful?' when she rushed on to the stage and cut me short. 'She is tired,' she said, her cheeks red, and dragged me off the stage.

I did not want to leave: I had enjoyed the singing and the attention. The man who had led the meeting appeared and clasped my hands. 'Comrades, our small general has set a good example for us. See how many revolutionary songs she knew and how she sang them with real feeling.' That was my most glorious revolutionary moment. But I remembered it because it had made Mama happy.

As we left the stage, the first man returned to the subject of the weather. Mama gave me a hug as we sat down in our seats, and sighed heavily. People all around us ignored the lecture and turned to us: 'Doesn't she look lovely? What a good voice she has. You must be so proud of her.'

'No, no, no,' was all Mama seemed able to say, much to my annoyance.

The talk drew to a close, and we headed for home. She strode ahead, pulling me along, and I struggled to keep pace with her. 'Mama . . .' I moaned.

She stopped abruptly. 'Why don't you do as you're told?' she shouted. 'Why did you sing the sad song when I told you not to? Do you know how naughty that is?'

I bit my lip to suppress a sob. I had thought I had made her happy. In the hall she had beamed with pride, but now her mood had changed.

When we arrived, the door was wide open. Uncle Thunder's wife was talking to Baba outside our flat. Her eyes were red, and she seemed agitated. 'Baba.' I let go of Mama's hand and ran to him. 'Baba, where is my pheasant?' I was so pleased to see him.

He picked me up and slung me on to his shoulder. 'Just a minute, Taotao.' He turned to Mama. 'Did you come by the factory road?'

'Yes, why?'

'Did you hear the gunshot?'

'No.'

'Thunder killed a man.'

'What?'

'We were passing the factory from the hills, when a man from the Die Hard Association of Defending Chairman Mao's Honour ambushed us. He had a knife. You know how Thunder feels about that Die Hard bunch. I tried to calm him down but he pointed the gun at the man and fired. I am sure he just meant to frighten him off, but the bullet went right through his heart.' Uncle Thunder's wife was crying and Baba put me down.

I clung to his legs and rubbed myself against him impatiently. I thought Uncle Thunder's wife looked ridiculous with tears running down her face. 'Where is my pheasant? Where is my pheasant?' I chanted in a low whisper, hoping that Baba would hear and Mama would not.

She did, though; she shushed me and frowned. 'Where is Thunder?' she asked.

'With Group Leader Shun at the factory. He said it was nothing to worry about. The Die Hard lot killed one of our factory men a few days ago so now we are square.'

Mama went into Uncle Thunder's house with his wife to comfort her and Baba picked me up again. 'So, how did it go?' I had his full attention now, but my nose felt sore and the tears I had hidden from Mama flowed freely in front of Baba. I felt so wronged. The tighter he held me, the sorrier I felt for myself. 'There, there,' he soothed. 'I'm sorry we haven't got you any pheasants for your birthday treat. But maybe Mama can cook you an egg.'

She did indeed cook me an egg, though she and Baba ate noodles with cabbage. I hated cabbage. We ate it all the time, nothing but cabbage for breakfast, lunch and dinner. In summer we ate it fresh and in winter we ate it pickled. Mama had a big store of it in the corridor and it smelt. I could smell it now as I ate my egg, hoping I would never have to eat cabbage again. Mama and Baba pretended they were enjoying their meal. Mama said she didn't like eggs, but I thought it tasted so good that I almost forgot how she had upset me earlier.

Later, as I lay in my bed, I heard Mama crying. I picked up words like 'movements', 'storms' and 'background'. More weather! Baba spoke softly to comfort her. The sobbing stopped and her talk turned to the 'songs' and 'our child's future'. I didn't know what 'future' meant. Was it a special kind of storm? But I knew her tears had something to do with me. Was my singing upsetting her again? Those sad songs?

I dreamed of a storm that night, heavy and frightening, with lightning and thunderclaps, but when I began to sing it died away. I kept on singing to protect my Mama, who cried as she walked through the storm, her back bent just like Uncle Beneficial's.

Chapter 2:

A Snake

After my birthday Mama began to behave strangely. I suspected it was something to do with that big weather meeting. When she was in a good mood, she would hug me when she got home in the evenings: so-and-so at work had said what a clever girl I was. She told Baba I was famous in her hospital, and I felt proud. Some days, though, she was snappy, lashing out at me and Baba for the smallest things. 'Chicken feathers and garlic skins,' he said, meaning it was nothing to worry about. Usually on such days they talked long into the night and I heard again those weather words that puzzled me.

Once while she was holding me, Mama started shaking as if she wanted to cough, but could not. I was anxious. 'Are you all right, Mama?' I asked. She nodded, but her face was turned away from me. I struggled out of her arms and was startled to see tears in her eyes. 'Mama . . .' I touched her arm, afraid, and tears came to my eyes as well. Her crying was so frightening.

That night when Baba came home we had some delicious fried eggs. After dinner he and Mama sat down to watch me doing my jigsaw puzzle, a picture of Tiananmen Square, where I dreamed of going one day. I knew it well and had no problem finishing it, but to my annoyance they wanted to help me. A couple of times I caught them exchanging glances and I knew something was afoot. I had seen that look before between adults, when they were plotting something bad that they tried to tell you was for your own good. Like sticking a needle into you. I did not like it, and although I pretended to be calm, I was prepared.

But not for what Baba asked me next. 'Taotao, are you a good girl?'

'Yes,' I said slowly, watching him.

'So you would not make your Mama and Baba unhappy?'

'No.' I shook my head.

'So if I tell you that Mama is very ill ... and ...' He stopped, looking at Mama.

'And we have to send you to your grandmother's so that she can look after you,' Mama finished quickly.

She was sitting upright, grinding some peppercorns, and did not look at all ill to me. She did not want me to be her child any more, I knew it. She was not sick, she just wanted to punish me for singing the wrong songs. I began to sob: my parents were deserting me. I was going to be an orphan.

Baba took me in his arms. 'Taotao, your grandmother lives not far from here. I promise we will come to see you every weekend, every six days.' He took my fingers and counted them. 'Let's see, how many fingers have you got? One, two ... How many has Baba got? One, two ... nine. Where has the tenth finger gone?' It was one of our favourite counting games, the magic one where he pretended he had a finger missing. Despite my tears I laughed and pulled out the finger from its hiding place. 'That's better,' he said, and hugged me. 'And as soon as Mama gets better, we will come and get you from your grandmother.'

Mama had disappeared into the kitchen and was clattering pots and pans. She did not come out until Baba had switched off the light and tucked me into bed. I tried to stay awake because I wanted to see her. Just as I fell asleep her face was hovering over mine. I knew she was there, even with my eyes shut, because I could smell her face cream.

My grandmother lived on the other side of town, and Baba took me there on his bicycle. It was cold, and he stretched his big jacket to cradle me to him, like a baby kangaroo in its mother's pouch. Whenever he saw a policeman, he jumped off – it was against the law to carry a passenger on a bicycle, although everyone did it.

We arrived at my grandmother's house in the late afternoon and Baba parked the bicycle outside the two-storey building. His forehead was sweaty from pedalling and my feet felt numb from sitting in the cold wind. I clutched my rubber skeleton – it had come free with Mama's medical textbook and she had made a dress for it. My eyes were red from crying. Baba pushed the door open and called, 'Ma,' then whispered to me, 'Don't let Nainai see you cry.'

We stepped into warmth, and a delicious smell floated to us. It was dark inside but when my eyes grew used to it I saw Nainai, sitting with her head bent on a low stool in front of a huge fire. She turned towards us slowly. When she saw Baba, her back straightened and a smile lit her face as if somebody had struck a match. Her black hair was combed smooth. She wore a dark blue jacket with buttons like little butterflies. 'Nainai,' I whispered timidly. Although she was no stranger, and I had been to her house before, the thought of living away from my parents made me apprehensive. Nainai stretched out her arms: 'Come to Nainai,' she said. I went up to her slowly and was embraced. She drew corn-on-the-cob out of the fire, warned me that it was hot, then stuck a chopstick through the centre and held it out to me.

I dropped my doll and took the fragrant sweetcorn. 'What is that?' Nainai pointed at Dolly, horrified – Dolly always had that effect on people when they first saw her.

Baba explained with a smile, 'This is Taotao's Dolly.'

Nainai closed her eyes, opened them and stared at Dolly, whose hollow eye sockets stared back at her.

Nainai and Baba chatted. I ate my sweetcorn and looked around the room curiously. Now that I was going to live here, I wanted to know it well. The floor was concrete, as it was in my parents' flat, and spotlessly clean. From where we sat I could hear the traffic outside, for the house was beside a busy road. There was a door to my left and another to my right; both were shut. A third door ahead of me had been left ajar. I remembered that it led to the garden, peered at it then looked at Baba.

'Go into the garden, my child,' Nainai said. 'Go and see your grandpa.' She nudged me towards the opened door.

I stepped outside. It was a big garden, but nothing grew in it. The ground was covered with frost. I turned back, disappointed. Then I heard movement in the little shed to the left. I poked my head in. An old man was squatting by an upturned bicycle. 'Yeye,' I said. He nodded at me, then carried on with his work. I stood and watched, fascinated by the wheels, the metal sticks and Yeye's hands moving among them. After a while he looked up, realising I was still there. 'Go back to your Nainai, it's cold in here,' he said.

Baba and Nainai had gone into the bedroom, the room on the left. It was warmer and brighter than the kitchen, where Nainai had been when we arrived. As in my parents' house, and everyone else's, there was a big portrait of Chairman Mao hanging in the middle of the wall with red silk around the frame. Below it were some framed papers, which Baba explained were Yeye's award certificates. Baba had some too. They were printed in red and decorated around the edge with red flags and stars. Underneath the certificates were family photographs. Nainai took one of the big photograph frames off the wall. It contained a picture of a fat baby. She pointed at it. 'That was you, Taotao.' I glanced at the baby with disgust. It could not have been me! I shook my head and made a face. Nainai and Baba laughed.

I climbed on to the bed – we called it a *kang* in the

north-east: it was so big it occupied one whole side of the room and it was warm from the fire nextdoor. I lay down on it and fell asleep, listening to the voices of Baba and Nainai. When I woke up it was dark. I got up and went into the kitchen where a table was ready with food on it. Baba said, 'See, she wakes up just in time for dinner.' I was hungry, even after the whole sweetcorn.

At the dinner table my grandparents and my father were sitting with two more members of Nainai's household, my young aunt and uncle, whom I called Gugu and Shushu. I remembered both of them vividly, especially Shushu, from my previous visits.

After dinner Gugu sat by me and plaited my hair like hers, and Shushu demonstrated a series of martial-arts moves he had learned from a neighbour. The room was too small for this and he nearly knocked down Yeye's model-worker cert-ificates. Yeye sat with his eyes closed, holding the radio. When he opened them he frowned at Shushu. I was so fascinated by everything that I did not mind when Baba rose and said goodbye. My eyelids fought a furious battle as I tried to stay awake. There was too much fun to miss.

We all slept in that big bed. I lay between Nainai and Gugu, clasped Dolly to me and dreamed of home.

The next morning I woke early and went to sit by the big fire in the kitchen. Nainai was out in the garden, and I saw that the door on the right was open a crack. 'Come in,' a voice said from inside the room. I froze. Who was it? 'Come in,' said the voice again, impatiently this time. It was dry and crackly, as if the person had sand in their mouth. I could not tell whether it was a man or a woman's voice. 'Come in, and I will tell you a story,' the person said, invitingly.

I hesitated and Nainai came back in. 'Nainai,' I pointed at the door timidly, 'there is a voice in that room.'

'Oh, she's awake,' Nainai said. 'That is your great-grandmother. You haven't met her before – she's just come down from the countryside to stay with us. Come and say hello.' My heart pounding, I followed her in.

An ancient woman sat cross-legged on the bed smoking a pipe. Her sharp eyes sized me up. 'Lao Da's [Eldest Son] daughter,' Nainai shouted. She turned to me: 'Call her Tainainai. Shout, she is deaf,' she added.

Someone knocked at the door, and Nainai went out. I stood beside the bed where Tainainai sat. 'Have you heard the snake story?' she asked abruptly.

I started. 'No.'

'Well,' she held my gaze, 'a man in the village killed a snake, and he was afraid, because as soon as you kill a snake all the other snakes know.' She stopped and coughed. Her toothless mouth seemed like a huge hole. I climbed up on to the bed to sit next to her. Tainainai smiled, pleased. Another puff at the pipe. 'So he tried hiding everywhere. If someone knocked at the door, his wife would answer it and say that her man had gone away for, you know, snakes can change into humans like you and me, and there is no way you can tell them apart from real people.' I shuddered. A chill shot down my spine, and I moved closer to Tainainai. 'But if you can find the snakeskin they leave behind, you can ask for anything, anything . . .'

In the dark, smoky room, I watched the shadow of the giant pipe in the dim light and felt small.

Nainai opened the door, brandishing a broom, letting in the light. 'Don't tell her old tales. They're not correct nowadays – they call them superstition.'

Tainainai yawned and agreed: 'Yes, yes, these are old stories, no good.' She leaned towards me. 'Don't tell anyone else!' I nodded earnestly. I was too frightened to tell another soul. That night, I went to bed without Dolly. Suddenly I was tired of her.

I didn't entirely believe Tainainai's story but I dared not disbelieve it either, just in case. I was careful where I trod, lest I disturb a hibernating snake. But what if I found a snake-skin? What would I ask for? I had no idea. I went back to

Tainainai's room to hear the end of the story, but she shut her eyes and pretended I wasn't there.

During the day, I attached myself to Nainai like a dog. Shushu and Gugu called me Gen Ding Chong – (Bottom-following Bug). They chanted the chorus whenever Nainai wasn't around, but I soon saw they meant no harm. My real threat was Yeye, who before my arrival had enjoyed his precise ration of food from Nainai. He handed Nainai all his money, did whatever she asked him to, and in return was given what he desired most: good food – peanuts boiled in soy sauce and tea leaves, with a saucer of warm rice wine; dumplings with different fillings; fried eggs with chives. Nainai was a wonderful cook. Before I arrived, he was the only member of the family who had a steamed egg for breakfast. Now I had one too, and Yeye was jealous. Nainai saw to it that we ate separately so that Yeye could not complain about my egg being bigger or better cooked or hotter than his.

Mama and Baba did come to see me at the weekends. The first few times, I cried when they left, clung to Mama's legs and would not let go. But as the weeks became months and their visits became less frequent, I started to enjoy being spoiled by Nainai and did not miss my home.

As the weather became warmer, Yeye accepted me as an egg-sharing partner. He made me a little bicycle, out of bits and pieces he had kept from his former trade. He had run a bicycle-repair workshop before the Communist Liberation in 1949. Afterwards he had handed his business over to the government and volunteered to work for free as an honorary consultant to the same workshop, which now employed ten people. Nainai didn't like it when she saw Yeye disappearing into his shed – she had a horror of anything old. She never told me stories of the family, not even stories about herself. Her past was closed to me like an old well, hidden, but still there.

I practised in the garden on my new bicycle. The snow had gone and the ground was muddy and wet. By the end of each day I was dirty and exhausted, but happy. Nainai watched me from inside the house through the window as Shushu held me while I found my balance. Soon I could ride on my own.

One mild spring day Yeye took me out for my first proper cycle ride and I pedalled fast to keep up with him. The early-morning streets were wide and misty, empty except for street-sweepers. They wore large white face masks, wielding their huge brooms from left to right, like a marching army. The dust rose, mingling with the morning mist, and they looked like figures in a dream. Yeye rang the bell as he cycled past them. It sounded crisp and clear.

Yeye's destination was the People's Park, built by the Japanese after they invaded this part of China and named by them Cherry Blossom Park. I had been there several times with Shushu on Sundays, watching the *T'ai chi* master teaching his disciples. Yeye came to watch the chess players who sat motionless, as if they were trees. I did not understand chess and was soon bored and started whining. After complaints from other onlookers Yeye sighed and got up, muttering that he would never take me out again.

On the way back we passed an avenue of cherry trees. '*Sakura*,' he murmured.

'What?'

'It means cherry blossom in Japanese,' Yeye said softly as we cycled, and he reminisced about some colourfully dressed Japanese women he had seen as a young man. They had been clustered around the blossoms in April for a festival, their faces painted white. Fascinated, Yeye had hidden among the crowds and watched them. But I wasn't interested in these Japanese women from long ago: I smelt breakfast. Forthright and Bright, Nainai's brother, my great-uncle, was coming that morning, and he and Yeye did not get on.

I had learned my great-uncle's name during an argument between Nainai and Yeye that I'd overheard. Yeye had made slighting comments about 'that younger brother of yours', but Nainai had excused him – 'Forthright and Bright is proud . . .'

As it was considered rude for a child to address a senior relative by name, I had never known the names of many of mine.

Forthright and Bright's arrival was signalled by a burst of coughing. He leaned on the door frame, gasping for air, while he banged impatiently on the door with his stick. I was both intrigued and frightened by him: his expression was serious and intense. He was an expert on bone conditions. Nainai told me that in Shandong where they had come from – where Confucius was born – Forthright and Bright had been a famous herbalist and revered like a saint. He had a bad temper, had married three times and did not get on with his present wife, who sometimes came crying to Nainai: 'What secret is he keeping from me?' she wailed. 'He prescribes remedies behind a black veil and never lets me look in! He doesn't trust me!' Nainai was silent, but when the woman had gone, she told me that he must have had a reason for behaving like this. Nainai was always supportive of her brother.

That morning, Forthright and Bright was in a good mood. 'Which one is this?' he asked.

'Eldest Son's daughter,' Nainai replied.

'How old are you?'

He pointed at me with his stick.

'Five and a half,' I whispered.

'A snake?' He counted the years on his fingers. 'Yes, a snake.'

'No, small dragon,' Nainai corrected. 'Our Taotao is a small dragon.'

'You women,' Forthright and Bright jeered. 'It's the same thing. It's going to be school time soon, isn't it?'

When he had gone, I asked everyone what they were. Nainai was a horse, Yeye a pig, Shushu a monkey, Gugu a cross between a horse and a sheep, but Tainainai was a snake like me. She told me so herself, grinning. She said there were twelve animal horoscope signs. It wasn't by coincidence that

21

we were born in certain years and under the sign of a particular animal, it was all preordained by fate. You could not escape your destiny. Those born dragons were 'the great ones, emperors, like Chairman Mao'. She pointed at his portrait on the wall behind her. 'Rabbit people are timid, monkey people naughty and rat people ambitious.'

'And the snake people?' I asked anxiously.

'Well . . .' She put aside her pipe, placed both hands under her thighs to warm them and closed her eyes. We were sitting in her little room, speaking in whispers. Nainai was not to find out what we were talking about.

Tainainai opened her eyes, the only feature of her face that did not look old. I thought this was because she winked so often. 'Snake people can be as great as dragons, but they also have the potential to hurt people – perhaps because they are very clever and often proud. They possess great powers.' She leaned close to me and said in an even lower voice, 'And the female snakes are usually very beautiful, so you have to be extra careful.'

I considered this for a while. 'What about your snake story? Did the snake wife find the man?'

Nainai pushed open the door and came in. We both straightened up. 'Telling her stories again? You'll give her nightmares.' Tainainai said nothing but as Nainai went out she threw me a grin, which made me giggle. 'Go and play outside in the garden,' she urged, and settled down on her bed.

The garden had been transformed: it was green – and I had seen it happen. Since the snow had melted, Yeye had put some horse manure on the soil and broken up the earth. Then he had ploughed it and divided it into rows. Nainai had planted some seeds, and now we had vegetables from the garden, like spinach and spring onions, delicious with fried eggs. Each time my parents visited, Nainai picked fresh vegetables for them.

On the last weekend before I was due to start school my

parents came for lunch. They didn't stay long. Mama had brought some pork with her: they had a bigger meat ration than Nainai because they both worked. Nainai cooked some pork with the spring onions, and put the rest of the pork away carefully. The dish was delicious.

Baba took out a school-bag. 'Look, Taotao! Look what Mama has made for you.' I took it. It had been an old bag of Baba's, a green army one, and Mama had sewn a small pretty flower and my name on the cover. I liked it, and threw a grateful glance at her.

Nainai smoothed the flower. 'It's beautiful,' she said.

'Do you know why you are called Taotao?' Baba asked. I shook my head. 'You were born in the year of the snake—'

'I know that,' I cut in impatiently, then realised that I did not know what signs my parents were.

'When I saw you, you were lying with seven other babies all looking the same, each with a number tag around your ankle,' Baba went on. 'You were number six. I picked you up. You cried and cried, and looked pinker than the other babies, like a little fruit. So we called you Taotao – Peaches.'

'What did I look like?'

'Just like a little peach. I told you.'

They all laughed, but I blushed. 'Can I go and sit with Tainainai?' I asked Nainai. She nodded, and I was gone like an arrow.

Tainainai looked as though she had been waiting for me to arrive. 'So the wife tried to hide her husband, underneath the bed? Behind the dressing screen? In the kitchen?' I asked. 'I know, underneath the quilt.' That was where I would have hidden.

Tainainai put a finger to my lips and stopped me. 'No, he hid in the big rice jar. His wife put the heavy lid and a big stone on top. They thought he would be safe.' She took a few puffs on her pipe, and I sat closer. I felt cosy, and I loved Tainainai. 'The next morning someone knocked at the door and his wife went to open it, knowing that he would be safe in the jar. She knew it was the snake wife despite her human appearance, but she had no fear.'

I closed my eyes and imagined a thing with a woman's face and a snake's body. I was sure this one had a big mouth.

'They sat and chatted. The snake wife said, "I'm very thirsty, could you get me some water?" The man's wife said, "Yes," and went to fetch some water in a gourd. While she was in the kitchen, she glanced at the jar with the heavy stone on top and felt pleased with herself. The snake wife drank the water, making a lot of noise, and looked satisfied. She thanked the man's wife and left.' Tainainai stopped again.

'And?' I begged. Had the snake wife been merciful and left the man alone?

'Well,' Tainainai continued, 'the man's wife came back to the house and called to her husband, "Come out, the snake wife has gone." When she heard no reply, she took the stone off the jar, lifted the lid and looked inside. All that was left of her man was a pair of shoes. The snake wife had sucked away his blood and flesh.'

I gasped, engulfed in delicious terror. 'You mean . . .'

'Yes.'

'Tell me more,' I pleaded.

'No, not today.' Tainainai pointed at the door. 'Your Nainai . . .'

I understood. 'Tell me how you wish on the snakeskin next time,' I said, before I left the room.

My parents had gone.

Chapter 3:

The Goose

———◅▻———

The school was just around the corner, and on my first day I was accompanied by Gugu. We had to walk past a big goose kept by a neighbouring family. As I walked by it, the goose eyed me leisurely, as it had all the children before. I knew it had killed them all, and it knew I was afraid.

Gugu greeted the family, and spoke flattering words to the goose, which sat cosily by the gate, feathers tucked in neatly, pretending to be small.

Gugu left me with thirty other children and Teacher Lee. The classroom was square with a big blackboard at one end, above which hung a portrait of Chairman Mao. This one was the biggest I had ever seen. Chairman Mao smiled down at us benignly and I felt at ease. His lips looked too red, as if he was wearing lipstick.

Teacher Lee was standing in front of the blackboard. She was a tall, thin woman of around thirty, with long black hair in a plait and soft gentle eyes. She started taking the register. 'Red Army, Patriotic, Red and Handsome, Small Soldier, China Blossom, Born in Beijing, Love the People, Peaches.' She looked up, and the whole class burst into laughter. I knew there was something wrong with my name. The teacher continued, 'Red Army . . .' She frowned. There were two Red Armys in my class. She decided that one had to be called Big Red Army and the other Little Red Army, according to their height. Big Red Army agreed with a grin, while Little Red Army sulked. 'Lotus Blossom! Lotus Blossom!' The class laughed again and started to look around. No Lotus Blossom.

During break some of the boys sitting at the back chanted, 'Lotus Blossom and Peaches, juicy fruits,' until Teacher Lee stopped them. But when she went out, they started again. I hid in the girls' toilet until the bell rang for lessons.

Later I headed for home, my school-bag filled with new books. My heart pounded as I approached the corner. I could see Nainai's house now, my bicycle leaning against the door, but from the corner of my eye I could also see the goose waiting. Inside I trembled but I walked straight on. I told myself that if I did not look his way, perhaps he would ignore me.

How wrong I was! The goose sprang with its long neck stretched and charged towards me with a look of hatred in its small eyes, its fat body wobbling from side to side. I was paralysed. I wanted to run, but my legs wouldn't move. The goose pecked my ankle and pain shot up my leg, breaking the spell. I ran home, panting with terror and fury.

'How was school?' Nainai asked.

'Why am I not called Red Army?'

'That's a boy's name.'

'How about China Blossom or Love the People?' I asked.

Shushu said, 'I think your name is the best.'

'But they laughed at me.'

'They are jealous.'

I was only half convinced.

I poked my head round Tainainai's door to say hello but I had not come for more stories. I had homework and the goose to worry about.

The next day I asked Nainai for some thicker trousers. Once I was outside, I found a big stone and held it tightly in my fist. I went towards the corner, my palm sweating. I was not alone; an old man was walking slowly ahead of me and I ran to catch up with him. The door of the corner house was open.

I tiptoed past cautiously, with the old man as a shield. No goose, but I caught a glimpse of white feathers on a fat tummy just inside the house.

It was not until the third day of term that Lotus Blossom appeared. We were in the middle of a maths lesson when there was a knock on the door. Teacher Lee said, 'Come in,' and in strode a tall, tough-looking girl. 'Hello, I am Lotus Blossom,' she said. The boys at the back laughed, but she stared hard at them and they quietened. 'My mother was ill. I had to look after her, and that is why I am late,' she blurted out, not looking at Teacher Lee.

In the playground during break, I went up to her. I wanted to be Lotus Blossom's friend: I admired her toughness in dealing with the boys and hoped it would rub off on me. She seemed flattered, although we made an odd pair – one small and thin with neat hair, the other tall and strong with wild looks.

I told her about the goose, and she walked home with me, excited. But the goose stayed indoors, pretending to be asleep, playing for time. I wished Lotus Blossom was not so tall – I had to look up at her when we spoke – and I was anxious because we lingered at the place I dreaded, pretending to be chatting while we waited for the goose to attack. But it didn't even look our way: it was dreaming of a pond full of rice.

I took Lotus Blossom home to see Nainai, happy to have a new friend, but Nainai frowned at her – I knew she did not like her messy hair, but she didn't say anything about it. Instead she sent us to get some soy sauce from the shop beyond the school.

A makeshift shed stood next to the grocery shop, and an old man in rags was sitting outside it. As we walked by, two boys from our class, the ones who had laughed at our names, approached him. One stopped, spat at him and shouted, 'Old counter-revolutionary.' He ran away, but the other boy waited for a reaction. The old man did not bat an eyelid. The boy who had run away approached him slowly. He kicked a basket that was lying next to the old man, whose gaze was fixed on his shoes. 'Old counter-revolutionary,' the boy said, 'where did you hide your secret book of revenge?' He sat up and glared at the boys, but still did not utter a word. They circled around him and started a chorus: 'Counter-revolutionary, counter-revolutionary, confess, confess.'

A crowd gathered, but no one interfered with the boys. Counter-revolutionary, class enemy, I knew these were things to be condemned, but somehow the old man looked dignified. Lotus Blossom marched up to the bullies, defiant. 'Stop picking on him,' she said, glaring. They recognised her and fell silent.

The boy who had kicked the basket glanced back at the crowd that had gathered around him. 'Are you sucking up to a counter-revolutionary?'

'No, I am trying to stop you tormenting this man,' she said, shaking her fist. 'I will report you to Teacher Lee for what you have done.'

Now all eyes were upon her, but she did not flinch. 'Go on, tell! We're not afraid,' said the boy, edging away.

Lotus Blossom sneered at them and picked up the old man's basket for him.

It wasn't long before Lotus Blossom found out about the school entertainment troupe. It sounded fantastic: you could miss classes, go to perform all over town and wear makeup. To join, we had to be interviewed by Teacher Luo, with five other boys and girls. He was a pale-faced, middle-aged man, who wore a worn but clean army jacket and smelt strongly of cigarettes. 'Let me see your hands,' he said simply. I was self-conscious, and couldn't help feeling that mine were the ugliest ones, fat and short, whereas Handsome, who was next to me, had long, slender hands with fingers like spring-onion leaves. Lotus Blossom stuck out her tongue and frowned at her filthy fingernails.

Teacher Luo admired Handsome's fingers. Then he said,

'Dismissed,' and we scattered like water in sand, released from his penetrating stare. Teacher Luo chose Handsome to play the violin, he would teach her himself, and I was assigned to the singing and dancing troupe. Lotus Blossom was left out, but it did not seem to upset her. When I told Nainai the news, Nainai said, 'Of course Lotus Blossom wouldn't be chosen! That girl is too naughty. You mark my words, she'll come to no good with wild hair like that. Hasn't she got a mother to scold her? Don't go about too much with her.'

We usually performed at school functions, but occasionally we ventured outside. On 1 October, National Day, we performed at the Happy Residents Socialist Courtyard, on wasteground near to where the goose lived. Nainai and Yeye brought small stools to sit on while they watched us, and left Tainainai to look after the house.

We wore skirts and shivered: the night was cold even though it had been a hot day. I was to introduce the programme, and when I appeared under the gas-light, made up and dressed in my red skirt, I heard Nainai, Yeye and our neighbours cheering and whispering my name. I made my first announcement: 'Dear Happy Residents Socialist Courtyard, the entertainment of Loving the People Primary School now begins. The first item on the programme is "We Love Tiananmen Square in Beijing".'

Afterwards I went home with Nainai and Yeye enjoying my fame. For once I didn't notice the goose, although it had had a good view of the show and, no doubt, had formed its own opinion about my performance. When we went inside I noticed the house was unusually quiet, as if something was missing. Nainai went straight to Tainainai's little room. She was not there. This seemed strange – I had hardly ever seen her anywhere else. Nainai's voice trembled as she called, 'Ma.' The sound echoed in the house, which suddenly seemed bigger. I was scared: I had never heard Nainai call Tainainai Ma before.

29

We found her in the back garden, dead. Perhaps she had felt lonely and gone out for a stretch. It was rare for the house to be empty as it was that night. Nainai was almost always at home. 'She was ninety-four,' Yeye said, comforting Nainai. 'It's a good thing that she died now. It was painless, you can tell by her face. It's a red thing, something to celebrate.'

'I shouldn't have left her alone. I brought her here from Shandong so that I could look after her and be there when she died. All this time I've wanted that. Who'd imagine this would happen?' Nainai wailed.

That night I crept into Tainainai's room, and studied her face closely. Yeye was right – she did look peaceful. Earlier I had asked him to explain his words to Nainai. He said we should celebrate her long life with gratitude: 'She had a good life, but like an old tree she had to die to make space for new life to grow in her place.' This was a long speech for him, but I was not convinced by his philosophy. To my young mind, death was mysterious and terrifying.

At school I told Lotus Blossom about Tainainai's death. She was not impressed: 'My grandmother died, my aunt and uncle died, my mother nearly died.' She counted her fingers. 'Your Tainainai, she must have been ancient. She should have died long ago.' I winced. 'I'm sorry, I didn't mean to be nasty,' she added.

Suddenly I was seized with terror. 'But I don't want Nainai to die!'

'We all die,' Lotus Blossom said coldly, her big bright eyes glittering with excitement. 'In different ways.'

At night I clasped Nainai tightly. After school I followed her around the house. She couldn't understand it and asked me what was the matter, but I dared not tell her and pretended I had a tummy-ache. She made me some fish soup.

Soon, the dance rehearsals drew me out of my secret fears, and with this distraction from lessons, time passed quickly. The new term saw us ready and well rehearsed. When the big day came for the city-wide school entertainment competition,

I got up at dawn and rushed to school for the makeup session. That morning I hardly noticed the goose hiding around the corner. It charged but missed, and I escaped. The dance was entitled 'Happy Harvest'. We were to take the roles of a group of young North Korean peasant girls, dancing to give thanks to the Communist Party for the bumper crop. Today, for the first time, we rehearsed in costume. I wore a bright yellow top and a fabulous pink silk skirt. Nothing in my life was as soft and smooth as that skirt – except maybe Nainai's soup. Teacher Luo gave a signal and the band struck up the prelude. Handsome smiled at Teacher Luo, who did not look at her. I couldn't say why but I had goose pimples about Teacher Luo and Handsome.

After the rehearsal, in the little room annexed to the dancing hall, under the dim light, we put on our makeup. To see myself transformed, a glamorous face with bright red cheeks, lipstick and heavy eyelids, was dreamlike. The fragrance of the powder filled the room, as we giggled and helped each other. From the corner of my eye, I could see Teacher Luo doing Handsome's lipstick. They stood right underneath the yellow light and he held up her chin. Her eyes were closed and her lips slightly parted. Teacher Luo wet his lips with his tongue as he drew the outline of Handsome's lips. I felt embarrassed and looked away.

The People's Palace was the biggest entertainment hall in town. As we were marching there, it started to rain heavily, so I put my spare clothes around my face to protect my makeup from the rain. I waved at Nainai when we passed the house on the way, but didn't cross the road to say hello. The People's Palace was vast and that night it was filled to capacity. The only other time I had been here was with Yeye to watch the Korean Friendship Delegation from Pyongyang. We had sat in the back row in speechless awe of the glittering performance. The Koreans had sung Chinese songs at the end and those had gone down best with the crowd. Something about the foreign accents had captivated me, even though the songs were the everyday ones we knew so well.

I peeped from behind the curtain at the audience, and felt apprehensive. However, I took comfort from the perform-ances before ours: one dancer tripped on her skirt, fell and could not get up; another came on stage without her hat and had to rush back to get it. Backstage I giggled hysterically with my friends.

We won second prize. As our own clothes were soaked with rain, we were allowed to wear our costumes home, 'Just this once,' Teacher Luo said, eyeing Handsome in her pink dress. Bright silky colours dispersed into the sea of worn blue workers' jackets and green army ones. I could have spotted my brightly dressed friends miles away and others stared at us, perplexed. I shivered from excitement and cold. Walking alone in my yellow and pink outfit, holding a huge pink fan, I hid under my heavy makeup and felt safer. It was like wearing a mask, and no one could see me blush.

At the rail crossing, the barrier came down and a train came whistling by. I walked past the Korean noodle bar at the corner near Nainai's house, and glimpsed myself in the window. The Korean woman working inside the restaurant stood up to look at me; her mouth dropped open. She was a real Korean, wearing a plain old blue jacket, and I was wearing a bright silk Korean costume. I wondered what she made of it. I started to run, past the goose, which did not recognise me in my finery.

I got home, panting. Shushu took out his old camera. 'Don't take off your costume. Go and stand in front of the house,' he ordered proudly.

'Come,' I shouted to Nainai.

'No, no, I have dinner to cook,' she said, smoothing her hair. 'Oh come on, Ma,' Shushu cajoled her; but to no avail.

A group of neighbours appeared to see me in my bright costume and to watch Shushu take my picture. Nainai peered out at us, and was caught in the photograph, as we saw when it had been developed.

Everyone came to inspect the photo. Nainai stroked it with the tip of her finger. 'If only Tainainai could see you in this,' she murmured. 'She'd be thrilled.' Shushu wrote on the back of the photo 'Taotao at seven and a half'.

Forthright and Bright examined my costume. 'They let you wear that home, did they?' He tossed the photo aside contemptuously.

'Yes,' I answered timidly. 'It was raining, so . . .'

He saw the balls I had been playing with. 'And why are you not at school?'

'It is winter vacation.' As usual, Nainai rescued me.

Chapter 4:

A Little Red Guard At Large

After our late dinner on the night before the Spring Festival, Nainai and I sat in Tainainai's room with the light on until midnight. It was an old custom that Nainai kept to ensure the smoothness of the coming year. When the clock struck twelve Nainai straightened her back, as though she had woken from a dream. She got off the bed to turn out the light. 'Bedtime. Come on, Taotao.' She sighed: she would have liked to leave the light on all night, but it would waste too much expensive electricity.

After she had left the room I lingered on the bed where Tainainai used to sit. I closed my eyes and smelt her and her pipe. I found it hard to believe she had simply vanished, and wondered if one day she would come back. Perhaps it had all been a dream. There were stories she had started but had not finished that I wanted to hear. What happened to the fox spirit that eloped with a young scholar? What happened to the brave thief who stole from the rich to help the poor? What about the stories of Nainai, when she was a little girl, which Tainainai had promised to tell me, along with Nainai's real name, which was a big secret?

Through the window I saw Nainai squatting in the garden. Tainainai's room was so dark that I could see everything outside clearly, especially with the snow. There was a brief flare of light as she set a match to a pile of papers. I ran out to find her. 'What are you doing, Nainai?' There were tears in her eyes, and I reached for her hands, which were cold and stiff. She watched the papers burn into ashes and started to bury them in the snow with her foot. 'I am sending Tainainai some money. I dreamed that she was very hungry and poor.' I only half understood what she meant, so I stood by her and kept quiet. 'You are shivering, poor child, let's get in.' As she shut the door and switched off the kitchen light, she turned to me: 'Taotao, I want you not to tell anybody what Nainai did tonight. Do you promise?' I nodded.

That night I could smell Tainainai strongly. She was around us. I was sure Nainai knew it too – I sensed it as I held her in the bed. Did the paper money Nainai burned reach you, Tainainai? I miss your naughty winks.

Spring Festival was the time of the winter vacation. We did not go to school, but we had a lot of homework to do, which included collecting horse dung from the street. When we handed in a basketful, we were given a ticket for it. Horse dung was good fertiliser, as Teacher Lee pointed out. Nainai agreed: the peasants in the countryside needed it to enrich the earth to produce more grain. In fact, she wouldn't have minded some for her little vegetable patch in the back garden. That vacation I was haunted by the sound of horse's hoofs and cartwheels. Whenever I heard them, I stopped what I was doing, and dashed outside with a spade. Sometimes when I got there the children from the other side of the street had already picked it up, and at others there was nothing to collect. Often I followed the horse a long way with high hopes that were dashed. The drivers on their high seats teased me all the time.

I watched the holiday drift away and panicked about how few tickets I had accumulated. Then Lotus Blossom came to the rescue. She had lots of tickets as she was always the first to get to the dung, so she gave one to me and I did her homework. Her horse dung was always top-quality pure manure, unlike much of the rest, which was usually mixed with ashes and chicken droppings. The woman who issued the tickets was curious about where I found mine. Naturally I did not tell her. Nainai saved my collection of tickets behind the frame of Yeye's model-worker certificate.

One afternoon Lotus Blossom and I came back from the street carrying our spades and baskets. We had fought off the boys from the street opposite and had won the freshest horse dung – it was still steaming. We giggled with excitement.

'Leave those stinking baskets outside the house!' Nainai shouted, when she saw us through the window.

'But I can't,' I said. I was worried that the boys might come and steal it.

'Do as you're told!' It was a familiar, sterner voice and came from behind Nainai. I looked up and saw Ma emerging from the house. She frowned when she saw us and covered her nose. I put the baskets and spades outside and peered at Lotus Blossom. With her knotted hair and ragged clothes, she would not make a good impression on my mother. Lotus Blossom seemed to read my thoughts. 'Is that your Ma?' she whispered. I nodded. 'I . . . I will come back later,' she said, and left.

Inside the house Ma looked me up and down. 'She seems quite healthy,' she said at last.

'Oh, yes,' Nainai said proudly. 'Taotao is never ill. She is strong as a horse. Look at her red cheeks.'

Ma wore a blue coat over her white hospital gown. A white face mask hung on her chest. I stood near her and breathed in the smell that used to make my legs tremble with the fear of injections. I hadn't been to the hospital for ages: I had been fit. With my parents I had been in and out of hospital as if it was my second home. Ma could always find something wrong with me, and she fussed whenever I felt unwell. Nainai just laughed it off and, funnily enough, at her house I never seemed to be ill anyway.

'She's grown.' Ma felt my shoulders with her hands.

'Of course,' said Nainai. 'She's nearly eight, a big girl.'

Ma asked me to try on a new jumper she had knitted. It was white. I didn't want to wear it, but dared not refuse. I tried it on: to my delight, it was too small. 'Look,' I said, turning to Ma and Nainai to show them how poorly it fitted.

'Go and see your mother off,' Nainai said, as Ma was leaving. She stayed inside. I followed Ma out – I didn't know what to say. Ma lingered at the door, also lost for words. At last she took the spades and handed them to me. 'You'd better take those in,' she said, and walked away.

I watched her back. I felt like running after her to hold her, but I didn't. She took a few more steps, turned and waved at me. 'Go in and be nice to Nainai.' Then she hurried away as fast as if somebody was chasing her.

A few days later, when we were doing the spring cleaning, I found a picture hidden behind Chairman Mao's portrait poster in Tainainai's room. It was old and faded, depicting a terrifying man in strange clothes. I called for Nainai to come and see. She frowned. 'Where on earth did you find it?'

'There, behind Chairman Mao's portrait.'

'Oh, that mad woman!' Nainai muttered, and snatched the picture from me.

'What is that picture, Nainai?'

'It's the Kitchen God. We used to believe he was the god in charge of our fortune. But all this is superstition! Tainainai should never have put it up, she knew it was a bad thing to do.' There was anger in Nainai's voice. After a long while she sighed. 'But she is dead, so let's not speak ill of her.' Carefully she folded the picture of the Kitchen God.

At the start of the new term, Nainai took my horse-manure tickets from behind Yeye's model-worker certificate and I put them in order. When Teacher Lee counted them and checked Lotus Blossom's homework, she looked at us both suspiciously. Lotus Blossom held her stare, but I blushed. 'How could she know?' Lotus Blossom laughed. 'She'll never find out.' Nainai was more tortured than I was. She did not approve of cheating like this, but neither did she want me to spend too much time following horses' bottoms, so she kept quiet.

On account of my horse-manure tickets and my good schoolwork, but mainly the horse-manure tickets, I was made a Little Red Guard and wore a red scarf around my neck. At the initiation ceremony, I raised my hand above my head and read after Teacher Yong, the political teacher, 'The red scarf is a corner of the red flag, which is red because it was stained with the blood of our revolutionary martyrs. I swear to be a good pupil and devote all my life to the Communist cause.' The blood of our revolutionary martyrs. The word blood scared me; I hated the sight of it. But the whole ceremony made me feel proud. I was on the side of the good, the Red Guard, from which I would proceed to become a Real Red Guard, a Youth League Member when I was older, and then, when I was properly grown up, a Party Member, like all good people in the world.

Lotus Blossom was not made a Little Red Guard. She sat at the back of the class with all the naughty boys and joined them in teasing the new recruits. I knew that this time Lotus Blossom was disappointed. The more noise she made about not minding, the more I knew she did. She had collected far more horse manure than anyone else.

We new recruits were treated to a cinema trip by the school. As we marched on our way, we sang song after song in high spirits. Inside the cinema, the sound of our voices came like waves, rising and falling, as one class took on another's singing challenge. Then the bell rang, and the film started. Four Liberation Army soldiers lost their way, became separated from the main army, fell into the hands of the Nationalists and were tortured to death because they refused to betray their comrades. Blood, torture, tears and more tears. The whole cinema was a heap of sobbing children.

Outside, I wiped my eyes. Now I knew what it was like to be a revolutionary martyr. All that blood and suffering had been too much for me. I doubted that I would ever be as brave as those four heroes. I felt burdened by this new discovery and looked around at my classmates to see how they would react.

With tear-stained faces they yawned in the bright sunshine and jumped around to stretch their legs. Teacher Lee scolded some over-excited pupils for stepping into the traffic. Back at school, we wrote our film reviews. Little Red Army wrote a list of additional methods of torture the film could have employed – he had this on good authority as his dad worked in the Army Special Branch. His essay was passed round and read in awe, until it reached Big Red Army who contradicted him: his dad worked at the Central Intelligence Unit so he knew otherwise. I tore up my review several times, convinced that were I to find myself taken captive I would turn traitor as I knew I could not endure such torment. In fact, I had shut my eyes during the more violent scenes and had only caught a glimpse of them.

Lotus Blossom read Little Red Army's essay with interest, although she had not seen the film. In the playground she came up to me. 'That goose,' she said, 'is it still bothering you?'

'Yes,' I said, remembering my fear, to which I had now become accustomed.

'Have you ever thought of doing something about it?'

'What?'

'Well, you know, make it suffer, kill it.'

The idea had never entered my head, but suddenly it seemed the right thing to do. It bothered me so much that perhaps it deserved to suffer. 'How?'

'I don't know,' she said, slowly. Then she laughed. 'Ask Little Red Army. Try one of his special methods.'

We used the simplest one. At the back of the playground near the construction site, the workers had piled up a huge heap of small stones from a house they had demolished. We each gathered a pocketful. The sun slanted, the air thickened, and our shadows loomed large. The goose saw me from a distance, and I knew that it was going to charge. It was just as well that I was prepared. I ran, but not too fast, to lure it away from the house to a spot where no one would see us. It followed without suspicion.

Lotus Blossom emerged from behind a parked truck, laughing. She whistled and threw a stone at the goose, but missed. I stopped running, and turned to look at it. Its eyes were red with anger. 'Come on,' Lotus Blossom shouted. I felt in my pocket and threw what I had in my hand. I hit it right on the head. It squawked, tilting its head to one side, as if it was trying to shake away the pain. Then it charged again, angry now. Lotus Blossom threw another big stone at it, and missed again. The goose flapped its wings and puffed itself up, as if it was ready to fly. I took out a handful of stones this time and threw them as if I was spreading a fish net, ensnaring the goose which was running towards me. They caught it, and it wobbled from side to side. Lotus Blossom and I jumped for joy. She threw more stones at the goose, until it flapped its wings more in defence than attack. It looked terrified and beaten. I felt so excited that I started giggling.

A small girl stood looking on behind the truck. I recognised her as the school door-keeper's granddaughter. She waved at us. 'Someone is coming,' she warned.

Lotus Blossom shouted, 'Run,' and set off for the school. I followed. I ran so fast that my knees felt weak. Then Lotus Blossom stopped, rushed back to where the small girl was standing and halted dead in front of her. 'If you dare to tell anybody . . .' I heard her say.

The little girl looked afraid. 'No, I won't. I promise to Chairman Mao.'

Lotus Blossom grinned; a vow made in the name of Chairman Mao was the most sacred imaginable and nobody would dare break it.

At the school playground we collapsed in the sandpit. 'That should finish it off,' Lotus Blossom said, breathing quickly.

I remembered how the goose had dodged in its terror. 'Serve it right.' I was elated now that the danger of discovery

41

was past. 'Let's go back and make sure.' I stood up, encouraging Lotus Blossom.

'No,' she sighed deeply, 'I'm too tired. Besides, I used up all my stones.' I still had half a pocketful and looked down at them regretfully. 'You'd better get rid of those before your granny finds out,' Lotus Blossom warned me.

That night, I went to bed early, pretending to Nainai I had washed my feet when I hadn't. I dreamed of an enemy aeroplane flying low to catch me, like the scene in the film. I ran through small alleyways to hide, but the plane always found me and dived at me. I could see that the face of the pilot was full of hatred as he aimed his guns.

When I woke up, Nainai was standing over me with a bowl of hot water. Then I heard the outpouring of abuse that flowed from the mouth of a woman standing outside underneath the street-light: 'I know who you are, you coward, tortoise egg, the thing that neither your mother nor your father wanted to keep. Show me how you did it. You've no morals! You'll come to a bad end.'

Nainai washed my feet. 'Some naughty child . . .' she said softly, as she splashed water over my feet. It felt nice and cosy.

'You will become a goose yourself in the next life, bullying us poor defenceless people, you daughter of a bitch and a crippled dog!'

The voice outside had got louder and Nainai stood up to shut the window. She looked worriedly at me, but I closed my eyes and pretended to be fast asleep.

The woman's harangue went on for nearly half an hour. I listened with excitement and dread. A dog approached and barked at her, but she barked back, undeterred. A child cried, and was soothed by an adult. A voice shouted: 'Shut up, you! The children are trying to sleep!' This prompted a further torrent of abuse.

In the morning when I walked past the goose house, I was surprised at my disappointment. My victory did not taste as sweet as it had the previous day.

Chapter 5:

A Zou Zi Pai Is Exposed

We spent the remaining part of the new term reading reports on the progress of the 'movements'. I enjoyed studying the 'movements' even though I did not understand what they really meant. They had nothing to do with the weather, I knew that much. So far as I could gather, they were concerned with criticising undesirable people, as had happened at the meeting I had been taken to when I was five. What about Uncle Beneficial? Surely he had not been bad. He hadn't seemed so to me. But our political teacher explained that bad people did not always appear evil, and that was why we needed movements, to expose them.

We had been through several movements at school, and they suited my buoyant mood. At movement after movement, we criticised people I had never met. Compositions were easier to write – I could simply copy my essays from the newspapers and change the names. In political lessons, we exercised our rhetorical skills. My school did so well that we were termed a model school, and teachers from all over the region came to learn from us. A 'demonstration day' was held and twenty or so teachers from other schools sat in on our class.

The text of this particularly well-rehearsed lesson was how angered the masses were by the reactionary words of Deng Xiao-ping, described by the newspaper as 'the biggest capitalist in power'. Even if we could not answer the questions we were told to raise our hands: Teacher Yong, the political teacher, knew who could respond, and the visitors were impressed by the spontaneous and enthusiastic participation of the students. We ran through the lesson beforehand in front of our school director, who was generally pleased with our performance, but suggested that Lotus Blossom, one of the chosen, should smash her fists on the table as she burst out: 'He is such an idiot.' Lotus Blossom obliged happily. Big and Little Red Army overcame their differences for once and united in supporting Lotus Blossom with all the necessary background noises. When Teacher Lee came to sit at the back to listen with the other teachers, even she looked surprised at our acting ability.

The days of no goose, and continual movements lasted for ever and I was happy. I slept like a pig and ate like one too. We had criticised Lin Biao, Deng Xiao-ping, Confucius and Liu Shaoqi, all top-ranking officials except Confucius who, we learned, had died more than two thousand years ago.

When Forthright and Bright came to visit one morning, I was holding a piece of paper and hovering around Yeye. Nainai was dusting the room, and Yeye had turned up the radio volume to try to drown my voice: 'The Central Broadcasting Station announces good news . . . grain production is at record levels . . . the harvest this year is one of the best in history.'

My great-uncle spat on the floor. 'Rubbish,' he said. He refused a stool offered by Nainai, and leaned on his stick. Coughing, he pointed it at me. 'What have they been telling you at school?'

'Look at this.' Yeye spoke up, grateful for somebody to share his burden. 'This girl has been pestering me about some Zou Zi Pai list that I don't have. Ask your great-uncle. Maybe he can help you.' I walked reluctantly to Forthright and Bright.

'What is a Zou Zi Pai anyway?' he roared.

I lowered my head and whispered, 'People [Pai] who

walked [Zou] on the capitalist [Zi] road. It's our political homework, to find out names of Zou Zi Pai from our parents.'

'There are none left in my factory,' Yeye said. 'They have all been exposed and criticised, so would be of no use to you.'

'But we have to have a name, it's our political homework,' I said, a bit wary of Forthright and Bright.

He waved his stick impatiently at me. 'Away with you, and don't talk back to adults.'

Nainai changed the subject. 'How is my sister-in-law?'

'Rotten woman, she is,' Forthright and Bright said shortly. 'Gone back to her sister's. We had a quarrel, silly woman.' Yeye offered him some steamed bread, which he accepted.

I sat apart, chewing my pencil. The smell of food tempted me, but I resisted going to sit with them because Forthright and Bright was there. I had never liked him much, and liked him even less today. I wrote down his name absent-mindedly on my piece of paper. I looked at it and thought it was a shame that his name did not sound like that of a Zou Zi Pai.

'Small Strong handed in his third application to be sent to the countryside,' I heard Nainai announce to Forthright and Bright – Small Strong was Shushu's name. 'What can we do?' She sounded sad. 'Children don't listen to us nowadays.' Shushu was the youngest son and had been allowed to stay in town with Nainai and Yeye instead of being sent to the countryside like the rest of his friends, but he wanted to join them. I knew how frustrated he felt. He had had several arguments with Nainai about this. Nainai sighed. 'The countryside is so poor. I heard they only have soy sauce with rice.'

Forthright and Bright grunted. 'It might be rather a good thing. The countryside is not all bad. You and I came from there, remember? The children need to learn to work hard and respect people.'

Back at school, I checked with my classmates on the progress of their homework. 'Have you got a Zou Zi Pai?' I asked anxiously.

Little Red Army shook his head, then changed his mind and nodded.

Lotus Blossom said, 'No,' with a short, careless laugh. I handed in my note with uncertainty. I was worried now, but it was too late to take it back.

'Does your grandmother know whose name you have given me?' Teacher Lee was collecting our papers to be handed in to the political teacher.

'Yes,' I said, looking away.

At home after school, I found Teacher Lee standing at the doorway of Nainai's house. Nainai smoothed Teacher Lee's long plait approvingly. 'Come again, Teacher Lee.' Her eyes followed Teacher Lee long after she had disappeared around the corner.

My heart pounded. I stole a glance at Nainai, who fixed her eyes on me. It was a strange look, one that I had never seen before. There was no reproach but surprise. I was scared. I ran into Tainainai's room. It had always been my refuge: whenever I felt wronged, I would come here to be consoled by Tainainai. Somehow her smell had lingered long after her departure from the world.

To my horror the room had changed. Tainainai's smell was gone: instead of tobacco, I smelt Gugu's fragrant face creams. I sat down in front of a huge poster of a woman worker sitting by a weaving machine. She had a big grin showing her white teeth, and wore a red band on her left arm bearing the words 'model worker'. Suddenly I saw everything in black and white.

'Taotao.' Nainai had followed me. Her tone was gentle and I glanced up: her eyes held the expression they always did when she looked at me, full of love and concern. I cried with relief and self-pity.

At the next political lesson, I lowered my head as the names of those who had not written anything on their Zou Zi Pai list were read out. We were kept in for ten minutes while the others played outside. I saw Lotus Blossom walk out with Little Red Army and anger rose in me. Liars, I thought, and despised them. Everyone seemed to be against me. Teacher Lee had hijacked my paper and told on me to Nainai; Lotus Blossom and Little Red Army had lied to me. I felt wronged, and raised my hand. 'It's not fair,' I said timidly. 'I have a list.'

'Yes?' Behind her thick glasses, Teacher Yong's eyes looked interested. 'What happened to it?' I was silent. I dared not mention Teacher Lee's name. 'Come to my office for a chat after the class,' Teacher Yong suggested.

When I told Shushu about Teacher Yong's suggestion, he sounded doubtful. 'To write a big poster criticism of Teacher Lee?' he exclaimed in surprise. 'But I thought you liked her.'

'Yes, I do . . .' I hesitated. 'But she has made a mistake and perhaps I can help her. Teacher Yong said sometimes people learn from being criticised.'

'I don't like it at all,' he said.

'OK, I won't do it.' Then I added hastily, 'Don't tell Nainai.'

Shushu had enough worries of his own. Every night I saw him add something secretly to the luggage he was packing. I was his conspirator, and helped him. He told me he had a feeling his latest application to be sent to the countryside would be granted. He had resorted night after night to sitting through the dinners of the chairman of the neighbourhood committee, but had been told that the biggest obstacle to his leaving for the countryside was the objection of Nainai and Yeye.

It happened one morning in the summer term, while we were all at home. The doors of the house were open, as was always the case in nice weather. Nainai had a constant stream of visitors: neighbours, relatives, sometimes strangers – anybody was welcome, she said. But she did not welcome this visit, I was sure. She was weeding in the garden, Yeye was in his bicycle shed, and Gugu was sitting at her little dressing-table. I was watching Shushu pace up and down the garden path, peering at Nainai occasionally and sometimes at his watch. I knew that something was going on.

Nainai straightened her back and smiled at us. Then we heard the truck. I was the first to run out, and saw the neighbours poking their heads out of their windows and doors. It was such a big truck, with red flags and red posters hung all around it. There had been trucks like this before, covered in banners and accompanied by drumming, sometimes stopping a few doors away from our house. I had seen Nainai shrink in terror at the sight of them, and close the windows to shut out the noise. This time, it had come for us.

Shushu, in a smart green uniform, got on to the truck to join the other young men. They were smiling and cheerful, with a look of otherworldly serenity on their faces as if they were leaving for paradise. Nainai stood rooted in the garden, her hands above her eyes to shade them from the sun. She did not move until the truck started up. I ran after it as it turned round. I waved at Shushu, buried now among his comrades. After they had gone, I felt as if I had sent off a hero on an adventure.

That summer holiday was less fun without Shushu. Nainai was withdrawn and often sat staring at the ceiling. I knew she missed him. 'Eldest grandchild, youngest son, the treasures of an old woman,' Yeye whispered in my ear. Her youngest son was gone, I was the only treasure left. I felt this responsibility keenly.

One of the shock discoveries of the new term was to see my big character poster pasted on the wall opposite the assembly hall. I had almost forgotten about it. It stood out as the only poster that mentioned somebody's name: 'Teacher Lee', it read in startling black characters. I had written it at the last political class before we broke for the holiday, where Teacher Yong had asked us to write a big poster criticising 'anything that is wrong about anybody, including your own teachers or parents'. She paused. 'You can even criticise me, if you think I have done anything wrong.' Walking around the classroom, she tapped on my table. 'Now is your chance to write about *that . . .'*

So I did.

Chapter 6:

'Dream of the Red Mansions'

Shushu's letter arrived in late autumn when all the leaves had fallen. He was staying with a peasant family and they treated him well but the work was hard. He had become popular as the village 'barefoot doctor', treating common illnesses. Many people in the area were illiterate, so he made himself useful composing letters and writing reports. I read out the letter to Nainai and Yeye, who were also illiterate: 'The countryside is poor and wild. Just the other day a wolf came down from behind the mountain where we live and took some hens away. There are many snakes as well, most of them harmless, fortunately. The girl next door found a snake on her bed one night and that created a stir. Anyway, really missing you all and the food at home. I will be coming back for the Spring Festival. Small Strong.'

Nainai stopped sewing and turned to Yeye, who sat with his back to the wall on the bed. 'Isn't our little girl clever? She recognises so many words. She will be a scholar when she grows up.' Yeye nodded.

There were a few lines at the bottom of the letter for my eyes only. I scanned them quickly: 'PS Taotao, don't read this to Nainai, but have you written your big poster criticism of Teacher Lee? I feel strongly that you should not do it. You might end up hurting Teacher Lee rather than helping her.'

His warning was too late and unnecessary anyway. I had

51

seen no sign that Teacher Lee was in distress. She smiled at me as usual, was still our class teacher and, if anything, gave me more attention than before. Apart from Teacher Yong, no one else knew that I had written the criticism, not even Lotus Blossom. We had chatted about the poster. 'What a coward!' she said, pointing to where I had written 'a student' instead of my name. We were standing beneath the now discoloured poster and I blushed. Teacher Yong had advised me not to put my name on it. 'If I were him, I'd write my name down in big red letters,' Lotus Blossom continued, running her finger down the poster.

'Do you think it's a he?' I asked.

'Sure, probably Big Red Army. He's always getting into trouble with Teacher Lee. It must be him.'

I was silent. Her words had made me keenly aware of what I had done: it had been like stabbing somebody in the back.

I dreaded the political lessons. I was convinced that one day Teacher Yong would declare before the whole school: 'She did it.' I was about average height in my class, but now I wished I was smaller, so small that nobody would notice me. The term seemed to last for ever, and I lived like an ant on a hot wok.

At last just one political lesson remained before we broke for the holidays – and we were to take a trip to the army camp next to the chemical factory, for 'better understanding of our liberation army'.

We stayed at the camp for a whole week, learning every-thing from folding our bedding to correct marching tech-nique, going to the toilet at the right time and, of course, firing accurately into a target; the enemy was in the shape of an 'American Imperialist' with a big nose. Little Red Army was proud to show off: his father was the camp captain's boss. 'He has to salute my Ba when they meet,' he announced to our class, and interrupted the shy soldier teaching us so many times that Teacher Yong had to scold him.

Shooting was the highlight of the training. We all loved it. Lotus Blossom stood out among us: she stripped the machine-gun even quicker than Little Red Army could. On the fourth day, we loaded the heavy rifles and fired. Many of us missed the target, and the Imperialist's face began to look disfigured and evil. Then it was Lotus Blossom's turn. She fired the best shot, hitting the tip of the Imperialist's nose. That day she wore red proudly.

All through January, Nainai busied herself preparing for the Spring Festival. She had a big family to feed, and the rationed amount of pork was hardly enough. As each day passed, she counted on her fingers the days until Shushu was due back from the countryside. Gugu was jealous: 'I will leave home, too, so that you miss me.'

Nainai stopped scraping mud from the dried mushrooms, her hands red from being in water for too long. 'You will, one day. All girls go away one day.' Gugu twisted her mouth in protest.

'Why?' I asked, bewildered.

Nainai sighed, and touched my hair. She did not answer my question.

The day before the Spring Festival Shushu came back. He had grown up a lot, his accent had changed, his hands felt tougher, his face glowed and he smiled a great deal when he talked about one particular peasant woman, the daughter of his landlord. At night he stayed up late and read a big thick book against the dim light. I had heard Nainai ask him what it was. 'Chairman Mao's words,' he replied impatiently.

Ma and Ba came to eat with us on the day of the Festival, with my other relatives. Together they bowed to Nainai and Yeye. I looked all around me and thought what a huge family I had. Ma looked much thinner. She helped Nainai to make the dumplings but did not say much to me. I couldn't bring myself to call her Mama: she had become almost a stranger in the years I had been away. I was nervous with her and clung to Nainai. She and Ba stayed late that evening and Ma talked with Nainai about my 'returning' when I started secondary school the following year. I listened with dread: I didn't want to leave Nainai's. As they were saying goodbye, I hid in

Gugu's room and refused to come out. When they had gone Nainai scolded me for not being 'a nice girl'. I was upset and went back to Gugu's room. There I found Shushu reading his Chairman Mao's words. He put the book down quickly when he saw me. He looked shifty.

A week after the Spring Festival Shushu left without his book – I had stolen it. I had always found Chairman Mao's words so dull and wondered how Shushu could devour them so eagerly. I went to Gugu's room with the book. She was not there – she hardly ever was nowadays. After work she spent hours in front of the mirror, putting on foul-smelling face creams, then disappeared for the evening. I climbed on to the bed and sat where Tainainai used to sit, with my back to the Chairman Mao portrait, now without the Kitchen God hidden behind it.

I opened Shushu's book. A new world, the world of a large extended family, the Jia family, and the lives of its young people, unfolded before me. So it was not Chairman Mao's words that had had him so enthralled, after all, but *The Dream of the Red Mansions*, a classical novel that was considered a bad influence on the young. It was not exactly banned, because Chairman Mao himself had read and quoted it. It had been written by a Qing Dynasty author nearly two hundred years ago. The characters were like ghosts, who lived parallel lives to the people around me. The boys and girls of my age spent time dressing, composed poetry, held parties, gossiped, got on each other's nerves; they were petty-minded, generous, heroic; they lived, they cried, they loved, they killed. They felt so real that I could smell the incense they burned and feel their pain. I became involved with this parallel world and took sides. I identified myself with Black Jade, the slender girl who wore a long silky dress and composed sad poetry.

It was, above all, a world of indulgence and luxury: we had meat once a week, but Black Jade's banquet took two months to prepare. The only silk I had was a thin ribbon to tie my hair, Black Jade had layers trimmed with fur and adorned with jewels. Each garment she carelessly tossed away in melancholy, I picked up and put on in my imagination. Melancholy – the ultimatte emotional indulgence. I relished the word, feeling the luxury of it without knowing what it meant. In my world all feeling had to be positive. We were encouraged to express only four emotions, and Chairman Mao himself had written a song about them: 'To our comrades we must be warm-hearted like spring, to our work we must be as enthusiastic as summer, to individualism we must be as cool as autumn sweeps the fallen leaves, and to our enemy we must be as cruel as winter.' But none of the approved emotions suited the way I felt. For me the real world was the world of the book, a world that was long gone, yet still alive. It aroused and fed my imagination. Suddenly I no longer cared about what happened around me. I did my homework quickly and carelessly in my eagerness to finish the book before term began.

Discovering *The Dream* was like making a new friend, a friend in whom I could confide. Together we discovered Gugu's big secret. One day I looked up from my book when I was sitting underneath a tree in the People's Park at dusk, and I spotted her walking with a bespectacled young man around the goldfish pond. Their clasped hands separated when they saw me. Soon the bespectacled young man was introduced to the household. He came with a bag of sweets and cakes and sat in the middle of the room, while Nainai, Yeye and two aunts chatted with him. Gugu was in Tainainai's room with me. Curious, I tried several times to go into the other room, only to be told to go away as soon as I entered. Gugu sat quietly beneath her model-worker poster.

After his first visit, the young man became Gugu's official boyfriend. But when I saw them again in the People's Park, I was shy and backed away to watch them from a distance. Sometimes they held hands, but mostly they just walked side by side, in the cool spring dusk, their shoulders hunched as they disappeared slowly into the darkness. I tried to imagine what they did together, and scenes from the book appeared in my mind, making me blush. There were some passages that I did not understand: somewhere it said, 'They made cloud and rain together passionately,' and I racked my brain trying to figure out what this meant. Why was it that things I did not understand were always expressed in meteorological terms?

I had not seen Lotus Blossom all holiday. She had vanished, and I was angry with her for not telling me beforehand. She had never mentioned her family or invited me to meet them, even though she had stayed for meals at Nainai's. Luckily the task for this winter holiday was not picking up horse manure, but collecting scrap metal, so I had not missed her assistance. Any metal would do, even a rusty nail. I had stolen some brand new ones from Yeye's tool box, and would have liked to take Nainai's shining wok to hand in. That would have counted for about a dozen tickets. But Nainai had said an emphatic NO.

When term started I had finished the first volume of the book – there were three in one thick folder. I was obsessed. I spent more and more time hiding in Gugu's room reading after school. Teacher Lee was often ill now, so Teacher Yong took our classes. Her lessons were dull and she was strict with us. We did not like her. She and Lotus Blossom in particular did not get on.

Lotus Blossom was distant to me now. I asked her where she had gone in the holidays but she replied, 'I went to the countryside with Ma to rest,' and refused to elaborate. She seemed taller and thinner, and her face was darker, like that of a peasant girl who had spent too long in the sun.

When we started the summer holiday I was on the last volume of the book. Now the characters were like my own family. I was especially anxious to find out whether Treasure would marry Black Jade, his true love, or Precious Hairpin, the girl his parents intended for him. Tragedy loomed because Black Jade was unwell. I read underneath the grapevine in the garden: the weather was too good to stay indoors and Gugu and her boyfriend made me feel unwelcome there. I couldn't understand them, hiding in a dark little room talking rather than being outdoors in the breeze.

Black Jade died. As she sobbed and cried Treasure's name with her last breath, he, in a delirium, had been cheated into marrying Precious Hairpin by his parents – thinking she was Black Jade. My tears dropped on to the page. I closed my eyes. The injustice filled me with anger and sadness. How could this have happened?

'Taotao?' Heavy footsteps came towards me up the path. I jumped up and hid the book beneath my seat. A dark shadow fell across me, and I looked up with tears in my eyes. It took me a moment to recognise who it was – I had been lost in the world of the book. 'Ma,' I sobbed, and ran up to her. She stood still and waited for me to reach her. I wrapped my arms round her and buried my face in her chest.

She did not move. After a while I looked up at her. She was frowning down at me. 'What is the matter, Taotao?' She freed herself from my embrace and walked back to the house. 'You're a big girl now, you mustn't cry so easily.'

I followed, furious inside. Talk to me, Ma. I was upset. Didn't you see? Nainai appeared at the end of the path. 'Goodness me, Taotao is almost as tall as you now,' she said, squinting at the two of us.

'Would you like to come home with me?' Ma said, after a while. We had sat down in the kitchen, where Nainai was cooking. She must have thought I was crying because I had missed her. I shook my head: I was used to living with Nainai. This was my home.

Chapter 7:

A Person Now

———◦◆◦———

Our first lesson of the new term was maths. The door opened and Teacher Yong walked in. She wore a new jacket and was smiling broadly. 'Students, from this term on, you will no longer be taught by Teacher Lee. I will be your class teacher and maths teacher.' Watching our bewildered faces, she added, 'Teacher Lee has been transferred to another job.'

When the bell rang, Lotus Blossom, Big and Little Red Army and I got together. 'What happened to Teacher Lee?' Lotus Blossom stared at all of us.

'She should at least have come to say goodbye to us,' added Little Red Army. 'I want Teacher Lee, I don't want Teacher Yong to be our class teacher.'

Big Red Army loomed behind Little Red Army and grimaced. 'Didn't you hear, you ignorant lot?'

'What?' We all turned to him.

He wagged a finger. 'Teacher Lee was sent to be re-educated in the countryside because she corrupted students.'

We all fell silent. My back felt chilly.

Lotus Blossom kicked a stone at her feet. 'But what on earth for? She is such a good teacher. Teacher Yong should have been sent away, not Teacher Lee. We should organise a petition to get Teacher Lee back. I'll draft something we can all sign.'

The next day, Teacher Yong made further announcements. I was appointed cadre in charge of propaganda. I followed the movement of a fly through the room so that I could avoid Teacher Yong's eyes. I was petrified. I had had no warning of this, and as the former cadre, Little Red Army, lowered his head, I lowered mine. I felt as though I had been pecked by the goose again, for I was frozen with fear, unable to move.

When Lotus Blossom marched up to me after class with clenched fists, I thought she was going to hit me. 'Sign here,' she said simply. I saw that half of the class had already put their names to the petition. I signed and heaved a sigh of relief. 'Are you all right?' she asked briskly. My face was red again.

'Oh, it's nothing, just a headache,' I said, and she walked away.

Food lost its flavour for me and Nainai became concerned. I sank deeper and deeper into my book – my escape in a confused world. I wanted to believe that nothing had happened, that it was just a rumour that Teacher Lee had been sent to the countryside. If it was true I was responsible for her downfall. My conspirator was Teacher Yong, and I did not like her. There was no one to turn to, to confide in. I was too ashamed to talk about it with Lotus Blossom or Nainai, so I consoled myself with *The Dream of the Red Mansions*.

On 9 September, only a few days into the new term, Lotus Blossom had persuaded and bullied almost the whole class to sign the petition. She showed me the signatures and I was nervous. 'Are you going to hand it in today?'

'Yes, I shall give it to Teacher Yong in the afternoon, during the political meeting.'

I ate little at lunch – I was worried about Teacher Yong's reaction when the petition was handed in. Somehow I knew that although she was always smiling she had a terrible temper and would take her revenge, like the snake wife. How I wished I could use a snakeskin. I waited with dread for the afternoon. Lotus Blossom's determination and Teacher Yong's temper would create a storm that nothing could stop, unless the sky fell on us.

It did.

In the afternoon, before I went back to school, I helped Nainai to spread the washing in the garden. Nainai's strong red hands raised a dripping sheet from the bowl. I held the other end and we twisted it in opposite directions so that more water was forced out. 'How is school?' she asked.

'OK,' I replied.

Nainai stopped and looked me in the eye. 'Are you sure?'

I blushed. 'Well . . .' I began, and licked my dry lips. Nainai waited. I put the wet sheet back into the bowl, and rubbed my hands together to warm them. Then I opened my mouth. At that moment there was a sudden shrieking, crackling noise. A cloud floated into the glorious sky. There was another shriek. It came from the loudspeaker installed high above the telegraph pole. Nainai still clutched the wet sheet. There were some muffled noises from the loudspeaker and then we heard: 'Please pay attention. Please pay attention. This is an important and urgent announcement. Our great, wise and best-loved Chairman, the great proletarian revolutionary comrade Mao Zedong, died . . .'

Nainai and I stared at each other. Then Nainai looked up at the sky, and the sheet dropped to the ground. I looked up too: the cloud had moved towards the sun and now covered it swiftly. The sky grew dark and everything seemed to have stopped – even time. I knew that I would never forget that moment.

I sped round the corner to school. Many of my classmates were running there too, a one-way traffic on the streets as we streamed in. We gathered in the playground, perplexed, to listen to the loudspeaker, which had started playing 'Aiyue', the solemn mourning music. I saw Lotus Blossom down by the sandpit, with the petition in her hands. My headache of a few hours ago was no more now than a scrap of paper with names on it, like a piece of homework. 'Can it be true? Did you hear it too?' we asked each other. All around us, the same words echoed.

It was the afternoon, so not all of the teachers were at school. Those who were seemed to have lost their authority. They spoke in hushed voices, and we obeyed as if we were good citizens rather than herded sheep, as if the seriousness of the news had made us grow up.

When we assembled in the classroom, Teacher Yong entered, a black band on her left arm, her eyes red from crying. 'Students,' she sobbed, 'there will be no lessons this afternoon. You can go home now.' She broke down and wept openly.

She walked out of the classroom, and slowly we got up and left. At the corner I stopped to hear the mourning music coming out of the goose house, echoing the loudspeaker in the street, and followed it home, hearing the echo from each open door, like a general saluting a band. I found Nainai, who always worked in the kitchen at this time of day, sitting by the bed, sewing. 'We'll all have to wear a black band now,' she explained. She made one each for the whole family from a piece of black cloth she had saved when she had made the lining of Yeye's winter jacket. Yeye sat on the bed, dozing, apparently unconcerned.

All around me the world was plunged into mourning. Everybody wore a black cloth band on their left arm as though they had lost a close relative. The school organised trips to different mourning functions in town where we cried and cried. It was easy to lose track of time.

One late winter afternoon, I sat by the window and picked up my novel. Soon I had escaped into that cherished other world. Treasure had forgiven Precious Hairpin and was playing with her. Outside the sun was setting, and Nainai called that dinner was ready. I put down the book and sighed deeply. What a cruel world this was! How could Treasure forget Black Jade so easily? I blew my warm breath on to the icy window. The frost melted to reveal the outside world and

I peered out lost in my thoughts until . . .

Something was trickling down my thighs. I touched and saw red on my hands. I shook my head: perhaps I was still in the world of the book. But the red stuff kept coming and I was horrified. I dared not tell anyone during dinner and that night got up several times to wipe away the blood. I thought I was going to die as punishment for reading forbidden books like *The Dream of the Red Mansions* during the period of mourning for Chairman Mao. On the third night Gugu caught me washing my pants, and my misery ended. I was depressed to learn that this would happen every month, but at least it was not a fatal disease.

I was no longer a carefree child. My new-found status of womanhood burdened me. I started to join the girls who were last to leave the toilets. I found out who among my friends had experienced the 'good thing', as we called it. I was convinced that Lotus Blossom hadn't yet – the telltale sign was that one asked permission to miss sports lessons, and she never did, but then she wouldn't, would she? She loved games as much as any boy.

One night I overheard Nainai and Gugu talking about my 'good thing' in the kitchen when they thought I had gone to bed. 'It's happened,' Nainai said.

'There is a lot going on in that little head,' Gugu said.

'I can't believe how soon it's come,' Nainai continued. 'She is a person now.'

In bed I hardly dared breathe in case they remembered I was there. Nainai's words had sounded so final and prophetic. I chewed over the word 'person', and was filled with pride and apprehension.

Slowly the terms went by. Teacher Lee faded into the background, though we continued our silent vendetta against Teacher Yong. When she asked questions, none of us raised a hand. We feared her, but we could show our defiance as indifference. We took our final exams and spent the summer waiting for the results. We had no tasks to do, no homework. I supposed we had done our bit for the Cultural Revolution: we had collected horse manure, scrap metal, killed flies and collected their bodies in matchboxes. I had supplied the name of one 'class enemy' – my great-uncle – causing the disappearance of a teacher I loved. Had I done right, or wrong?

One afternoon I agreed to meet Lotus Blossom at Chairman Mao's statue in Red Flag Square so that we could cycle together to the river-front. The square was at the centre of our small town: public rallies started and ended at the foot of the statue, and during the mourning period, when it had been covered with a huge veil, I had gone with my school to lay wreaths there. The day was bright and sunny, with not a cloud in the sky. As I cycled to the square, I could feel the breeze on my bare arms and legs. My legs had grown so long that I no longer had to sit at the front of the bicycle, I could sit properly on the seat. I arched my back and pedalled fast. The speed was exhilarating. The official mourning period was over and I started to sing. It was a relief not to have to disguise my laughter. 'I love Tiananmen Square in Beijing,' I sang as I approached the statue. Chairman Mao's benign face smiled to the east, his hands outstretched.

A small crowd had gathered there. Two children with kites in their hands gestured to me, yelling excitedly, 'A lunatic! A lunatic! Come and see!'

I got off my bicycle and pushed my way through the people. A middle-aged woman was standing in the middle struggling with a young girl – Lotus Blossom! One look at the woman and I knew it was her mother. The two could not have been more alike. The woman had taken off her red jacket, revealing her soft white breasts, and Lotus Blossom was trying desperately to cover her. Her mother had a savagely beautiful face and her eyes sparkled like those of a trapped cat, while her hair was long and messy. She giggled and dodged away from Lotus Blossom; 'Can't catch me, can't catch me! I'm a snake.'

Lotus Blossom was red-faced and her hands were shaking. She glared furiously at the crowd and turned away when she saw me. I heard two men chatting: 'She must be mad to disgrace herself in front of the Chairman.' I found my bicycle and, head lowered, cycled away fast, almost colliding with a police car coming round the corner. I sped along the wide street that led to the sea-front, keeping my eyes fixed ahead of me until I was about to turn left. Then I glanced back. Beneath Chairman Mao's statue I could make out a figure in red being carried away by two blue-uniformed policemen. As the car headed away, it looked as though Chairman Mao was waving farewell.

I turned down the riverside road and felt the force of the wind. The sun shied away and the waves beat on to the bank. Lotus Blossom's mother was a snake. A snake, a snake, a voice chanted in me, as I pedalled. Of course, this did not mean she was born in the snake year, but that she was one of the disgraced categories, 'the cow-head devils', *niugui*, and 'the snake gods', *sheshen*, an untouchable to be spat on and despised, like the old shoe-mender. 'Beware of female snakes,' Tainainai had warned. 'They are usually beautiful and proud. That is their downfall.' Lotus Blossom's mother was beautiful, and her daughter was certainly proud. I wondered if the same fate awaited her. Now I understood why I had never met Lotus Blossom's mother, and why she herself was so tough: she had to defend a mother who was both a lunatic and a class enemy. Suddenly a chasm gaped between us: she was from a 'bad element' family – we ought not to be friends. And yet she was the girl who had defended me against the tough boys and the bully goose, the girl whose hand I held when we marched out of school. If only she didn't have wild hair and a snake mother. For the first time it struck me that not only bad people were class enemies. The world was just as unfair as it appeared in my book.

The bridge that connected our city with North Korea was in plain view. A train was running across it from the other side.

It passed the old broken bridge in the middle of the wide river, left unrepaired as a reminder of the wickedness of the American Imperialists who had bombed it. Two soldiers, border guards, saluted as it rushed by. This was the sight Lotus Blossom and I had often come here to see, the solemn salute, the mysterious train from another country, North Korea, whose people were like us but not us. The scene filled our hearts with a sense of drama and awe.

It got windier. I stopped and sat on my bicycle. Now at last I could cry safely, right in front of the broad river. I wished I was holding Lotus Blossom and watching the flowing water with her, as we had planned.

TWO

However Beautiful the Sunset Is

人閒桂花落 夜静春山空
月出驚山鳥 時鳴春澗中

唐王維诗鳥鳴澗

Birds Sing at the Creek

A person at leisure watches
laurel blossom fall,
The night is still and the
spring hill empty.
The moon emerges, startling
the birds,
Who sing intermittently in
the spring creek.

Wang Wei (701–761)

Chapter 1:

Home

I sat with my feet dangling out of my bedroom window, watching the peasant woman opposite feeding her pig, a baby strapped to her back. I could smell the sunshine that had been baking me for the last hour, making me sleepy. From this angle the yard reminded me of a board game I had loved to play when I was younger; the difference was that I did not move the playing pieces, they moved themselves to amuse me. The woman was chewing sweetcorn.

A narrow dirt track divided my parents' house, the Workers' Residential Block of Number One Textile Mill, from the peasant woman's, Number One Red Flag Commune. My world and the one that began just beyond the dirt track couldn't have been more different. Everything on my side was suburban, neat and tidy: Number 28, Block 5, Neighbourhood Committee Number 34, Sunny District, read the inscription on our door, which was blue, made of cheap wood, and exactly like eight hundred others. We were not allowed to change the colour, and could not have afforded to anyway. On the peasant side, all was chaotic: the peasant woman's house did not have a number, or even a proper door. Her belongings were littered about. Her family didn't draw their curtains so at night I could see how they sat together to eat at a round table, and how the small girl was slapped by her mother. I never spoke to the peasant woman, though we watched each other closely.

Dark clouds gathered above the hill-top behind the peasant woman's house, so thick that it seemed as if they would crush the hill with their weight. Soon I could hear dull thunder. A roaring tractor stopped at the roadside to drop off a young man, who hopped like a rabbit on to the dirt track and ran beneath my window. The thunder followed him, giving rhythm to his running as he tried to get ahead of the storm. As he sped past, the peasant woman looked up. Her eyes passed through him and lingered on me; her stare was uncompromising but not unfriendly. I willed the boy to beat the rain. Lightning flashed – and then it poured. The woman with the baby ducked indoors, the pigs scrambled back to their dirty shed, the hens to their coop. Heavy raindrops splashed on to the dry yard, and the air smelt of dust. In the distance, I saw that the young man was sodden, and he was jumping up and down in the wet. His long limbs danced along with the raindrops. I watched him disappear – I stuck my head out to keep him in sight until I, too, was soaked myself.

As yet I had made no friends. I had been at home for only a week, and had been heartbroken to leave Nainai's house after six years. But Nainai had been firm: the new school was nearer to my parents' house, and my parents wanted me back. She was adamant that this was for the best.

Wet from the rain, I gazed round my new room. My parents had moved house since I had gone to live with Nainai, though their new home was still within the factory dormitory complex. Now they had an extra bedroom for me. A room of my own, a space of my own – I had not experienced this before. It was a cosy room; on the wall there was a photograph of me, a studio shot, taken when I was four, holding Chairman Mao's *Red Treasure Book*. Could that really be me? I examined it: I looked too eager and too dressed up – it was embarrassing.

The doorknob turned and I jumped. I had already been

scolded once for sitting like this by the window. 'Behave properly,' my mother had said, though I had not understood what I was doing wrong. Now she was wet and loaded with shopping. I rushed to help her, but she snapped, 'Where were you when I was struggling with the rain and the crowds in the shop? Nobody in this house helps me.' She stomped into the kitchen and started cooking. Moments later a lovely smell drifted out of the kitchen.

A tall bearish man poked his head through the open kitchen window: 'What's cooking? Smells good.'

'Pork chive dumplings. Taotao's come back, this is her favourite,' Ma replied.

Outside the kitchen, I was almost in tears. I started dusting the furniture frantically. If there was one thing that made Ma happy, it was a clean house, and I wanted desperately to please her. I could smell the dumplings boiling, as my mother clattered around in the small kitchen. I moved about the room trying to find things to dust. We were awkward with each other – we had been apart for too long.

In the evening, Ba came back from work smelling of engine oil. He gobbled down the meal and made appreciative noises. Ma's dumpling tasted different from Nainai's – too much ginger, not enough salt. 'Ma,' I said. Both Ba and she looked up in surprise – it was the first time I had called her Ma since my return. 'Who was that tall man outside?'

'Oh,' Ma softened, 'don't you remember? That's Uncle Thunder, our neighbour. He used to spoil you when you were small. He shot pheasants for us sometimes.' I recalled a much younger version of the man, with a lot of beard, carrying a gun. 'Didn't he kill a man?' I asked.

There was a silence. Neither of my parents looked at me, but went on eating as though I hadn't spoken. After dinner, Ma picked up some dumplings and we went next door. Uncle Thunder seemed much older than his wife, who was thin and dry like a fallen leaf. I could see that Ma liked him: her sulky face glowed in his presence. 'Hey, what a big girl you are!' he roared, and turned to his wife who stood silently behind him. 'Do you remember when we first saw her? She was this small.' He held his hands a short distance apart.

After dinner, Ba and Uncle Thunder brought out chairs to sit underneath the huge street-light in the square yard of the dormitory complex. I followed them, carrying the heavy chess box. Ba had explained that they always played late on Saturday nights – they had the next day off work. Lots of men were already there, in groups in white vests, waving bamboo fans to keep off the mosquitoes; they were all from Da's factory. I sat watching the wooden chess pieces move, hypnotised. Then I counted the moths that flew around the pale light like phantom dancers, banging their wings. But soon I was bored. I told Ba I was going home. He was too intent on the board to speak and just waved.

I missed Nainai's house. I missed being the centre of attention. On hot summer nights like this we would all have sat out to chat together, not just the men. Nainai, Yeye, Tainainai, Gugu and I watched traffic in the street, or were sometimes joined by neighbours. Evenings always ended like a party with half the street gathering at Nainai's house.

Away from the street-light, the tall blocks surrounding the yard towered menacingly above me. I ran quickly up to the third floor and our flat. At home the bright fluorescent light greeted me. Ma was sewing and I did not know what to say to her. I stood for a while, feeling the coolness of the house and its stillness. There were no mosquitoes here – Ma had made sure that not a single one survived to give us disease. I wanted to be close to her, to talk to her, but the silence was unbreakable.

Reluctantly I went to my little room and sat down to read. The new term hadn't started yet, but I liked the look of the textbooks and had read them all. The work seemed too easy. Next door Ma started singing, a low hymn. I stood up, moved to the door and listened. Now I felt close to her: I loved her voice, which seemed gentler than she was. It was the voice of love. I had heard the song before, and joined in with it. Stealing a glance inside the room, I saw that she looked dreamy, as if she was in another world, and felt sick with longing to touch her. I walked towards her as if enchanted, but she stopped singing and eyed me suspiciously. I went to the toilet.

Once the door was shut, I sobbed in humiliation. After a while, I peered through the blurred window to where two figures sat alone under the street-light – Ba and Uncle Thunder, still engaged in their chess battle. I watched. Thunder made a kill, and the sound of the piece falling was a splash in the still night. The moths were their only audience now, but the pair were oblivious to all around them.

I sat in the toilet for a long time, nursing my wound. I went back, past Ma who had stripped to her underwear and lost that air of otherworldliness. She asked whether I had washed, sounding normal and reassuringly concerned, and I went to bed. But I couldn't sleep – I was unused to sleeping alone in a bed, let alone in a room of my own. The darkness made huge shadows that frightened me.

Chapter 2:

'Poor City Folk'

———◁►◁———

The factory complex was a self-contained unit. It had its own shop, barber, hospital, post office and public bath-house. In the morning streams of bicycles flowed out to work; at dusk they flowed back. My dad was one figure among hundreds. We lived on the third floor, below us was the director of production and next to us the chairman of the trade union – Uncle Thunder. There was no privacy: we knew about each other's lives, possessions, children, rooms, furniture, salary. A trip to the public bathhouse revealed the most personal details of all.

There were no shops here in which I could idle away my time. The suburbs consisted of one big factory after another. Poisonous fumes from the chemical factory rose like huge dragons above the battered blue bridge and, as if to compete, the mountain of rubber outside the shoe factory gave off a foul stench in the heat of the sun. Waste flowed into the river under the bridge, and after a brief treatment, ran eventually out of our tap. The water tasted sweet if it was not boiled. My father's factory, a textile mill, was a big skeleton against the skyline. Beyond it spread the countryside, which felt strictly forbidden. Our house was among the outermost rows of suburban residential blocks.

At the end of the first day of term I came home with the student registration form. Both Ma and Ba examined it carefully. Their attitude contrasted hugely with Nainai and Yeye's: when I had asked Nainai what I should fill in for family background on the registration form for my old school, she had turned to Yeye. 'What are we, old man? Peasants?'

I read out the possibilities cautiously: 'Lower or upper-class peasant, or very poor peasant.'

'Put "lower",' said Yeye from his bed. 'The lower the better.' So that was what I wrote: 'Lower-class peasant.'

Ba led Ma aside and they talked earnestly. I heard Laoye, maternal grandfather and Laolao, maternal grandmother, mentioned. Ba came back to the room with a list of family members, mainly on Ma's side, all with their backgrounds, in neat writing. 'In future, you might need to fill in your family background many times. Be careful not to copy it wrongly.' He was a soft-spoken man, but his voice carried authority, I felt it now. I wrote down our designated category: 'Poor city folk'.

It was nice, though, to write my parents' name under 'guardian'. I had previously had to write down Nainai's name and after it 'jobless'. I copied their details diligently: Ma, Autumn, doctor, and Ba, Lucky, designer – very grand indeed. I carried on: 'Laolao, Field of Jade, and Laoye, Smart Scholar.'

'What is Laoye's background? What does *zhi yuan* mean?' I asked.

Ma's eyes were downcast as if she was chopping cabbage leaves; her long eyelashes sheltered her eyes like a screen. 'It means someone who works in an office.'

I had never met my maternal grandparents, but remembered receiving letters from them, sent from the countryside. It sounded fantastic: they lived near the Chinese-Mongolian border and had their own chickens, dogs, a cat and a field with fruit trees. A paradise.

A few days into the new term, I helped Ma to clear out the cupboards. The radio was on – a Revolutionary Peking Opera performance, one about a tea-house hostess who acted as an underground agent for the Communist Party during the Civil

War. The sound was fuzzy, and Ma stood up to tune it. As her hand turned, the sound of the opera disappeared down a dark tunnel as a Korean chorus rose up steadily and clearly. One of the few dubious benefits of living so near to the Korean border was that the Korean channels often came through more strongly than our own local stations. Ma tried to retune the radio, but the Korean chorus followed her. She heaved a heavy sigh, switched off the radio and turned to me abruptly. 'Have you been accepted?'

'What?' I was startled.

'Your registration form, is it accepted?' She watched me eagerly.

'Of course.' I shrugged my shoulders absentmindedly. Surely there was nothing to worry about – we were hardly class enemies.

'Is there a landlord or a rightist in your class?' she asked, in a low voice, almost a whisper.

'No, of course not.' Sometimes Ma asked the strangest things. I found her so puzzling.

She went to the kitchen with a dirty bowl and I heard her singing a piece from the Peking Opera we had just heard. Somehow the news of my registration had made her happy.

I wanted to please her more. I turned on the radio and searched for the missing station with the precision of a searchlight on a dark night, starting from the left and moving little by little to the right, with a patience I never knew I had.

Chapter 3:

The Earthquake Might or Might Not Happen

M y new school was much bigger than the old one. It had an impressive gate that opened on to the road and a massive swimming-pool at the back. With the nearby hospital, the medical school and the department store, it was in the centre of the district and the most prestigious school in town. Only students with the highest marks were allowed in, or children from the nearby air-force ground troops. They were big fat bully-boys who came on special buses looking down from their high seats at the rest of us. There were even more pupils called Red Army here – you'd have thought we were a military camp. I made friends quickly with two girls, and together we were nicknamed the Gang of Three. Our friendship was founded on sharing secrets, telling each other things we would never tell our parents – or indeed, anyone else – just like other twelve year olds. We laughed at the rest of the school, and at our Chinese-language teacher most of all, a pale-faced middle-aged man from Beijing. How he had ended up in a small town like ours was a mystery, but he was sulky, probably on account of his exile. He had an annoyingly proud manner, exaggerated by his impeccable Beijing accent, which we mocked. Often he came into the classroom with blood-stains on his clean-shaven face. He would glance at the rows of pupils, impervious to the hostile atmosphere around him, and announce, 'Page thirty-four, "The Farewell on a Wedding

Night",' and read on, soon lost in his own world of literature.

Strangely, he seemed to like me, perhaps because I had read a good deal. 'The Farewell on a Wedding Night', by a Tang dynasty poet, was hard for most of my classmates to understand, but my earlier reading, especially *The Dream of the Red Mansions* helped me with classical Chinese, his favourite subject. When lessons went badly, he would ask me to translate aloud, then say, 'Sit down, good. You, the rest of you, do you see how it should be done?' I hated his praise, which marked me out from the rest of the class, because I was desperate to conform, and joined all the more enthusiastically in his persecution. I began also to neglect my Chinese study, and decided to do deliberately badly in the exam.

But the exam was cancelled, because of the earthquake.

Or the rumour of an earthquake. The thing about it was that no one knew for sure when and how or, indeed, whether it would strike. In Ku Shui, Bitter Water, a city not far away, an earthquake had killed many people so when the warning came we were dismissed from school, 'pending further notice', with no homework.

I idled at home. I should have enjoyed this unexpected freedom but the lurid tales about earthquakes haunted me. I thought often about death and was scared. The army sent men to help erect tents for those who were too afraid to sleep indoors and it was like a festival: the soldiers came with their tools in their uniforms, the children from the block following them like dogs. Ba and I went to stay in the new tent, but Ma refused to join us. She cooked us dinner, brought it to the tent then went back with the dirty dishes to sleep in the flat, passing tent after tent that housed families whose squalid situation she frowned upon. 'I'd rather die in my own warm bed than of pneumonia,' she declared.

The factory leaders issued pronouncements that urged us not to panic. The earthquake might not strike us, they pointed out, and in any event we would be given plenty of warnings. Twice a day, during the lunchbreak and after dinner, the loudspeaker broadcast a plea for 'common sense about the earthquake'. The neighbourhood committee came up with a song about the signs of an imminent earthquake and copied it on to a blackboard which they placed where people could see it every day. We were told to remember it by heart.

During the day we lived normally in our flats because, we were told, earthquakes happened at night. After darkness fell we lived with the other families in the tents, where all sorts of rumours and horror stories circulated, along with tales of arrests, executions and public parades of those who were caught robbing houses.

'Don't panic,' the radio advised.

'Don't panic,' the factory leaders pleaded.

'Don't panic,' Ba said to Ma, who had just heard from Uncle Thunder's wife that the earthquake would reach seven on the Richter Scale, bigger even than the Bitter Water quake, and that it would strike around Spring Festival time.

Her pale face like blank paper, Ma took out our food-ration coupons for the whole month. She sent Ba with big sacks for all the rice. She gave me the meat-ration tickets, which looked flat and brand new (she had kept them hidden underneath their mattress), and a big handful of money. I had never done any shopping for her before – Ma did not trust me; she said I would get the figures wrong and be cheated. We could not afford mistakes. I looked up at her hesitantly. She smiled and touched my shoulder gently. 'Go on, you can do it. You're a big girl now.' She handed me a huge bowl – I couldn't believe the size of it. Our normal amount of pork, about the size of my fist, lasted us a week. I imagined the big lump of meat I was going to bring home, and my mouth watered. I took the bowl and went out.

That winter there had been no snow – no snowmen, no skating, no fun – but the wind had lost none of its bite. The meat and egg shop around the corner from the earthquake board looked unusually quiet. 'No meat this week, all sold out,' read a hastily chalked sign. I stood before it, not believing what I saw. Perhaps it was an old sign. I pushed open the door and went in. A woman sat behind the counter; shivering at the cold air I brought in with me. I brandished my ration tickets. 'Didn't you read the sign?' She yawned.

'But it's only Tuesday today.'

'Yes, and it was Monday yesterday, the day the meat sold out,' she snapped, turning to retreat behind a curtain, the back of her white apron stained with dried blood. I lingered, not wanting to relinquish the vision of a huge piece of juicy meat. 'Come back first thing next Monday, very early if you want to get anything,' she called from behind the curtain.

On my way home I stopped beside the earthquake board. It was as big as a door, rectangular, made of clay painted black and set into the wall. It looked well weathered. A board like this had been built into every building, and always bore a quotation from the sayings of Chairman Mao. They varied depending on the movement of the time. Ours bore the command 'Never forget class struggle', a favourite of our propaganda director. Director Zhang was a famous calli-grapher who specialised in free-style calligraphy and I had needed some help from Ba to work out what it said when I first saw it. The earthquake song was written by Director Zhang's secretary, who wrote like a model pupil. I had seen it so often I could recite it: if you see panicky rats crossing the streets in swarms, you will know that an earthquake is imminent. When you see lightbulbs shake, run to the door. I stared at the words: EARTHQUAKE, CLASS STRUGGLE, EARTHQUAKE, CLASS STRUGGLE. When it happened, a huge chasm would open in the ground and swallow us all, even the class enemies. Each and every one of us would be buried alive.

Behind me a child bleated, 'Ma, Ma.' I turned back. A toddler stretched out her hand to her mother, who held a hot sweet potato, teasing the little one. When real tears appeared, she gave in: 'Here, here.' She soothed and held her. The little girl smiled – she had her sweet potato, and was happy. But still we would all die, I saw it clearly, and not all the sweet potatoes in the world would make any difference.

My fingers were numb from the wind – I had forgotten to put on a pair of mittens when I left the house – and I had bought no meat. I felt despondent, yet we were alive. In that moment I knew I did not want to die now. I was only twelve and I hadn't done enough running, singing, lying on Nainai's lap, getting closer to Ma, rereading *The Dream of the Red Mansions*. There was more fun to come, fun I couldn't even imagine yet. I was not going to be swallowed by a hole in the ground. I gripped the bowl tightly and ran home wildly.

We had barely woken up on Monday morning when we heard a piercing cry. Ba had had a fever the night before, which meant we hadn't slept in the tent. All around us I could hear screams and bangs and the floor shook. My heart jumped. The earthquake had struck at last! Ba rushed to the door and listened. Then he laughed. 'The meat is being delivered,' he called, and Ma burst into tears. For a while we sat in our flat and listened. Shrieks from downstairs spiralled upwards as the whole building whipped itself into a frenzy. 'Find the bowl, the ticket, the money, quick, run to the queue, run.' A stream of cursing, rushing women and girls flooded towards the small shop. Ba turned to Ma: 'What are you waiting for?' Ma and I jumped up, dressed quickly and joined the stream, laughing hysterically, glad it was not an earthquake, and that we had been spared for another day.

Uncle Thunder's wife was on duty at the shop. She saw us at the end of the queue and winked at Ma, who went round to the back quietly and returned to me a few minutes later. 'Come on, I've got it,' she whispered.

We ate like kings that week – meat, the fat juices of meat. Ma made noodle soups and red stewed meat, deep fried meat, boiled meat dipped in soy sauce and vinegar with garlic. It was my best Spring Festival ever. We had so much meat that we took some to Nainai's as a festival present. That, and seeing me, made Nainai's day. Her house had changed, and I noticed that Gugu's things had gone from Tainainai's room. Nainai told me she was living in her new factory dormitory near her boyfriend's house. They were going to get married just after the Spring Festival. She said lots of my old school-mates had come to see her and asked about me, including Lotus Blossom. 'Poor girl, her ma died. She was wearing a black armband. She's very tall and pretty now, but still has that messy hair.' Nainai sighed. 'Too young to be without a Ma.'

Chapter 4:

A Wolf in the Suburb

A fter the Spring Festival we were told that the wave of earthquakes had passed us by and we could go back to live in our houses once more. School resumed. It took us some time to get used to sitting still in class again after so much time away. During this extended vacation our muscles had grown but not our brains, our Chinese teacher said.

In the summer term I had a surprise visitor: Lotus Blossom. I saw a tall girl jump off a truck and wave at the driver. I wouldn't have recognised her but for her particular way of walking: she always tucked both her hands into her trouser pockets and swayed from side to side in that way Nainai disapproved of. She wore a bright yellow nylon shirt with the top button undone, and her trousers were tight around her thighs but flared at the ankles. I had never seen anyone dressed like that and was glad Ma was not at home.

She had got my address from Nainai, she said, and hadn't come before because she had had to look after her mother. We cooked lunch together or, rather, she cooked for me. She walked round our house pointing at and commenting on things: the flame on our gas cooker was too small, we had too much furniture – what? You have a room of your own? Lucky pig. What does your Ba do? Your toilet is so clean! She made me dizzy: she just couldn't keep still.

After lunch we sat by the window looking at the peasant

woman's house. She said she would like to go and live in the countryside and stay there for ever. 'I'm sorry about your Ma,' I said.

'Well,' she dangled her legs carelessly from the window, 'it's been a long time since . . .' She stared at the peasant woman and seemed lost in thought. After what felt like hours, she whispered: 'It's nearly a year now since she – she stepped in front of a train in one of her wanderings.'

I didn't know what to say so I asked, 'Where is your Ba?'

'I haven't got a Ba. I never had one.' She shrugged her shoulders and tapped on the window. The peasant woman looked up at us. 'Hi.' Lotus Blossom waved at her, and the peasant woman stared back, but did not return her greeting. 'I never had a Ba, I don't have a Ma or any other relatives. Well, I have an aunt, who is living with me at the moment. She said she would look after me, but we don't really get on.'

In the afternoon heat we crossed the railway line to Ba's factory. We attracted much attention – at least, Lotus Blossom did. Ours was a small, closed world and nobody dressed like she did. Everyone knew me, but she was a stranger. Walking next to her I felt half excited, half jealous. In one year apart our lives had diverged dramatically: now there were much bigger differences between us than that in our heights. She had always had strong opinions and now seemed almost adult in her decisiveness. Losing your parents made you grow up quickly, I realised.

Huge red posters were pasted along the factory wall: 'Never Forget Class Struggle!' I thought of the earthquake song and shuddered. We went to Ba's building. He sat with his back bent over his slanting desk drawing diagrams of machinery in a huge room full of maps and graphs. He showed us round.

We reached the edge of the factory ground. A junk heap, the end of it joining a waterweed marshland, extended to the sea. Skeletons of rusty-looking machine parts were scattered around, some half emerging from the water. Dragonflies dipped in and out of the wavelets and their transparent wings shone in the sunshine. I dipped my fingers into the warm shallow water and a frog leaped out. Lotus Blossom shrieked, the first playful noise she had made since she arrived. Ba said he had to go back to work, and we waved to him. Now the real fun began.

We climbed over the fence and walked along the river-bank for a long time until we reached the sea, and watched a fisherman at work. We tried to guess what the Koreans were doing on the opposite shore. I told Lotus Blossom the song Ma had taught me, the one about waving to our Korean comrades. We sang it and waved blindly. I was pleased to have given her a taste of my life here. For a while she seemed to have lost that distant adult air and became noisy and relaxed. We took off our shoes and paddled, then dammed the stream so that we could tickle the fish.

We lay back on the bank spreadeagled, our eyes to the blue sky. I sang another song, and saw that she had closed her eyes. When I finished they were still shut, but she spoke to me. 'Carry on, don't stop. I love your voice. It's so beautiful. Did your Ma teach you this one as well?'

'No. I learned it myself. When I was older, she stopped teaching me songs. I think the older I get, the less she likes me somehow.' I had never spoken so openly about Ma with anyone, though I wasn't sure why I had chosen this moment to confide.

'My Ma had a good voice too . . .' She trailed off and sat up. 'Your Ba seems really nice.'

'Yes.' I laughed. 'Ma said he spoils me.' I wanted to tell her more about him but remembered – her father was a taboo subject.

She stared at the sky. 'Some men are really bad, though. They take advantage of you.'

I was puzzled. What did she mean?

She turned to face me. 'You know I sleep in the street sometimes?'

'No!'

'When my aunt and I quarrel, I just want to get out of the house.'

'So where do you live?'

'All over the place, stations, cinemas, mainly stations. Sometimes I go to sleep in other people's houses. And,' she avoided my eyes, 'I don't go to school any more.'

'How?' Now I was really shocked, I had never known anybody of my age who did not go to school.

'It was easy enough. Remember, I have no parents now. Ha,' she said, with a grin.

I did not like what I was hearing. She was a truant. Truants were bad. Orphans were unlucky and sad, but truants had only themselves to blame. I sat up and inched away from her. She laughed. 'I knew you'd disapprove. I suppose you're still reading all the time? Is school fun?'

School was not always fun, but that was the only life I knew, the only life I could lead. What choice did I have? But here in front of me was Lotus Blossom, orphan, truant, homeless and dangerous to know. She slept in strangers' houses, she had told me. I was curious. Exactly what advantage did they take of her?

The sun was going down, and the sky was cloudy. We tickled the fish for one last time, and caught three. We were so excited. This will please Ma, I thought.

At the foot of the steps to our flat I saw Ba's bike. 'Where are you staying tonight?' I asked Lotus Blossom.

'I don't know. I haven't thought about that yet.'

'You can stay here with me . . .' I paused, imagining Ma's reaction to my friend's appearance. 'I – I'm sure my parents would welcome you.'

'OK,' she replied, so quickly that I had no way out. I nodded and tried to look pleased.

When we showed Ba the fish he was very impressed, and almost as excited as we were. 'Lotus Blossom is staying with us tonight. Is that OK, Ba?' He smiled. 'Of course. Your friend can stay as long as she likes. You're on holiday now too, aren't you?' Lotus Blossom nodded, without looking at him.

When Ma came home she went straight to the kitchen to wash her hands. She always did that – to get rid of the germs she collected on the bus, she said. When she came out she saw the three fish: 'Where did these come from?'

'We caught them in the river! And this is my friend Lotus Blossom, who helped me catch them,' I said breathlessly, wanting Ma to like her. Lotus Blossom was even taller than Ma. They nodded awkwardly to each other. Ma went back to the kitchen.

I followed. She sniffed the fish suspiciously. 'It's very fresh,' I assured her. She ignored me and started to scrub them vigorously with a brush. Then she took out a purple bottle containing the vile-smelling liquid she poured on to summer fruit to disinfect it, and applied it to the fish. She looked as if she was performing an anatomical examination rather than preparing food.

I helped her, passing the bowls, handing her the knives, and pouring away the dirty water. When she had finished, I whispered: 'Lotus Blossom's Ma has just died. Can we have her for a night? We haven't seen each other in a year.'

Ma clattered the pans, then nodded to me. 'OK.' She turned her attention to the fish. 'I'm still not sure about these. Where did you say you caught them?'

'In the river by Ba's factory,' I said, pleased she had agreed that Lotus Blossom could stay. 'They are fine to eat. Ba said so.'

The fish would have tasted lovely, had they not been disinfected and rubbed so much. Ma ate in her usual precise way, carefully picking the flesh off the fine bones. Lotus Blossom ate her rice and vegetables heartily. Like Ba and me, she tasted little of the fish. She ate quickly, shovelling food into her mouth. Sweat shone on her forehead.

'Lotus Blossom is a curious name,' Ba remarked. 'We don't have lotus blossoms in the north.' He was right. I had never seen a lotus blossom; our climate was not warm enough for it. It grew in lakes mainly, and there were no lakes around us.

'My Ma was from the south, from Hang Zhou,' Lotus Blossom told him.

'Hang Zhou?' Ma and Ba exchanged a glance, and Ba smiled. 'Hang Zhou is famous for two things, its garden and its beauty. Your Ma must have been very beautiful.'

'She must indeed.' Ma smiled a rare smile. 'Look at her daughter.'

I peered at Lotus Blossom, who blushed and said, 'She was a Peking Opera singer, before . . .' She lowered her head and the smile vanished from her face. Then she looked up defiantly at us. 'Before she was criticised as a snake, and . . .' She trailed off, and we all fell quiet. I feared that Ma would turn her out of the house.

Ma didn't say a word and carried on eating. Once in a while she glanced quietly at Lotus Blossom, at her face, at her shirt. I noticed that she was picking up food and putting it in Lotus Blossom's bowl. We finished the meal like wind sweeping away loose clouds. After dinner Ma surprised us by suggesting a trip to the factory's public bathhouse. This was usually a treat we reserved for special weekends, and the idea excited us. Ba said he would not come: 'You girls go.' Ma chose an old shirt of mine for Lotus Blossom and we took all our wash-things and left.

The bathhouse was across the railway line near the factory ground. Here we stripped off in a great rush in front of a fat woman sitting in the middle of the changing room on a stool. I always thought of her as an animal spirit of sorts, exuding hot steam from her back. We were given a key to a locker for our clothes.

Lotus Blossom and I ran to the big hot pond, a huge bath of almost scalding water. We sat in it for a while watching other naked bodies all around us. Ma had a deceptively strong pair of hands. After I had soaked in the bath, I was subjected to a good scrub, which hurt, but she persevered and would not stop until she was satisfied that I was thoroughly clean. I winced but secretly enjoyed this brief, intense physical contact with her. She scrubbed me with the same attentiveness with which she cleaned her fish and vegetables. She sweated and sighed with satisfaction as she watched the dirt roll down my back in thick little balls. Then it was Lotus Blossom's turn.

I watched Lotus Blossom's bosom heave up and down with Ma's scrubbing. Her breasts were upright and firm, bigger than mine. Her body reminded me of a statue in a picture book I had once seen that belonged to Shushu. I liked especially her feet, the toes small and pretty, perfectly formed, like tiny bamboo shoots. Some grotesque bodies were on display, which, try as I might, I could not avoid seeing, but Lotus Blossom's soothed my eyes and gave me pleasure.

I went to the shower to wash away the dirt. Ma did not go into the bath, believing it to be swarming with disease. She preferred the showers, but showers did not come easily: both patience and quick wits were required to secure one. Lotus Blossom was more successful than I was and soon I heard her clear, bell-like voice: 'Taotao, Auntie, I've got a shower.'

Afterwards, we walked home slowly with wet hair. The coal dust near the railway lines invaded our nostrils, and we covered our heads with towels. Ma started singing; Lotus Blossom and I listened. When we crossed the railway line, Ma turned to my friend: 'You know, Lotus Blossom is a lovely name. You have heard of the saying: "Out of the mud but not stained"? That refers to you.'

Lotus Blossom nodded. 'My Ma taught me that. She said I was to be beautiful and . . .' she lowered her head and whispered '. . . pure.'

At home we brushed our teeth quickly and pretended to my parents that we were tired so that we could be alone in my room together. I gazed at Lotus Blossom's skin under the moonlight. It looked fine like the porcelain figure on my Ma's cupboard. Her breath was heavy and close to my ears. 'How did the men take advantage of you?' I murmured.

She stared at me, her eyes bright and watery. 'Do you really not know?'

'No.' I shook my head and blushed in the dark.

She opened her mouth, then closed it again. 'They . . . they touch you.'

'Where?'

'Well . . .'

I waited, my heart pounding.

'Places. I don't want to talk about it, really. Haven't you had biology lessons?' She turned away from me, her chest heaving. There was no more sound from her for a long time.

'What kind of men are they?'

'Just men, all men.' She tossed in the bed. 'You don't want to know. It's not all bad, I liked it sometimes.'

What did she mean? I was almost mad with confusion. Men? All men? Including my Ba, my Shushu? They were men. Our Chinese teacher, he was a man. Men were different.

'Yes. They are all the same . . . You remember Teacher Luo? The entertainment teacher?'

'Yes.'

'Well, he was caught doing his man thing to Handsome.'

'No!' I exclaimed, still uncertain as to what the man thing entailed, but surprised nonetheless by this news.

'Yes, they were caught in his house and he was sentenced to ten years. Served him right. I never liked him.'

In a biology lesson the class had been split into two, boys and girls, and we had half an hour each. We had been shown diagrams of the human reproductive organs. The biology teacher was a man, and we lowered our heads and looked away, but he seemed unembarrassed. Sperms and eggs – these had nothing to do with my body, the body I knew so well, which I lived with every day. But there it was in the book, and on his chart. When the bell rang, we all heaved a deep sigh of relief and escaped as quickly as we could.

After that lesson, things went on as before. We still drew

lines between us and the boys sharing our desks. If his elbow stuck out my way just a tiny bit, I pushed it back hard. We never talked to boys, not willingly. We were girls. We laughed at their silliness. But the glimpse of the chart had made an impression on me. It came back to me in unexpected places and at unpredictable times, always with a sensation of shock. Lying there with Lotus Blossom, my mind was full of the colourful biology map as I tried to figure out what they did, she and the strange men – which apparently all men did to women.

When Lotus Blossom left I was both relieved and sad. I wanted to return to when I had thought nothing of men. I did not want to feel embarrassed in their presence. But Lotus Blossom had made me restless.

One sleepless night, long after Uncle Thunder and Ba had finished playing chess outside, I pushed open the door and stepped on to the balcony of our flat. There was nobody in the square but the moths fluttering playfully. The area was enveloped in the white mist of the street-light. Somewhere I could hear a buzz and a train whistled by, but nobody stirred. Facing the empty square, I felt cold, desolate, clear-headed and alone. I was about to go in when, out of the corner of my eye, I saw an animal. I knew instantly that it was a wolf, even though I had never seen one before. It was a sudden and clear revelation, appearing as if from nowhere, like destiny. It looked around the block, as if it had been transported from another time and place. Then it spotted me, eyed me. I shuddered, and ran inside. Breathless, I tiptoed past my parents' room, heard their breathing and felt reassured. I went back to my own bed and tried again to sleep.

I dreamed of Tainainai for the first time since my move to the suburb. The old woman who had told me fox and snake stories told more stories in my dream, but when I woke up, I could remember only the wolf, and was not even sure whether it belonged to the world of sleep or of waking.

Chapter 5:

'A Heart Pure as Ice in a Jade Pot'

The next time I saw Lotus Blossom was in winter, when I was at Nainai's house for the Spring Festival. This time Nainai was not so pleased to see my friend: she had heard rumours, she said, after Lotus Blossom had gone, that she had been hanging about with hooligans and criminals, and stealing things. 'Look at the clothes she wears! I mean, trousers tight as that, and her hair, too long, too long.'

Lotus Blossom was offhand with me, and again I felt at a remove from her. She spent the evening huddled up to my other old classmates, Big and Little Red Army, listening to their talk. When we found ourselves alone briefly, there was no mention of our last time together. It was almost as if she regretted having been so intimate with me and now wanted to withdraw.

Spring came slowly that year. It snowed on the first day of the Spring Festival, which was a good omen, Nainai said. Then the snow melted and it felt very cold. It never seemed quite so bitter when it was snowing, I noticed, perhaps because you were too busy making snowmen or having snowball fights to notice. I hated the thaw, when it was wet and muddy and there was nothing to distract us from the cold.

Sometimes the weather surprised us with sudden warmth. On one such morning, in late March, we peeled away the newspapers that sealed out the draughts and opened the windows, which had been shut all winter. I breathed in fresh air, and peered down at the peasant house. The baby had grown and was running around now, helping to feed the pigs. The hills beyond the peasant house looked beautiful, all the more alluring because I was forbidden to go there.

That day, when Ba came home from work he handed Ma a letter. As she read it her face lit up. 'Ma and Ba are coming to see us. They don't live in the countryside any more, thank goodness. They're back in Ri Cheng, the Sunny City, this month.'

I was disappointed to hear this: it meant I could not see their earthly paradise. 'Ten years, they've been away.' Ma sighed.

Finally, after several telegrams confirming their dates, Field of Jade and Smart Scholar, Ma's parents, came to stay with us. I called them Laolao and Laoye, and they told me that they had seen me when I was very small, although I had no memory of this. I watched Laolao and saw how much Ma resembled her. They both had oval faces and eyebrows that arched like a crescent moon, but where Ma kept her eyes downcast and frowned, Laolao's wrinkled face always bore a smile. She moved about gracefully and slowly, and was a great storyteller. She smoked heavily, and unlike Nainai, she was talkative. Before long, she was telling me of her own childhood and that of Ma and my aunts. Ma chatted to Laolao all the time – I had never known her talk so much. Ba set up a bed for me in his and Ma's room and Laolao and Laoye slept in mine. Sometimes Ma and Laolao talked deep into the night in the kitchen when we were all asleep.

On the second day of their stay, Laolao took me for a walk, leading the way even though I was the hostess. We passed the peasant woman's house, and Laolao stopped to relight her pipe. She admired the sweetcorn growing in the yard. A dog barked and leaped at us ferociously. I was about to run, remembering rabies, but Laolao stopped me with one hand, swooped down to pick up a stone with the other, straightened and said to the dog: 'Stop.' It stood still, and remained at a distance.

The peasant woman came out with her baby. She gazed at us blankly. Laolao stepped forward. 'Your sweetcorn looks good,' she said.

The peasant woman's face lit up. 'The weather has been fine.' She nodded to me, and turned back to Laolao. 'You're not local, are you?'

'I'm here to visit my daughter. This is my granddaughter. Do you own this field?'

They chatted, and I took the opportunity to scrutinise the peasant yard. The colours were more vivid, the animals more alive. The dog wagged its tail now and circled around me, breathing heavily. The baby's face was rosy but dirty.

I enjoyed walking with Laolao, who talked to everybody and was interested in everything. Visitors poured into our home, friends she had made – numerous old women from the neighbourhood, a bus conductor, a gate-keeper and a butcher. The peasant woman came once, without the baby.

Laoye was like a god, or so it seemed to me. He was tall, handsome and dignified. In contrast to Laolao, he spoke little but did a lot. Something strange was going on between Ma and Laoye. She hardly ever talked to him and whenever she, Laoye and I were alone, they addressed me but not each other. They prepared our meals together, though: he did the preparation and she the cooking. He cleaned the food thoroughly and beautifully: he had exquisite hands. When we sat down to our meal, he ate carefully and slowly, chewing each mouthful, as if he was counting each grain of rice. Ma talked almost exclusively to Laolao, and only turned to Laoye to ask if he needed more rice.

It was warm enough to sit outside. One afternoon as the

sun was going down I sat next to Laoye, watching him prepare a fish in the yard. He skinned it carefully, then separated the head from the body, his eyebrows close together. He put the cleaned fish into a separate bowl with clean water to wash it. There was elegance in his actions, unlike Ma's: she cleaned the fish as if she was performing surgery. Laoye's concentration was perfect: he never stopped to look around him. Finally, he raised his head, only to wrinkle his eyes at the sunset beyond the top of the opposite building on the hill in the distance. He murmured something, and I followed his gaze. 'What did you say?' I asked loudly.

' "However beautiful the sunset is, it is still near the dusk",' he replied. 'It's from a Tang poem, you will understand when you are my age.'

In the evening Ma and Laolao chatted while I did my homework. Laoye came up behind me and took the calligraphy brush from my hands. I was annoyed. 'What are you doing?'

'If you cannot grip it when I try to snatch it away from you, it shows you aren't holding it properly. Hasn't your teacher told you that?'

'No,' I replied, impressed, although the character I was writing was a mess now.

'What was that supposed to be?' he asked, pointing at the black smear.

'To fly,' I replied.

His eyebrows arched as he exclaimed: 'Is that to fly? You are humiliating the word.' He sat down, adjusted his breathing for what seemed hours, straightened his back, dipped the brush into the ink, stirred it lovingly, took another deep breath and started writing on my notebook.

I was transfixed. I heard waters fall in the distance, my own breath followed his, and his followed the movement of the brush. I felt lighter as the brush moved swiftly up and down, the curve twisting and turning as if it was dancing to a tune. The smell of the ink was like edible flowers. When he

stopped, I picked up my notebook and saw five flying characters, like butterflies, adorning my book. 'Ba, why don't you
teach her?' Ma asked him. It was the first time I had heard
her call him 'Ba'.

'I'd love to.' He nodded eagerly as she looked away. There
were little pearls of sweat on his forehead, which he wiped
away with his hand.

The next day I did not go out with Laolao; I went with
Laoye. 'Let's go and catch the sunset,' he said.

After an early dinner we set off, and walked further than I
had with Laolao, beyond the peasant woman's house and into
the hills. The air was pure and the hills fresh with a spring
wind. We were alone. I did not know why but I told him that
I had read *The Dream of the Red Mansions*. He rubbed his chin
and laughed. 'There is a saying, "If you are old, you don't
read *The Three Kingdoms*. If you are young, you don't read *The
Dream*." '

'Why?'

'Because *The Three Kingdoms* is all about plotting and
scheming. Old men are already shrewd, they do not need to
read something that makes them even more so. *The Dream* is
all about romance, and when you are young you are already
romantic enough, so you don't need to be made even more
foolish by such books.' He leaned forward and put a finger to
his lips. 'But I believe you should read as much as you can,
especially *The Three Kingdoms* and *The Dream* because these are
two of our four greatest classic novels. I was discouraged
myself from reading them when I was young but, like you, I
devoured them all and . . .'

'And?' I watched him expectantly.

'Look what an old schemer I have turned into.' He winked
at me. 'Don't tell your mother I told you this. Let it be a secret
between us.'

I had never trusted any adult enough to tell them I had
read *The Dream*, and had always felt there was something
wrong and shameful about it. Now I had Laoye's approval

and praise. I felt him to be an ally.

The hills were not so intimidating any more. Ma never liked me walking beyond the peasant house and had warned me of all sorts of dangers; poisonous plants, biting dogs, stinging insects, strange men who did horrible things, unexploded bombs . . . The list went on. But Laoye walked on beside me, pointing at a flower, a bush, a path or an animal track. When he wasn't talking to me, he murmured to himself, something rhythmic and enchanting.

We stood on top of the hill – my parents' flat was just a dot in the distance. Laoye sat down on a big rock and I joined him. The sun was setting. I remembered the poem he had recited, something about a beautiful sunset: 'Laoye, that poem you told me the other day, about sunset, can I hear it again?'

He drew me to him. 'I don't think I should tell you that one, it is too sad. Let me tell you another poem, something more positive.'

He paused. The sun had gone down, and it was very still. Somewhere a bird sang like a flute.

> 'Ren xian gui hua luo,
> Ye jing chun shan kong;
> Yue chu jing shan niao,
> Shi ming chun jian zhong.'

Laoye's soft voice broke the silence.

I held my breath, captivated by the rhythm. He recited the poem again, then made me repeat it after him. We recited again and again until I could do it on my own. He smiled. 'You must be wondering why I am making you learn it without explaining it to you. But the beauty of poetry cannot be fully appreciated without speaking it aloud. You get the rhythm better that way. Can you feel it when you recite it, now?' I nodded.

Then he explained the poem to me. ' "A person at leisure

[watches] laurel blossom fall, the night is still and the spring hill empty. The moon emerges, startling the birds, who sing intermittently in the creek". Close your eyes and imagine the picture.'

I closed my eyes.

'Think of the word *xian* [leisure], and the word *luo* [fall], which describe the person and laurel blossom respectively. What strikes you as extraordinary about them?' I thought for a while and shook my head. 'Has it occurred to you that the person is passive, at leisure, and the laurel blossom is active – it falls?'

I began to see the picture. 'It makes the laurel blossom more alive.'

'Yes, it makes nature more alive, doesn't it? Now think about the word *jing* [startle], and tell me, how could a moon startle?'

I opened my eyes and looked at the moon in the sky. It was so pale I could not imagine it being startling. 'It could not,' I said.

Laoye gazed up at it too. 'Imagine that it is very, very still, and imagine you are a very careful bird.'

I imagined. I had to try hard. I supposed that for a very careful bird the appearance of the moon might be startling.

It started to get dark and we headed home. On the way I recited the poem again to myself. Even though the moon was still not startling to me, the night on the hill became more vivid. It was magical. It was as if I had been given an extra pair of eyes and ears. I took in more than I had before. I had not known that poetry was so simple and relevant.

We hurried along the path. Laoye's slow, quiet voice spoke: 'You know the Tang poems were written in the Tang dynasty when poetry in China was at its peak, don't you? You must have heard of the famous poets like Li Bai and Du Pu.' I nodded. 'But there are lesser-known ones, just as good, like Wang Wei, the author of the poem I taught you just now. It wasn't hard, was it?'

'No. it seemed easy to understand. But you have to think about the words to get their full meaning.'

Laoye nodded, pleased. 'The themes vary, but many of them are about parting. You can imagine those days when travelling was much harder than it is today. There were no cars, the roads were difficult, and there were wild beasts everywhere. It was a big thing to embark on a journey, to leave one's family and friends.'

Laoye said that when I could recite three hundred Tang poems, I would be ready to write poetry myself. I asked him if he had a book of them for me to read. He looked down at me sadly. 'They have all been burned. Nobody is allowed to keep them. I almost burned my fingers when I burned mine – I did not want to let it go. My collection of poetry books came from my parents.' He put his hands behind his back and gazed at the hills. 'Nobody can take the poems away from me, though. They are all in here.' He pointed at his head.

Each time we went out for a stroll I learned new poems from him. After dinner now I always helped Ma to clear the table quickly – she was pleased and said I had become a more considerate daughter. Little did she know that the reason behind my improvement was that I was eager for my treat – my poetry walk with Laoye.

Ba had been given some tickets by his factory for us to go to see *The Tale of the Red Lantern*, one of the eight revolutionary operas, which were the only ones allowed to be performed. He had just been named a model worker by his factory. We went to the People's Palace, where I had performed the Korean dance. The hall was half empty, and I was bored. I knew the story by heart – I had heard it on the radio many times – and it seemed ridiculous to have to sit through the play pretending I did not know what was going to happen next. I was impatient for the hero to die so that we could all go home. But he sang a song so long I began to fear he might be spared – had they changed the plot? Laolao and Laoye enjoyed it, though; their eyes half closed, they were in the world of the rhythm.

I explained my frustration to Laoye. He said, 'When hungry, one is not choosy about one's food. Laolao and I loved Peking Opera. If those eight model plays are the only ones ever put on, what can we do?'

I asked him how many operas there had been before the ban. He said he was not sure and that I could ask Laolao. 'What are they about?' I was only interested in the stories.

'You know some of them already. They are stories taken from *The Dream* and *The Three Kingdoms*.'

Ma got out an old gramophone record of a traditional Peking Opera she had kept and played me a piece. She was secretive about it and instructed me not to mention it to anyone. Laolao and Laoye listened to it with delight, and Laoye explained the rhythm and how the drums and other instruments worked. The record was of poor quality, as if the sound was filtering through sand, and I did not like it. I preferred the modern opera we had seen – at least I had understood the words. Laoye shook his head. 'Well, it's an acquired taste. You are too young to sit still and let the music sink in.'

After a two-month stay Laolao and Laoye left. I was devastated, but they had to go back to Sunny City to visit their other daughters, of whom there were three. They had not seen them for a long time. I made Laoye promise to find the other three classical novels and send them to me.

At the station we said goodbye. Ma held Laolao's hands with tears in her eyes. Laoye stood by, loaded with luggage. He kept opening his mouth as if he wanted to say something to Ma, but she did not look his way. 'Laoye,' I tugged at his sleeve, thinking how rude Ma was. He didn't notice me at first, so I tugged harder. When he finally lowered his head, I was shocked to see tears in his eyes as well. I let go of his sleeve.

Afterwards I went out for walks on my own. Ma said I could only walk in the daytime, so I went before breakfast rather than in the evening. I recited the poems Laoye had taught me when no one else was around. When I missed him, it was this poem about parting that I recited:

'Cold night rain enveloped the river as it entered Wu County. When day broke I said goodbye to my friend, who went alone
                             towards Chu Mountain.
If people in Luoyang ask about me, my friend,
Say my heart is still pure, as a piece of ice in a pot of jade.'

Chapter 6:

Smart Scholar No More

———⬥———

Despite my best efforts I still scored the highest mark in my end-of-term classical Chinese exam, and the teacher praised my translation. Since the earthquake year, our lessons had returned to normal and, with only a year left before the university-entrance exam, we were pressured to study hard. 'Read, read, and use your brains,' our Chinese teacher urged, but we were impatient for him to finish and let us get on with the summer holiday. This was the last day before we broke up, which always felt so long. I had my own special treat to look forward to: I was going to visit Laolao and Laoye in their house in Sunny City. Ba had asked a friend, who would be driving his lorry there on business, to give me a lift.

Sitting in the lorry, I had my first real sight of the country-side. We drove right past the peasant woman's house, and I was surprised to find that she had a front door, a proper one with red posts on each side, and thick green paint. The dog ran out to bark dutifully at us. As we went further into the peasant domain, it dawned on me that, just as my own flat was like so many others, the peasant houses were alike too. This discovery made a big impact on me, but I was ashamed to point it out to Mr Tian, who sat high in his driver's seat, fearing he would laugh at such a trivial observation.

I woke up at midnight. We had to be in Sunny City now, I thought. I could hear more cars driving alongside us and sounds of braking, and I could see the street-lights, even through closed eyelids. I sat up. Street-pedlars were packing up and although the buses were still running, gloriously lit up, they carried few people. There were trolley buses, too, which ran on tracks – I had never seen them before.

The truck slowed down on a side-street outside a three-storey red-brick building with a neon sign: 'Peaceful Guest-house'. Under the light, a thin man wearing a grey jacket stood with his back towards us. I recognised his hunched form. 'Laoye!' I shouted from the truck. Somehow this was the last place I would have expected to find him. The driver braked, and Laoye ran up and pressed his face to the window. Mr Tian switched off the engine and jumped down to get some sacks out of the back of the lorry.

Laoye and I stood silently and waited. He looked shabbier than he had in my memory of him. I held him in such high esteem, and this insignificant-looking guest-house didn't seem worthy of him.

The driver came back with two sacks, and hesitated. 'These are from your parents, Taotao. They are a bit heavy. Are you sure you won't let me drive you to your grandfather's house with them?' Both Laoye and I said no. It was very late when we got home and I was exhausted with excitement. I fell asleep almost immediately.

In the morning, I got up and found Laoye already gone. 'He's out selling cigarettes,' Laolao said.

'Why?' I was shocked.

'Silly child, we have to make money to live. He is working by the park. Why don't you go and find him?' Suddenly the food tasted bitter as I digested the words: my grandfather, so learned, with his fine calligraphy hands, reduced to selling cigarettes?

I bought an ice-cream from an old woman near the park and, licking it, walked towards the gate where Laoye would be. My legs felt heavy and the ice-cream did nothing to cool me. A boy cycled past and whistled at me. I stared at him hard, and he took off, leaving a lewd suggestion to linger in the air. I did not care. Then I saw Laoye in front of the north exit, sitting upright in his stiff blue clothes, serious and attentive – the posture he adopted when he wrote calligraphy. Not far from where he sat, an old woman was shouting, 'Ice stick, come and buy, good for thirst.' I felt my back creeping with goosebumps and hastily retreated to the flower-beds. I trod on a rose-bush and winced as the thorns scratched me. A serious-looking man with a red band on his left arm stole up from nowhere, demanding that I pay a fine. I ran home.

Laoye came back with a satisfied smile on his face. 'Not a bad day at all, all sold out.' He handled Laolao all the money, and added, smoothing his hair with his delicate fingers, 'You brought good luck, little Taotao.' I smiled, avoiding his eyes. At dinner he ate a lot.

The night was hot, so we took some chairs and sat outside. Next door, another family was sitting around, grandparents and grandchildren, fanning away the mosquitoes and the hot air. Occasionally, the wind carried over fragments of their conversation. The scene reminded me of times I had spent with Nainai. I sat with my face in Laolao's lap, and watched Laoye walking slowly but steadily towards the watermelon seller under the gas-light.

'Tell me a story,' I begged, seduced by the warm air.

'But you've heard them all.'

'Then tell me, again, the one about the oyster and the scholar.'

'All right.' So Laolao began. 'Once upon a time, in the south, along the grand canal . . .'

'Hello, we're here!' Neither of us had noticed the arrival of two women, my aunts. The youngest was only eight years older than me and was tall and strong. The other was also tall, but a bit thinner. Soon another aunt joined them on her way home from work.

Laoye came back quietly with a huge watermelon. Only the

second and third aunts greeted him: 'Ba,' they said.

My youngest aunt jumped to her feet and flashed out a brand-new tape-recorder. I knew it must have been expensive – only the army kids in my class had them. 'What's that?' Laolao scolded.

'It's a recording machine. Listen!'

Youngest Aunt was single and spent all her money on pleasure and gadgets like this. She played back the conversation we had just had and Laolao tried her best to look serious, but gave up when she heard her own voice: 'Who is that witch talking? That is not me.'

Youngest Aunt shrieked with delight. 'Let's sing a song and record it.' All the aunts loved singing, and Youngest Aunt was in the factory singing and dancing troupe. We sang, Youngest Aunt recorded it then played it back. We heard Laolao's voice telling us not to be so silly – 'look at the neighbours all watching us'.

I laughed with them, happy to be with my aunts. My Ma would never laugh like this. I wanted all of them to be my Ma.

Several passers-by stopped and watched us. Laolao noticed and shushed the aunts. I searched for Laoye's face. He still sat upright and I could not see his face clearly in the shadow. No sound came from him. Slowly, he rose up from his seat, dusted around his ankles and sighed. 'Come on, it's getting late. Second Daughter, you have to cycle to work tomorrow. Go home now.'

The next morning I lay in bed. Laoye was out selling cigarettes, and Laolao was shopping. I listened to the noises outside: bicycles, a neighbour washing up, somebody flushing their loo. I thought of Laoye. Before he had left in the morning, I reminded him of his promise to lend me the other classic novels he had mentioned. He said he had them somewhere, but couldn't put his finger on them. I stretched, yawned and decided to look for them myself. There were so many drawers in the room and they were all full of stuff, but maybe I would stumble across them. A drawer was half open. In it I found some thick old newspapers, and peered curiously at the date – 1958. The paper smelt salty and sandy, the way old newspapers do. I was about to put it back when my eyes caught what was wrapped inside it.

There were six copies of the same letter addressed to Chairman Mao in the handwriting I now knew so well. I blushed with excitement and a sense of doom. I read it, my ears cocked for movement from downstairs in case either of my grandparents came back and caught me. I understood even before I had finished reading, and only read on because I needed to confirm my fear. It was a letter appealing for mercy, for the crime of being a 'counter-revolutionary'. The calligraphy was beautiful, the tone fawning, that of a naughty child appealing to his parents. Smart Scholar, now a self-confessed 'class enemy', had been stripped of his dignity.

I wished I had never opened that drawer. I did not like what I had found there. I remembered the old shoe-mender around the corner from our primary school, how the bully-boys in my class had taunted him, and how I had stood by watching with pity. I remembered the old man staring straight at me. He had been a class enemy – one of those I was told to hate. But I felt no hate, only pity. Laoye was my hero – how could I pity my hero? I had always felt there was something mysterious about him – from Ma's nervous reaction to his arrival, to the rude way Youngest Aunt treated him. Now I knew.

Laoye came back, bubbling with his day's achievements, dusting his trousers. His eyes met mine and he asked if I had had a nice day. He even touched my head with his delicate fingers. I winced. I couldn't stand him now. I did not ask why he had been labelled a counter-revolutionary, I blamed him. I wanted him to be the hero I had worshipped, not this down-trodden old man. I wanted to be carefree, instead of being burdened with a class enemy as a relative.

He had committed the terrible crime of appearing dignified while being a fawner inside. I felt betrayed by the image of him in the letter. I should have admired his courage and sympathised with his suffering, but I was young and vain and knew no better. His suffering and humiliation added to my anger, as if he had created them himself. I despised him with as much cruel simple-mindedness as a fifteen-year-old girl was capable of.

The next day I walked to his stall licking my ice-cream. I checked his sales tally, and joked with the people who came along to buy cigarettes. He was unsuspicious and enthusiastic, explaining to me the methods he used to sell more. I interrupted him rudely. I saw surprise and hurt in his eyes, and enjoyed punishing him. When three off-duty policemen came over to buy from him, he moved excitedly to serve them, his voice rising, his eyes begging me to help with the change. I pretended I didn't understand and watched him apologising to the men for having given them the wrong money.

Laoye's return present to Ma and Ba was a whole card-board box of cigarettes, even though neither of them smoked. They could give them away as presents, he explained to me. 'Worth twenty yuan,' he boasted. On the truck, I sniffed at the offending smell, then kicked the box away as my tears dropped on the cardboard, which soaked them up.

In the late afternoon, the truck drove in the dust past the peasant woman's house and into my parents' block. Although I had been away only a week, it felt like years. I clutched the cigarette box and walked slowly towards home. I passed the board with Chairman Mao's words, and stopped. The setting sun shone its dying light on the words 'Never forget class struggle.' When he visited, Laoye had praised the calligraphy. I thought, with a shudder, how relevant the slogan was. My family were class enemies because my grandfather was a rightist, a Nationalist, a man with overseas connections. I had thought none of this had anything to do with me.

As I climbed up the stairs to my parents' third-storey flat, the strong, familiar smell of pork and chive dumpling came to me. I found it offensive, vulgar, and felt sick. Anger towards my parents rose inside me. They were to blame for this unwanted discovery. They had cheated me by not telling me about Smart Scholar.

Uncle Thunder caught me loitering outside the kitchen window holding the cigarette box. He called out to Ma, 'Look what your daughter has brought you from Sunny City!' I inched my way up to her. She looked radiant and loving, and smelt of my favourite meal. She gave me a motherly hug. Wrapped in the aroma of food and face cream, I felt a faint happiness – which was wiped out by a powerful pang of pain: this hug had come too late.

Chapter 7:

Lotus Blossom Stained

I felt driven to go back to Nainai's. I hitched a lift regularly to town with one of the drivers at Ba's work, all of whom I now knew well. Since my Sunny City trip my parents had trusted me to come and go to Nainai's on my own and even to stay a night there. 'You are a big girl, you should be able to look after yourself,' Ba had said. Nainai, delighted, had begun to expect me whenever a truck drove by. I always chose the big ones and stood at the open back like a peasant when I could have sat by the driver's seat. Nainai did not seem to grow old: her memory was as sharp as a knife – she remembered all my schoolfriends' names, and laughed at me for forgetting some.

On one autumn afternoon I went to Nainai's after school. The gutters were clogged with fallen leaves, and the road from my old school to Nainai's house was littered with sheets of black and white paper, some with red crosses. They danced in the wind as it swept them into the gutter to join the leaves. I walked past the goose house, surprised that I had to stoop down to look at my reflection in the window – if I did not bend, I could see only my legs. I must have grown, I thought. But the goose still loomed large in my memory.

Nainai was sweeping outside her house. I ran up and took the broom from her hands. 'What is this rubbish?' I asked, sweeping the papers into a heap with the leaves. Nainai watched me, smiled but did not speak.

When I had finished we went in. She gave me hot water to drink. I wandered about in the house, holding the cup to warm my cold hands. Tainainai's old room was now being redecorated. 'Your uncle is getting married,' Nainai said, behind me. 'This is going to be his room.' It was bare and painted white; the window with the view of the garden had been enlarged to let in more light. The air of mystery that I had attached to this room was gone, along with Tainainai, my storyteller.

We went to sit in Nainai's bedroom, where I felt more comfortable. Nothing here had changed. We sat on the big bed, and I put my head on Nainai's lap. She smoothed my long hair, which I wore in a plait. I looked up and saw Chairman Mao's portrait still there, faded now. 'You used to put my horse-manure tickets there.' I pointed at Yeye's framed certificates.

'Yes,' she said.

'I used to have so many of them. But, you know, I really did not do anything, it was Lotus Blossom who . . .'

'Ah, Lotus Blossom.' She sighed. I sat up.

'There was a public parade, just before you arrived. I'm surprised you didn't see it,' she said, holding my hand. 'Perhaps it's a good thing you didn't. Those bits of paper you saw, they were from the parade trucks. Lotus Blossom was on it, with her hair shaved, like a nun.'

I sat in Nainai's garden hugging my knees. My little bicycle leaned in Yeye's shed, rusted. The sunflowers Nainai had planted around the edge of her garden had bloomed, and now their heads were filled with seeds, the stalks the colour of gold, and dark brown leaves clung half-heartedly to them. I remembered the fun we had, Lotus Blossom and me, taking the heads off, rubbing out the ripened seeds with our palms. When a wriggly caterpillar fell into our hands we screamed. We watched the bowl fill with the black seeds, which still smelt of the sun when we took them inside to Nainai. We waited while Nainai fried them in the wok and the delicious smell made our mouths water. Then Lotus Blossom had had long hair like mine but, unlike mine, hers was always messy.

I tried to imagine Lotus Blossom without any hair, and could only see her as even more beautiful. It would show off her big eyes and high cheekbones. But a hairless woman, however striking, was not a desirable one. Only two types of women had their heads shaved: nuns and criminals, women in disgrace. Lotus Blossom, the flower that grew from the mud but should be stainless, had been stained.

She had been caught pilfering from a man after sleeping with him. Nainai recognised her even with her shaved head because she would not lower it like the rest of the criminals in the truck, all of whom were men. The young policeman kept pressing her head down, but she pushed it up again. A heavy board had been tied to her chest, weighing her down, with something written on it. Nainai had not been able to read it, but I could guess what it had said – I had seen parades like this before. It would have given her name, the crime she had committed, and perhaps her sentence.

Lotus Blossom, a thief and a broken-shoe – that was the word for a loose woman. What would be her sentence? Three years? Five?

I had no idea. She was only sixteen, a little older than me. Perhaps she would have been sent to a Youth Re-education Centre rather than prison. She should have been at school, doing her lessons, complaining about homework and her parents, sometimes feeling melancholic. But she was a truant, she had no parents, she had no home, and no time for melancholy because she had to survive.

'She is finished,' Nainai said. 'She has lost face, disgraced herself and her family. They will never be able to raise their heads in front of others. How could she do that to them?'

But she has no family left, I wanted to protest, then remembered. Nainai was not to know. I gazed at Nainai's hair, turning grey now but still smooth and shining. I knew I could never do wrong because it was not only I who would lose my honour but she too. To me, Nainai *was* the family whose face I must not tarnish, whose dignity I must preserve. I resolved never to forget that.

Nainai scrutinised me. 'You're getting fat, your mother is feeding you well.' She sounded jealous.

'I don't like her cooking at all, Nainai, I want to come back here, I want to eat your food all the time,' I said impulsively.

Nainai was shocked. 'Don't you say a thing like that.' She paused. 'Your mother knows what is best for you.'

Then she watched me eat the omelette she had prepared for me.

Shushu's wedding was held at Nainai's house, which took on a new lease of life as celebration filled each corner. The bride was a charming peasant girl.

I caught a distraught Nainai discussing plans for the house with Yeye. The town-planning department had decided to widen the road and change Nainai's building and others on the same road into high six-storey buildings. They had received a compensatory fee, and were temporarily housed in a shelter near the site. The money paid for Shushu's wedding. I stood beside Nainai when the bulldozer came in to flatten into a neat pile everything that had meant happiness and childhood to me. Watching the demolition made it easier to think about the future. I made my choice of university: on my application form I put 'Anywhere' to indicate that I did not mind being sent to other parts of China, although I believed that I would not be sent outside my own province.

Everyone panicked. A university degree guaranteed a respectable job for life and the competition was strong. Each time I did well on the mock tests, I felt as if I had pushed somebody else off the narrow path leading to a beautiful garden. We were all spurred on by our parents, whose ambitions for us made them ruthless. My day was timetabled both at school and at home so that I could cram in the maximum amount of revision. Even our trips to the toilet were limited to four a day.

The exam lasted three days. It was held in the Central Town Hall. Ba took me on his bicycle, with Ma sitting at the back, loaded with food. We set off early in the morning and saw others like us on bicycles – my fellow sufferers. Like everyone else we were two hours early. The queue went beyond the corner of the street. You'd think we were being sent to exile in Tibet from the look of our accompanying parents. Ambulances were parked outside the exam rooms, and white-uniformed doctors were chatting to each other. The sight of them scared me and my legs went wobbly. Police guarded the entrance and we were searched like criminals before we were allowed in. When I said goodbye to my parents, I felt as if I was leaving for the battlefield. I knew I could only win.

During the breaks, Ma stuffed me with boiled eggs and prawns, which she had bought on the black market. They were full of protein and good for the brain, she said.

I was constipated for the three days of the exam and did not eat eggs for a long time after that.

'How was it?' they asked, each time I finished a paper. Sometimes I responded frankly: 'Bad.' How could your performance not suffer under pressure like that? Their faces took on a doomed look. Sometimes I was more economical with the truth: I shrugged my shoulders and answered vaguely. It was as if they were the ones being examined, not me.

On the second day, I felt calmer, partly because I had got used to the sight of the doctors, partly because I was confident with the two subjects tested on that day – Chinese and English language. Strangely, the more nervous my parents got, the calmer I became.

I left the exam room early after I had completed the English, confident that I had done well. Ma and Ba were horrified. 'Did you check your answers?'

'Yes, three times,' I said impatiently.

'Did you hear,' Ma whispered, 'that one girl in another room fainted because she forgot to answer a whole page of questions? The ambulance took her away just now.'

'Are you sure you haven't forgotten to answer any questions?' Ba asked anxiously.

'No, I am not,' I tortured them.

Ma's face darkened and I stared back at her. Now I could afford to be less obedient. I knew I would be forgiven, that I could get away with anything. Just as I had predicted, Ba tugged at Ma's arm. 'Don't upset her. It will affect her mood. There's nothing she can do if she did miss any questions. She just needs to prepare well for the next subject.'

Ma brightened. 'Yes, have another egg,' she said eagerly.

The exam results were out sooner than I had expected. I went to Nainai's to open the letter. 'To the English Department, Yi Cheng University,' I read aloud, not believing it.

'Where is Yi Cheng?' Nainai asked frantically. Yeye got up and found the map. I studied it. 'Yi Cheng, Pleasant City, south of the Yangtze River, about 1,500 kilometres south of Beijing.'

THREE

'A Small Lotus Blossom Has Just
Shown Her Tiny Shoot'

Chapter 1:

To the South

Nobody in my extended family had ever been outside our province, let alone to a place as far south as Pleasant City. It was in the real South, the home town of Black Jade, my heroine from *The Dream of the Red Mansions*, a vast distance away: it was about 600 kilometres to Beijing, an overnight train journey, and from Beijing to Pleasant City was another day and a night on the train. I might as well have been sent to the moon. I trembled with excitement, but at night I could think only of how much I would miss Nainai and my parents, and my heart sank so low that it ached. What had I done? Why had I been so careless? Why hadn't I put: 'within this province only' on my application form?

It had been hard telling Nainai I was going so far away. She behaved as if she was never going to see me again. All my parents showed was delight that I had been accepted by a university. There was never any question that I might turn down the offer so that I could stay near them – it was too great an honour and too important for my future. My initial guilt at having almost planned this escape from them gave way to renewed anger at their lack of sadness at my imminent departure.

I leaned out of the train window, my eyes filled with tears. The late-summer sun had set and dusky light veiled everything with a thin mist. Until now my relatives had been

121

fussing over me on the train but now they had all got off and I was alone. Suddenly the distance to my destination seemed even greater. As the train started up I panicked, and for a moment I could not see them on the platform for the sea of waving hands and eager faces. Inside the carriage, sad parting tunes played over the Tannoy. I felt like a tree being uprooted. I blinked as tears rolled off my cheek, and saw Ma lower her head and lean on Ba, who held her in his arms. Was she crying? I imagined her tears and felt better.

Travelling was hard in China, and it always had been. The problem was distance. Poems of departure and homesickness flashed through my mind, but I could not grasp them, and fear took root. I was on my own: the older man was not an uncle, the older woman was not an aunt, the young people were not cousins. I was in a terrifying world of strangers. Some were less strange. Opposite me sat a couple going on honeymoon to Beijing. The girl heaved a deep sigh of relief that we were on our way. 'Only a thermometer for a present,' she sneered about an aunt. The young man saw my tears and pointed to a peeled apple. 'Want one?' In spite of myself I burst out laughing, and indicated my own gigantic food bags, which contained boiled eggs, biscuits, dumplings with different fillings, nuts, apples, grapes and lots of sunflower seeds.

At midnight the train stopped at Jiayu Pass, the furthest north pass of the Great Wall, which had once divided the North, where the 'barbarians' lived, from the capital, Beijing. I had been on the train for nearly ten hours. It was dark, but the station itself was well lit and full of people selling food. I slumped in my seat, sleepy yet excited. The young man opposite went to one of the stalls and chatted with the girl, who wore a white shop-assistant's uniform. She laughed and her white teeth glistened under the light. At the front of the train, the signalman stood alone before the darkness ahead. I felt vulnerable and small.

Many peasants boarded the train. They spoke with heavy

accents that made me think of Peking Opera. Suddenly it was full, and it was difficult to find a place for my feet among the luggage. A whistle blew, and the guards shoved the food-vendors off the train. A horn sounded. A man carrying huge baskets on a stick balanced across his shoulders leaped on from nowhere before the guards could stop him. No sooner had he got his balance than the train started to move. He put down his load and wiped the sweat from his forehead. I saw what he carried with him – downy yellow ducklings. One tried to escape, but the man picked it up gently and put it back into the basket. The light shone on the coarse hand that had held the soft wriggling duckling.

It was a hard night's sleep, if sleep you could call it. To be entitled to a student half-fare, I had to travel 'hard seat'. The peasant with the ducklings slept on the floor, face next to his basket, whose occupants had settled down. The loudspeaker, which had been on all evening, was turned off. Even the most enthusiastic card-players yawned and dozed. The train trundled into the darkness of the night, occasionally puffing and tooting loudly enough to wake the whole earth. As the night went on I drifted into sleep.

When the loudspeaker woke me up to announce 'Output of grain this year is three times what it was at the same time last year,' I thought I was at home with Nainai. There never was a year when grain production was reported to be lower than it had been the previous year. I remembered Great-uncle Forthright and Bright, who always spat at the news. 'Lies,' he would say bitterly. But things had changed since then: I was leaving the North just as life was beginning to improve. Preserved cabbage was no longer our only winter vegetable: the peasants were free to produce their own crops, which they could bring into town and sell. Each morning a group gathered just outside Ma and Ba's compound and sometimes, after furious haggling, Ma came back with some vegetables. I wondered what sort of food I would get in the South, and whether I would like it.

After the news, the train attendant announced that we were approaching Beijing. Standing in front of the dirty sink I examined my face. My every move was observed closely by a queue of people waiting impatiently to wash. I felt I had been transformed by the journey. It had made me more aware of myself, not as a daughter, a niece, a granddaughter, but as a person among strangers, with whom I had gradually become friendly. I thought of the young couple opposite me: we were not related but we had got along. I now had no choice but to move on, to meet strangers and befriend them. Was this part of what travelling was about?

I could no longer see the peasant with the ducklings. The honeymoon husband said the attendant had driven him off the train at the previous stop: peasants like him were not welcome in Beijing. I did not have long to feel sorry for him as I needed to obtain a transit ticket to my final destination. I squeezed through the crowd thronging out of the trains, and joined the transit queue outside the station. It was so long I could not see where it began. After two hours, it seemed to have moved backwards. I went up to the front and saw why. Crowds of people clustered around the window, pushing and jumping the queue. A young man in army uniform fought his way to the front – he reminded me of Shushu. I tugged at his sleeve, smiled sweetly and handed him my tickets: 'Please, I've got to catch the train to see my mother in Pleasant City. I haven't seen her for three years.' It worked. I got my ticket and, feeling shy, rushed away from him.

The gusty cold autumn wind of Beijing drove me into a restaurant selling dumpling soup. I had never eaten alone in a restaurant and I thought of Lotus Blossom. She of all my friends had eaten in restaurants, once in the Jade Light House, the most expensive restaurant in town, she had bragged. I had listened to her with envy. She could go in and order whatever she fancied, with her own money and some-times someone else's.

I clutched my purse tightly. It contained a collection of

money from all my relatives, including Great-uncle Forthright and Bright, who had been smiling and full of praise for a change. I was the first of my generation of the family to go to the university. I had 'gilded the family reputation', Nainai had said, amid her tears at my departure. My shoulders had felt heavy since that party, where I was praised but told to 'carry on setting a good example to your younger cousins'. As I mingled with strangers that weight had started to lift.

The restaurant was staffed by plump middle-aged women with pale fine skin. They shouted at the tops of their voices and were rude to bewildered travellers from all over the country who were not quick enough to understand their instructions. I sat down to join others who were slurping the hot dumpling soup. Soon I felt my energy return, and stretched like a cat. My first attempt at getting things done had been a success, and I congratulated myself on my cunning in obtaining the transit ticket. I was ready for more dealings with the big bad world.

Outside, streams of bicycles were passing, sounding their bells. How big and wide the bicycle tracks were, and how high the sky was in Beijing. I felt smug, and I felt free. For the first time I could decide when and where I went – I didn't need to tell anybody. Had I wanted to, I could have stayed in Beijing for ever. I had a list of contacts, my father's friends or friends of friends, in case things went wrong in the city, but having got my ticket stamped, I did not see any point in looking up any of these people, so I deposited my luggage and explored until the next train left that evening. I felt very small on the bus, jammed between two big Beijinese, who shouted to each other in the high-pitched nasal accent.

First I went to the Palace Museum, then to Beihai Park, but I did not enjoy them. I found the crowds oppressive and exhausting. It was in Tiananmen Square that I suddenly felt uplifted. People moved about slowly, took time to stop and look about them. A little boy flew a kite, an old man held his hand, a blond-haired foreigner took pictures of the old man and the child, and a colourfully dressed Mongolian watched the kite. The little boy did not know he was the object of so much interest. He attended to his kite.

I stood facing the huge portrait of Chairman Mao that hung down the front of the Tiananmen Building. It was the biggest picture of him that I had ever seen. I sang the song, like many others on their first journey to the square: 'I love the Heavenly Peace Gate [Tiananmen] in Beijing; the sun rises above it, our great leader Chairman Mao leads us on the way forward.'

On the train to Pleasant City, we crossed the big muddy Yellow River, which flowed down from the Yellow Earth Plateau. I had left the North, and with it my past and my childhood. I looked down at the river and thought of a line of Tang poetry: 'I cannot see any forefathers, nor any followers, thinking of the eternity of the universe; I alone shed tears.' I felt curiously heartened by my melancholy – it was such a grown-up feeling. Leaving my home town physically had created an emotional space where I could feel independently. I was homesick no more.

I spent a restful night on the train. When I woke up, the view outside the window told me that I was in the South. It was a different world: unlike the bleak North, it was green and lush, the fields cultivated. The people I glimpsed wore straw hats, and stood knee-deep in water, working, chatting, straightening up to see the passing train in the strong sunlight. As we went on, flat plains rolled ahead as the rocky mountains of the North receded. Lake after lake stretched before us, like mirrors reflecting the gentle green hills surrounding them.

I listened to the voices around me. This was a new accent, full of sibilants, making the voices softer, especially those of the women. I closed my eyes and felt as if I was in an aviary.

The ticket collector came to inspect my ticket. She smiled and tugged at my thick coat. She had spotted me as a typical northerner. I stripped the coat off, stretched and breathed deeply. My future lay ahead, like the tracks of the train. Where would it lead me? I felt like a young bird with new wings, ready for the blue sky above. I longed to soar.

At the station I persuaded a taxi driver to take me to the university. I could not understand a word he said until, what felt like hours later, he stopped in front of a shabby-looking gate. Then he made himself perfectly clear: 'Forty-five yuan,' he said, in a clear, standard accent, staring at me blankly. He sounded like a different man. I knew I was being ripped off, but I gave him the money – I was too tired to argue and if I had he would have started talking unintelligibly again.

I was escorted by a fat woman in slippers along a boulevard of trees with scented white flowers whose name I did not know. The branches extended a generous canopy of green leaves that sheltered us from the scorching afternoon sun. The pavement was patterned by the light that filtered through the leaves. We were accompanied all the way by insects chorusing in a tone I had not heard before. The air was thick with unfamiliar scents: the sweetness of the flowers, my own sweat, and something edible, which came and went with the breeze. The woman beside me yawned; she had been woken from her afternoon nap. A huge bunch of keys dangled at her waist, and she waved a big fan.

We walked in silence through the stifling heat. She took me to an old four-storey brick building. We entered the hall. I was struck by the sudden darkness after the brightness of the burning sunshine outside. The dark corridor seemed to extend for ever. We reached the furthest end and the woman stopped, opened a door and gestured to me to go in. Then, without a word, she walked away slowly, fanning herself.

I put down my luggage and observed my new room. It was narrow, longish, with four beds and four sets of tables and chairs. Three of the beds were already made up, with mosquito nets hanging over them, and the tables were spread with books, mirrors and hair brushes. The room smelt of face cream and incense. It was daunting to realise that I was going to share my living space with three other girls. For the last five years I had had my own little room, and now I had to live cheek by jowl with strangers. Would we get on? I hoped they didn't snore, like Ba.

As I started unpacking, the door was pushed open from the outside by a short, plump girl with wet hair and rosy cheeks. 'Hi, are you new?' I noticed her heavy southern accent and it took me a little time to adjust to it. 'Yes, I am Li Taotao.' I said.

The rosy-cheeked girl immediately switched to a not-so-perfect Putonghua – standard Chinese based on northern dialect: 'Ah, you are the Beijing girl.'

'I am not from Beijing, I am from the North.'

'You are the Beijing girl, then. I am Hair. This is my bed, next to yours. We are neighbours.' She pointed at the top bunk where a furry toy rabbit sat grinning at me.

I didn't have a mosquito net, so I spent the first half of the night fighting off the troops of attacking insects. They came in swarms and swirled around me like a fleet of enemy planes. After fighting in vain for hours, I broke down in tears. Hair's arm emerged from her mosquito net, and she murmured, 'Come inside my net.' I crept in without a word and fell asleep almost immediately.

Chapter 2:

'A Young Lotus with First Shoot Attracts Dragonflies'

T he next day Hair and I went to buy a mosquito net. When we returned, the other girls had arrived and the dormitory was noisy and lively. Hair knew them all so she performed the introductions. Willow, a lean, tall girl and good friend of Hair's, came from the countryside. Admiration of Rainbows was from a county town. She was a Party Member candidate. She liked to wear red, so that was what everybody called her. She smiled proudly as she was introduced and tilted her head on her long straight neck.

Hair took me to the college canteen. There were a lot of noodle dishes, and vegetables that were new to me. The rice was awful, coarse and difficult to digest, unlike the fragrant rice at home that I could eat without any accompaniment. I shouted to the man at the counter in my newly acquired Pleasant City accent, 'Rice noodle with pork and lotus root,' and he grinned. He gave me a lot. I told Hair, who stood behind me, not to get anything as I had enough to share with her. Red ate alone, which I thought strange. I would have felt so self-conscious on my own in a huge hall.

We were walking slowly back to the dormitory with our food bowls when a football shot straight into my bowl and knocked it to the ground. Hair laughed, and I glared at her crossly. A tall thin boy in trainers and a blue cap came running up to me, red-faced. 'Sorry,' he said, scratching his neck. I looked down at my new skirt; an oily stain had appeared just above the hem. He picked up my bowl, and held it out to me. I stared at him but refused to take it. 'Sorry,' he murmured again, in a low voice, glancing from me to his team-mates, who were waiting for him to retrieve the ball. I did not want to spoil their fun but nor did I want to let him get away with his mistake too easily, so I kept my eyes fixed on him, while his face got redder and redder.

'Steel! Look what you've done!' Hair exclaimed, playfully. Then she turned to me. 'Taotao, this is Steel, famous for being the clumsiest boy in our college. Forgive him this time. Look how he's blushing – if there were a hole in the ground he'd slip into it.'

I laughed and took the bowl from him. Steel scratched his neck again and smiled first at Hair then sheepishly at me. 'Don't worry about it,' I said, waved at him and walked away with Hair.

'The clumsiest boy I have ever known,' Hair continued her description of Steel as we entered our dormitory, 'but also the cleverest.'

After lunch all the girls in my dormitory crept under their nets for a siesta. As southerners, this was their habit. I stood by the window, too excited to sleep. It was open and the thick new smells of the South wafted in, that heady mixture of flowers, sweat and cooking. In the North the air was clear as water, refreshing and calming: this new smell made me restless, made me wonder. The playground was abandoned; even the most enthusiastic athletes had given up their games. The insects sang busily on the trees, the sound appealing to me. Our room was damp, on the dark side of the building, which intensified the aroma of the face creams.

I turned to look at our little room. My desk was still bare – I hadn't had time yet to unpack properly. Willow's was elaborately arranged: there was a small round hand mirror, with pictures of the flower-beds of Tiananmen Square on the back, a framed picture of herself dressed in a long skirt –

obviously taken in a studio, and a small glass that contained a branch of laurel blossom she had picked from the tree outside, which gave off a strong scent. Her drawer was locked – I guessed that she kept a diary in there. She seemed that kind of girl.

I walked past her desk and began to unpack. I tried to be quiet, but even the smallest movement sounded noisy in the prevailing peace of the afternoon. I heard people toss and turn and felt self-conscious. Finally I climbed up to my own bed, and stared at the new mosquito net. It was pink, the last one in the shop. I rather liked it, although Hair had said it would seem odd; she had insisted the shop assistant look for a white one, which they failed to find. Now I saw her point. Everyone else's was white and mine stood out, but the pinky-peach colour for a girl called Peaches seemed appropriate.

Red's bed was opposite mine. Her net was the whitest in our room. It wasn't the newest, though, because it looked worn from washing. Now I saw how practical the nets were: they fended off insects but also gave us a little privacy.

A bell rang for afternoon lessons. Red coughed, Willow moaned, Hair cursed, and I laughed, despite myself.

I was punished for not sleeping during the siesta: all afternoon I yawned and had a hard time keeping my eyes open. When I was called to comment on the theme of the poem 'The Peacock Flies South-East', my brain went blank. Steel, who sat a row ahead of me, scribbled something on the back of his textbook then lifted it up for me to see. 'Exposing feudal filial piety,' I read aloud, as if I was in a dream.

'Good, sit down,' the teacher said.

After the class I walked back with Steel. In the shadow of the trees his face appeared darker. As southerners, they were all darker than me, but Steel looked almost like an Indian, with his deep-set eyes and full mouth. 'I hope I haven't spoiled your lovely dress,' he said, pointing at my skirt – the same one I had worn in the morning when he had shot his football at my bowl.

131

'I had to scrub it hard, but the stain came out. And things dry so quickly here, it's amazing.' I smiled. 'Thanks for rescuing me today.'

'Oh, it was nothing. It's silly, isn't it, that we have to bother with this really basic stuff? It's hardly higher education.'

'Yes,' I responded eagerly. 'That's why I drifted off, you see.' I was anxious that he should understand that I had known the answer to the question. I added, 'I can recite practically the whole poem.'

'Really? That's better than me.' He paused. 'How many Tang poems can you recite?'

'Well, about fifty.'

'I can do about a hundred.'

'I don't believe you.'

'Try me.'

We dared each other and he won.

I had no idea when and how we ended up at the West Lake. Steel led the way – he seemed to know the geography of the college well, although we had been there such a short time.

The West Lake surrounded our college. It was one of the many lakes I had glimpsed from the train – the first and most constant reminder that I was in the South. Now I was right beside it. Black and white spotted cows grazed on the bank, and a man lay asleep in a little wooden boat in the middle of the water, surrounded by umbrella-like cool green leaves and giant pink lotus blossoms. It was picturesque. I sat down and Steel sat next to me. 'A young lotus has just shown her tiny shoot,' I murmured. 'Already there is a dragonfly standing on it.' Steel continued the poem with a slight accent.

'I know a real Lotus Blossom,' I said. 'She is a girl from my home town in the North, but her family is from the South.'

'What happened to her?'

'She . . .' I glanced at him cautiously. 'She got stained. She stole things and she slept with men.' I was amazed to find myself talking so frankly with a boy. I had always been shy with boys, but not with Steel. We talked as if we were not boy and girl but two people who had much to say to each other, who had much in common, who were friends. Friends. I had a new friend. I stared at the lake as joy spread through me.

There was no embarrassment or reserve in Steel. 'You were close, were you?' he asked.

'We were. I haven't seen her since . . . since she was paraded in public.' I hadn't seen that, but Nainai's description of it had been so vivid that I felt as if I had been there myself.

'But she is still a friend in your heart, because you still care for her.'

I nodded, speechless now. A big cow sauntered over, eating grass next to me. I turned to Steel. 'Lotus Blossom should be here, blossoming, living. Instead she is in some cold damp room, rotting. She stole and she slept with men, but what else could she do? She was an orphan, she had nowhere to go, no one to care for her. It's so unfair.'

'Life is not fair,' he said, and stood up.

At dusk we went back to the campus. On the way I learned that his father was a Chinese literature teacher at a middle school and had made Steel recite Tang poems since he was five, which was why he was so good at it. The afternoon was hazy with the heat. There had been no sunset but the cloud had darkened. We parted with a casual wave, but as I stepped into my damp corridor and stood still to adjust to the darkness, I felt as if I had unexpectedly found treasure.

For many days after our lakeside walk, I woke in the afternoon and couldn't remember where I was. The murmur of the southern accents and the fragrance of laurel blossoms puzzled me, then something would remind me of Steel, the thought of his gentle voice reciting a line of a Tang poem would bring a smile to my face. So many of the Tang poets were from this part of China: perhaps one of his ancestors had composed one of the poems for which we shared such affection.

On the night of the Mid-Autumn Festival, a Friday, I hid under my mosquito net and cried. I was pining for home. Mid-Autumn Festival had never meant much to me back in the North – the moon was full in the sky yet I never bothered to look at it – but today we had a party to celebrate it. The dean of the department said he hoped we would not be homesick at this special time. I thought he was referring to me, because I had come the furthest, and I was given two mooncakes instead of one. At the time it felt like a treat, but lying under my net peeping through the holes at the full moon I felt worse. I remembered Laoye's poems, the departure poem and the moon poem. I got out my Tang poetry book.

In the next bed, Hair was talking to Willow in their dialect about an outing to the town centre they were making on Sunday. I felt excluded and resented Hair for her betrayal – although I had known her only a few weeks, I already thought of her as my exclusive friend.

The light was switched off at eleven o'clock. After a moment of darkness, everyone lit a candle under their net. We kept to ourselves and did our own things: I read, Hair knitted and Willow wrote her diary. Red did not light a candle: her net was always dark. At times I heard her snore gently. I was curious about her: she was a friend to everyone, and no one in particular. Anyone could ask her for a small favour – 'buy lunch on your way back for me' and 'save a seat for me at the lecture' – without feeling obliged to return it. She was always happy to help by 'doing good deeds', which she was required to perform as a party candidate. She swept the dormitory floor on Sundays when the rest of us were either away or catching up on a week's sleep.

I was the last to blow out my candle. After a while I opened my eyes and saw a moonbeam seeping into the room through the window. 'Moonlight in front of my bed, I took it for frost on the ground. Lifting up my head I saw the moon, it reminded me of home.' My thoughts drifted to Steel: I was sure he knew this poem, written by my favourite Tang poet, Li Bai, about homesickness.

In the morning music blared from the loudspeaker down the corridor, and another day had begun. I groaned and did not want to get up. Red's face emerged from her net. She looked refreshed. 'Hurry up, it's morning exercise time.' She woke everyone in turn – it was just as well that we had someone to nanny us. I yawned and joined the toothbrushing queue.

We ran three circuits of the campus, which I quite enjoyed – it was the coolest part of the day. When we were praised for being there on time, we all looked at Red, who smiled proudly.

In the postroom I picked up two letters. One was from Shushu about Nainai's new flat. They had moved into the second floor of the new building, and it was clean, big and shiny. The letter said I should not miss home and Nainai wanted me to concentrate on my studies. But I knew she would not be happy in the new building – she had always been happiest in the garden, which no longer existed. The other letter was from Ma: Uncle Thunder, our neighbour, had been taken away by armed police one morning and charged with killing a man during the armed riots of the sixties. Ma said he was also charged with inciting violence and being a supporter of the 'Gang of Four' during the Cultural Revolution. The news was shocking, even though I had known about the killing since I was a child: I had never thought of him as a bad man.

The letters intensified my homesickness, and the southern accent seemed alien and offensive. I avoided Hair, and didn't wait for her to come to lunch with me. In the evening I bumped into her in the washroom. 'Taotao!' she cried. 'Why didn't you wait for me for lunch? I looked for you everywhere.'

Water dripped from the tip of her nose, her shirt clung to her and her hair was wet. She looked like a puppy, and I laughed. 'Why should I wait for you when you're going to town without me?'

'What?'

'Tomorrow. You're going to town with Willow.'

'Oh, that.' She turned off the tap. 'You silly thing, I was going to ask you to come along when we met at lunchtime today. I thought you were asleep last night. There was no sound from your net.'

'I was homesick.'

'Why didn't you say?' She put her arms round my shoulders and drew my face to hers, close to the horrible smell of her face cream and to her soft, smooth skin.

We set off after a lie-in. There was no morning exercise on Sunday – a treat. A man on the bus leaned too close to Hair and she screamed, 'A pervert! A pervert touched me!'

Willow and I rushed to her. 'Where is he? Who is he?' Our eyes finally settled on the man. He was red-faced and jumped off at the next stop. I was pleased with our power. Walking hand in hand with Willow and Hair, I felt as if we were sisters. We climbed the tallest pagoda to view the city and the Yangtze River. Willow recited a poem, Hair screamed with exhilaration and I looked on. A blind fortune-teller squatted beside us and shouted, in a coarse voice, 'Come and have your fortune told.'

We returned to our dormitory at dusk. Willow reached for her mirror and shrieked. 'Cockroaches!' She fled the room. The whole corridor stirred. Hair got a broom to open Willow's desk gingerly and found two huge cockroaches, one crawling past Willow's diary and another beside her handkerchief. She yelped, and we all joined in. No matter how we cajoled and dared each other, none of us could bring ourselves to go near the cockroaches. Eventually Red, brave and practical as ever, put on a pair of gloves and took the desk to the washroom. She sprayed the cockroaches down the drain.

Laughing hysterically, Hair and I packed to go to the college bathroom to wash off the sweat of the day's travelling. She was good at rubbing, just like Ma. Everything about her body was round: big round breasts, firm thighs, and a round, smiling face. I rubbed her back, though she complained that I only tickled her. Her breasts, soft and pink like two ripe fruits, heaved up and down in the hot steam as she giggled. I admired her curvy body and sensed she had had experiences that I could only guess at.

On the way back we sang, Hair's voice loud and high, mine low and soft. Before we got to the dormitory building she stopped, her face glowing in the dark. 'I like your voice and your accent. Do all northern girls speak like that?'

'I don't know. I like the southern accent, it's so soft.'

'No, really, everybody in our class adores your accent, and your voice, like a silver bell.' She paused, then giggled. 'Or, in Steel's words, "*zizheng qiangyuan* – words square and tone smooth".'

'What did Steel say to you about me?'

'Just that. He said your voice reminded him of flutes and nightingales . . . and . . .'

'And what?'

'Frogs.' She ran off up the stairs, with me in hot pursuit.

Somehow, she reminded me of Lotus Blossom – had Lotus Blossom been born into a different family, in a different place.

Chapter 3:

Lucy in the Foreign Experts' Building with a Double Bed

―――――◆―――――

In the middle of the term, a pretty Englishwoman, Lucy – the first foreign teacher we had had – came to take the English-conversation class. I saw her standing on the staircase in a bright red skirt. The weather had turned cold so we had all started wearing trousers and it was refreshing to see a skirt. She was young and walked fast, like the wind. She introduced a type of class called 'the seminar' and made us all choose English names. I chose Jane, as in Jane Eyre. Hair became Cleopatra, and Red was Elizabeth, like the Queen of England. Steel called himself Shelley. Others were Shortman, Whiteman and Longman. As she read the list Lucy giggled.

In the seminar, we held discussions. Lucy was full of whys. One Friday she asked us to come to her flat in the afternoon for a chat, but we couldn't come because we had to do 'Friday voluntary works'. Lucy couldn't understand this. 'But surely you don't need to go if it's voluntary?'

'Well,' we told her, 'it may be called that, but we really don't have any choice.'

'But why?' she asked. It was her refrain.

She asked us to teach her Chinese, but she was not a good student. We taught her phrases and made her repeat them, then laughed at her accent. She got upset and frustrated, but we told her this was the Chinese way – it meant that we thought of her as one of us.

Once she came to see us in our dormitory, when a girl from two doors down was arguing with another girl about some missing shirts, using colourful language. We all came out to watch. Lucy asked me to translate what they were saying, and laughed and laughed. More girls came out to watch the argument and the giggling foreigner, and soon the whole building stirred. Hair and I stood beside Lucy and laughed with her.

When Red came out, she said to Lucy, 'Please go away, and don't laugh at those girls making fools of themselves. Their behaviour is a disgrace to we Chinese people.'

'But I am learning Chinese,' Lucy protested solemnly. 'This is my listening exercise.' Hair and I burst into still more giggles, and I decided Lucy was fun.

Lucy said she would organise a party, and that we should all come dressed as the characters we were named after. 'Cleopatra,' she pointed at Hair, 'should come in a long robe,' and 'Elizabeth should wear a crown.'

I helped Hair to make her robe from two scarves. Red wore a paper crown, which made her look ridiculous, with a beautiful red blouse. I put on a traditional cloth-buttoned blue jacket that I had stolen from Nainai – Jane Eyre Chinese-style.

Lucy lived at the Foreign Experts' Building, overlooking the West Lake. By Chinese standards her flat was spacious. She lived by herself and had a bedroom, a bathroom, a kitchen and a sitting room. Once a week a woman came to clean for her. I knew this was her privilege as a foreign expert, but it made her seem bourgeois to me. I envied her the space.

At the party, she wore a dress that bared her shoulders and her long blonde hair fell on them like a waterfall: she seemed dazzlingly glamorous. Sometimes we dressed up for the balls held by the department, and as the foreign-language students were reputedly the prettiest girls in the college, we received all sorts of invitations to other departmental parties. But our dressing up did not involve long gowns of the sort that Lucy wore. She was like some TV actress. At first we couldn't relax: we huddled in a corner and watched the seniors chatting in English, seemingly at ease, in the centre of the room. The only English we could bring ourselves to utter was our names: 'Jane, Elizabeth, Cleopatra. Oh, look at you, Mr Darcy.'

'Shelley, you are standing on my toes,' Hair squawked.

In the end, though, we conquered our nerves, and had a hilarious – if slightly hysterical – time. We didn't stop gossiping and laughing about it for days. Steel was the only one not impressed: he hadn't enjoyed the party. I had seen him there, aloof and embarrassed, unsure whether to hold his glass with one hand or two. He told me later he had thought it was a waste of time, and such a decadent thing to do. When Lucy talked to him, he blushed and spoke to the ground.

Another snub came from our political teacher, Teacher Yan. Once a month we gathered together for a political briefing. It was very boring and predictable, so much so that it was quite safe to let your mind wander or be doing something else at the same time, as long as you appeared to be listening. The briefing took the form of a lecture and we were never asked to say anything.

I stared at Teacher Yan. She was not bad-looking, but why did she always wear the same white shirt? Did she perhaps have ten of them all in the same style? It always looked perfectly clean, but I knew I wouldn't last a day in white. How did she do it? And her hair was so short and bluntly cut you wondered if she had noticed that she had hair at all.

One day she had come to inspect our dormitory, and had seen my mosquito net. 'Why is this one pink?' she demanded. Although proud of it, I had enough political sense to tell her that I had needed one in a hurry and pink was the only colour they had had left.

Red, who had accompanied Teacher Yan on her inspection, rushed up to explain. 'Taotao is from the North. She did not realise there would be so many mosquitoes here.'

Teacher Yan softened. 'Taotao, let me know if there is anything you need. We are all one big family here and we should help each other.'

I must have looked especially faraway at this briefing, for Teacher Yan asked to see me after class. Oh, horror. I watched my classmates walking past and felt trapped. When Steel went past me, he shot me a concerned glance. But I need not have worried: it was just a lecture. I should be more open with my ideology, she said, and show solidarity with the wider mass of classmates, not just a narrow circle of people. We must show respect to foreign guests, but remember who we are. In dealing with them we must be neither fawning nor arrogant. 'Your academic record is excellent,' she said, 'but politically you are not very active. To be an expert academically is not good enough. One has to be red too. Both red and expert, that is the sort of student we require.'

I wondered how one became active politically. It would be too much to shout slogans, surely, but perhaps she was asking me to do as Red did, and here I guessed right. As if she was reading my mind, she nodded. 'You should learn from Admiration of Rainbows. She is both red and expert. A model student.'

I decided there and then to do deliberately badly in my studies so that I wouldn't be accused of being a 'white' academic worm.

No one talked enough in Lucy's class, and today she was cross. She didn't realise that for us silence was a way to show respect: she thought it rude and was offended. I decided to go and see her after class to explain. She wasn't in. The fat woman at Reception took down my name, the time and the purpose of my visit before she let me into the building. I was sure she knew Lucy wasn't in and only went through the formalities to annoy me. I did not give up: I took a walk around the West Lake, and went back an hour later. This time Lucy was in. But she was not alone: she was with an American man. After I had explained the purpose of my visit

she was pleased to see me. She turned to the man: 'This is my
star student, Jane. She has the best brains and an excellent
English accent.' I felt self-conscious and instantly failed to
understand what the American said to me.

They both laughed, and he said kindly: 'It must be my
accent.' Lucy started talking very fast to the American, and as
I couldn't understand them, I felt unwelcome and left.

In the South in autumn the leaves did fall but the campus
was still green. When December came, and it was cold, I was
surprised and depressed. After the scorching hot summer, I
had assumed that winter here would be mild. Of course, it
was not as cold as it was in the North, where water froze and
we wore thick coats, but here it was a different kind of cold,
an insidious cold, a cold that penetrated your skin, your
bones, and chilled you to the soul. I became homesick again
and missed the straightforward snow-white iciness of the
North. As we were south of the Yangtze River here, we did
not qualify for indoor heating, which in the North I had taken
for granted. We sat in our beds with quilts around us and
shivered.

One freezing afternoon I struggled out of bed to the library.
Lucy cycled past me. 'Jane, there you are.' She stopped,
perched on the seat, with one foot on the ground – it was
easy for her to sit like that with her long, foreigner's legs. 'I
would like you to come to my Christmas party.' I remembered the last time I had been at her flat and shook my head.
'Oh, come on, don't disappoint me. You must. I've only
invited those whose English is good enough. You're the only
one from your grade,' she insisted, her large brown eyes
squinting in the sun.

I went along without telling anyone in my class. As no one
else had been invited, I felt somehow as though I was
betraying them in going alone. But I was flattered by the
invitation: Lucy valued me, and I wanted to find out more
about this glamorous girl from the country whose literature I
had read so much of.

It was nice and warm in Lucy's flat. Many English students from other colleges were there. At first I wasn't sure I felt comfortable, but eventually I relaxed. In fact, I was the last to leave. I helped Lucy to carry all the plates to the kitchen, and offered to help her with the washing-up. 'No, don't bother, the cleaning lady will do it.' Again I felt the distance between us. I wanted to leave, but she stopped me. 'Can you stay a little while to chat?' She looked at me imploringly.

We sipped tea she made especially for me and she lit a cigarette. She told me about Oxford. 'It's a great city,' she said. 'You will like it there.' She sounded so sure that I would visit it one day. She showed me a photograph of herself underneath an arch. 'That's Oxford,' she said.

When I heard the clock strike twelve, I stood up abruptly. 'Oh, no!' Our dormitory gate was closed at eleven every night. 'Don't worry, you can stay the night here,' Lucy said casually. I thought, Why not? She was not a man, so surely it could do no harm. It would be nice to carry on chatting like this in bed, as Hair and I did all the time.

Lucy emerged from the bathroom wearing a silk nightdress. 'Would you like a bath? I'm running you one,' she said. Steam swirled out of the bathroom behind her, as if we were in a film set, with her the star.

I stared at the bath. It was fragrant, bubbly, foamy. I couldn't see the water. I put in one foot, then the other. It was such an odd experience. I sat upright and could not get over how strange I felt. Then it occurred to me that it was the first time in my life that I had had a bath alone. It made me stare at my body – I was suddenly so aware of it. Did Lucy stare at hers every day?

I had wanted to ask her more about England, about Oxford, but when I came out of the bath, Lucy was already in bed. It was a double bed, and I felt uneasy at sleeping in it. My proximity to her forced on me an intimacy that I found embarrassing. I could smell her scent. Soon she snored gently, but I tossed and turned. The moon shone on her body, enveloped in the soft silk. By comparison my skin seemed unfeminine and coarse. I missed the warm, familiar ritual of my dormitory. Eventually I fell into an uneasy sleep.

In the morning, I slipped away before Lucy woke and tiptoed past the fat receptionist's window. Her curtain was drawn. As I stepped outside, the cool air from the West Lake refreshed me. I took a short walk around it to clear my head. I was puzzled by my feelings towards Lucy. I realised that I liked living between worlds, and I wanted to have a taste of the unknown. Lucy represented the femininity and sophistication I was curious to experience, but when she had shown them to me, I had run away. I was like Lord Ye, who loved only false dragons.

The next day, at the political lesson, I daydreamed as usual. Teacher Yan's voice, piercingly loud, served as an inharmonious background. I heard the words 'sleeping with a foreigner' and looked up. She avoided my eyes and continued, '. . . corruption and bourgeois liberalism. I won't name names, but let the person be ashamed! Think of where you stand – sleeping with a foreigner.' She sounded indignant. Blood shot to my temples. Did she mean me? Had it been a crime to stay at Lucy's apartment? It had nothing to do with Teacher Yan. Conditioned to think only in terms of 'Chinese and foreigner relationships' or 'man and woman relationships', she was incapable of understanding the subtlety of the situation. I felt sorry for her.

Still, I didn't understand the mixed feelings I had towards Lucy. It was not as if there was anything wrong in sleeping with a woman: I slept in Hair's bed all the time. Whenever I felt homesick or lonely, I just crawled into her bed and had a good cry. Sometimes she came into my bed. It meant nothing. Perhaps I was too curious: crowds gathered in town to watch a big-nose foreigner's every movement and pinched his skin to see if it hurt, but I went deeper – I wanted their souls, I wanted to see what they were like inside.

My heart was heavy: I knew that my personal file, which would follow me wherever I went in life, would now be marred with a black dot. Teacher Yan, with a sinister twist of her pen, would have written, 'This person slept with a foreigner.'

Chapter 4:

'Dear Jane, I Love You'

I did not tell anyone, not even Hair, that I had spent the night with Lucy. No one suspected anything, and I puzzled over how Teacher Yan had known about it. Had I been reported by the woman at the door of Lucy's flat, or someone in my dormitory? It could only be Red, the Party Member candidate. But she did not look guilty and kept her impeccable smile.

On the last day of term I met Steel outside the library. I had just got out a copy of the Bible. During the night I had spent at her flat, Lucy had told me to borrow a Bible and read it, or part of it, over my winter vacation. 'You don't have to believe in God to read it. It's a very good book in its own right. Good for your English anyway.' She winked at me, then added, 'Which is already excellent.'

The Bible had been donated to our college by an American missionary group and had lain ever since in the library collecting dust. I was its first reader, and the librarian had peered at me suspiciously as I took it from him.

'What's that big thick book you're holding?' Steel asked. There was a gaiety in his tone that I associated with the end of the term.

'The Bible,' I said proudly.

He made a face. 'You're going to read that on your train journey home?'

I nodded – I wasn't sure that I was but I hoped it would impress him.

'I hope your family is well,' he said, sounding like an elder brother rather than a fellow student.

'Same to you,' I felt obliged to say.

'It will be cold now in your home town, won't it?' he continued.

'Yes,' I replied. I thought of the knee-deep snow and realised how much I had missed the fresh crisp air. 'The snow is wonderful. I wish you could see it. Hair told me it hardly ever snows here.'

'Almost never. When it does, which is rare, it's thin like dust. But I know that in the North . . .'

' "The snowflakes on Yan Mountain are as big as mats." '

We spoke the line simultaneously, then looked at each other and laughed.

'Goodbye, then.' I waved my Bible.

'Goodbye,' he said. Then he did a curious thing: instead of turning away, he glanced around, then stepped up close to me and pushed an envelope into my hand. 'Something else for you to read on the train.' He hurried away without looking back.

I guessed what it was: another poem he wanted to share with me. We had often done this since we discovered our mutual interest in Tang poems. Hair used to laugh at us and said we acted like KGB agents. I put the envelope inside the Bible, thinking what interesting company they made for one another. Then I went off to do last-minute shopping. This was my first trip back, so presents from the South were essential: local Pleasant City honey for Nainai; a packet of peanut sweets that I liked for Ma, and a key-ring I had bought at the Buddhist tower with an inscription for Ba.

On the train to Beijing I opened the envelope under the nosy gaze of a curious old man sitting next to me. I had to push myself further into the seat to get away from his prying eyes. 'Dear Jane,' it said. 'I have searched long and hard for a poem to express my feelings but have failed. All I can say is I feel deeply for you and hope you feel the same for me. I would like to be your boyfriend. Your good friend, Shelley. PS If you are not ready to talk about love, I can understand. Please don't hurry your answer as I can wait.'

My face burned as I folded the letter. I caught the eyes of the old man and felt as though he could see through the page. I stood up and pushed my way through the queues of people standing wearily with heavy loads. Finally I found a solitary place, the freezing space between two carriages. I leaned on the rocking door and read the letter again. A love letter. To me. From Steel, of all people. My friend, wanting to be more than that. I put my hands to my cheeks. Confusion was all I felt, mingled with a sense of pride that someone liked me enough to want to be my boyfriend. Did I feel love for him? I had no idea. I did not know what love was. I liked him, yes, but love? What was love? I had heard the word 'boyfriend' mentioned only once by Lotus Blossom. Had hers written letters to her? I suspected not.

I spent a long time in the freezing space rereading the letter and thinking things over. A ticket collector found me there and demanded to see my ticket. I told him I had left it on my seat. He followed me back suspiciously. A plump middle-aged woman had settled there and was asleep. The ticket collector nudged her rudely, and she opened her eyes, sighed and stood up reluctantly. I snatched my bag, flattened by her fat bottom, and handed the man my ticket. He checked it, nodded and left without a word. The old man sitting opposite opened his eyes and spoke to me for the first time: 'My child, if I were you I wouldn't leave my bag lying about like that. You can't be too careful when you travel, you know.' I was grateful for his concern – I had been careless. 'What is it that fascinates you in that big thick book, then?' he asked.

'It's the Bible.' He opened his eyes wide. 'In English,' I added.

His eyes opened wider still, and he whispered, 'I didn't know it was allowed.'

'Of course it is allowed. I borrowed it from our college library.'

'So, can you read it, then? Your English must be good.'

'Well, I'm trying my best,' I said modestly.

The old man said he had been a pupil at a Christian school in Shanghai, that he knew the Bible, and he told several stories from it. Soon he attracted the attention of other passengers and they listened to him attentively. By the time we got to Beijing we had extended the storytelling to Chinese ghost stories. I loved the train, and was reluctant to get off it. This, my second train journey, had not only run smoothly, but entertainingly. There was much that strangers could give each other that families couldn't.

But I had missed the food at home. I had missed my parents, and Nainai terribly. My first stop was at Nainai's and Yeye's new flat. She seemed happy in it, and she was pleased with the honey I had bought her, but told me off for wasting my money. Ma seemed to have aged. I asked her about Uncle Thunder, but she shook her head silently and took me to see his wife, who had shrunk even more and feared to go out now. Rude children followed her around and sneered at the 'murderer's wife'.

Within a week or so of getting home, I had had enough and wanted to leave again. Ma still scolded me as though I was a child and I no longer wanted to retreat to the toilet to sulk. I argued back, which incensed her, and Ba had to intervene. In the end I went to stay with Nainai. There, I lay in bed persevering my new book: the Bible.

Lucy was right. It was a good book. It read as if it was an epic rather than a religious book. Now and then I exclaimed out loud when I found the source of a phrase that had puzzled me in our literature classes: the Tower of Babel, the Garden of Eden, the snake. The snake – me, and Tainainai. Snake people were powerful and seductive: Tainainai had warned me of this. It seemed that the same was true even of foreign snakes.

'What is it?' Nainai poked her head out of the kitchen, whence came a delicious smell. 'What book are you reading now?'

'An English book.'

'What sort of book is it?'

'A bit like Chairman Mao's words.'

'Oh dear. No one is reading Chairman Mao's book nowadays. Is it your homework?'

'Well, sort of. My English teacher asked me to read it.'

'So it's a foreign chairman's book? Do they have chairmen in England?'

'Nainai!' I laughed. I didn't know what to tell her.

I was too distracted to continue reading, though, so I went into the kitchen and ended up eating there with Nainai. Nainai sang the praises of her new flat and took me around it after we had finished our meal. I could see why she liked it: it was bright, new and spacious. In winter she no longer needed to light a fire. There was central heating and she cooked over a gas fire, whose flame was strong and satisfying. Chairman Mao's portrait was gone and the walls were covered with family photos. My face appeared many times.

A few days later I got to the Book of Job. It depressed and fascinated me at the same time. So much of it was concerned with death. 'Like rivers that stop running and lakes that go dry, they will never stir from their sleep.' So true. I was so impressed by the language that I copied phrase after phrase into my notebook and read them again and again. Had Teacher Yan, my political teacher, been able to read this, I thought, with sudden generosity, she would never have been so dogmatic. It would have made her understand how short life was.

The trip South was easier this time. I managed the transition perfectly in Beijing. On the train to Pleasant City I shed all my thick winter layers, and felt spring pulsing in the air as the train trundled along. I was not nervous about travelling now. I welcomed it: it was good to be among the crowds. No longer timid, I felt empowered. Who would I fear? My reading, and the knowledge that I was being courted by a man I liked, gave me a new sense of maturity.

As I listened to the southern accent, I composed my letter to Steel. How should I put it? I loved him as a friend – I could even love him as a brother – but not as a boyfriend. Why? I had no idea. Love was a far-off, romantic thing, something I could think of only when I had fulfilled ambitions that were now forming. What did I know about physical attraction? I liked to hold a girlfriend's hand and smooth her hair. Men were unfamiliar, and I was not certain how far I wanted to get to know them. My memory of what had happened to Lotus Blossom, who had had dealings with men, had etched in me the notion that there was something forbidden and disgusting about physical closeness with the opposite sex.

I hoped he liked my letter. It was beautifully written, I thought, understanding, caring, but firm. 'I am sorry, I am too young to consider such things as love. I want to concentrate on my study.' I gave it to him in the library, a good neutral ground where we wouldn't be seen by classmates. While he pretended to read a magazine, I pushed it at him and left him there.

For a long time after that, he was withdrawn in class and would not chat with me and Hair as he used to. I was sorry for him but hoped that in the end he would get over it and we could still be friends. But the fear that I might have hurt him weighed heavily on me: I kept thinking about him and wondering whether I had done the right thing. Many girls, including Hair, found him attractive: perhaps I was being silly to push him away.

One night in the dormitory when the light was turned off I initiated a man talk. We all lit our candles and lay clean and snug inside our mosquito nets. 'What's your ideal man, Hair?' I called.

A ripple of giggles followed. 'What's yours?' Hair called back.

'Well, tall, handsome, intelligent and powerful, but pre-pared to wash my feet for me if I'm tired,' I rabbited.

Then all the girls were gabbling: 'What cheek! Where is such a man? I would never touch your feet.'

Then Hair said, 'Isn't Iron Army sweet?' He was her current favourite, a boy from the sports department who had strong arms like a wrestler's. He was so vain he wore T-shirts even on cold days so that he could flaunt his muscles.

Willow and I laughed.

'But he is so strong,' Hair argued.

'Yes, so is the buffalo that ploughed our fields,' Willow said. 'And he never argues, just goes "Moo".' We laughed hysteri-cally. Red coughed from inside her net and reminded us of the rules: 'It's time we slept.'

I lay in bed thinking of Steel. I felt sick to think of him fancying me. In truth, I did not want a man to wash my feet, or any other part of me, thank you. I was too ambitious for love affairs, right now.

Chapter 5:

The Losses

My first spring in the South. I felt it suddenly, like a hand stroking my face. I was used to waiting patiently for spring to come in the North. First the snow melted, then the wind grew warmer; each day you watched for small signs of green, and just as you thought spring had arrived, a cold spell killed off the new buds. Here it all seemed to happen overnight. Suddenly the cold was gone, the willow trees bore new green leaves and the girls started to wear colourful floral skirts.

On one of these beautiful spring days, Hair, Willow and I walked along the West Lake. ' "The south of the river is beautiful, the scenery I once knew so well . . ." ' I recited aloud, forgetting myself.

Hair turned to me. 'Steel used to recite poems like that. He hasn't done so for a long time. Do you know why?' She had penetrating black eyes, which bored into me. I looked away.

'Oh, Steel is full of poems,' Willow said quietly, beside me. She was chewing a long blade of grass.

After the walk, Willow went off to the reading room to do some work but Hair winked at me and I stayed behind in the dormitory with her. We sat on Willow's bed and chatted. Hair started plaiting my hair. 'You know this thing about Steel, don't you?' she said.

I was tongue-tied. How did she know?

'You know – Steel. The whole class knew apart from him . . . and you.'

'What?' I sat up, shocked now. 'What has it got to do with the whole class?' I imagined my worst fear: that the letter somehow got into the wrong hands and poor Steel was exposed as the one whose love had been rejected. Hair let go of my hair. 'That is just what I say. What has it to do with the rest of the class if Willow is in love with Steel? It's not as if the other girls have a chance with him. I mean, they're just plain jealous, because Willow is so much better-looking and better-natured than they are.'

I felt my face turn red. 'How do you know Willow is in love with Steel?'

Hair threw me a questioning look. 'How can you not know? Just look at them. Actually, don't look at Steel because I don't think he knows, but Willow is all over him. She does not know how to hide it. Everyone is talking about it. And I know for sure.' She turned over the pillow on Willow's bed and revealed a neat silk-wrapped notebook. Willow's diary.

The words in Willow's diary ran through my mind throughout the political-education class: 'His masculine shoulder and elegant hands. When he reads poems, how his voice echoes . . .' I had never thought of Steel as being masculine. He was far too skinny. But it was true that he had elegant hands, like Laoye's.

The term went quickly, and Steel avoided me. We no longer went for our lakeside walks, and I missed them at first, but gradually got used to it. The silent lake and the cows were my company as I watched spring deepen and the lotuses show young shoots.

However, I began to miss Laoye terribly, and whenever I thought of him I worried. Then I had a terrifying nightmare: Laoye got onto a train with many people in black clothes and hats. They looked solemn, and the interior of the train was dark. He waved at me slowly as the train pulled away. We both knew that this was a journey he had to take, and that the other men were there to make sure he didn't escape.

The dream haunted me all the following day. That evening I walked past the West Lake with Hair. It was misty, with no views to the other side, and the air was thick. A woman who lived in a small hut by the lake was burning some papers. The smoke added to the impenetrable smog. Hair whispered, 'Look, she is remembering her dead husband.' Suddenly it occurred to me that today was Qing Ming, Clear and Bright, the Day of the Dead, and that the widow was burning paper money so that her husband would be able to bribe the torturing devils.

I remembered my dream, and knew that Laoye was dead.

At the end of term, I was impatient on the train home. I wanted my suspicion to be confirmed. Ma told me the news while we chatted in the kitchen. Laoye had died of a stroke while out selling cigarettes, back in the spring. 'Why didn't you tell me then?'

'We didn't want your studies to be affected.' I didn't tell her about my dream: that had been a private message from Laoye to me. He had come to say goodbye.

Somebody knocked and came in to tell her that Ba would be late home. Ma's face darkened. 'Again,' she murmured. When the man left, she threw down the plates and burst into tears. 'I'm leading the life of a widow. See how your father treats me!'

I felt awkward, and went into the sitting room. She followed me. My eyes ran over the objects that were both familiar and strange to me now. There was the cupboard with the picture of the Korean girl with colourful skirts and long black hair; the door was ajar and I could see a box of sweets. As a child I had stared at the girl and fantasised about her life. The radio on top of the cupboard was covered with a piece of cloth to keep dust out of it. I remembered tuning and tuning it to steer it away from the North Korean channels, to find the Peking operas to please Ma.

I felt tears forming and turned my back to her. Suddenly

she spoke behind me. 'Do you hate me for sending you to Nainai for all those years?' I didn't say anything, and walked towards the window. She followed me and continued, 'You must. You refused to call me "Ma" when you first came back here. But do you know why I gave away my daughter?' The room felt hot. I opened the window. She grabbed my shoulders from behind and went on: 'It's all because of Laoye. If I hadn't lied and sent you to live with Nainai, who was from a poor peasant background, you would never have been able to go to university and become what you are today. Look at me – I lied about my background so that I could go to university. All your aunts were brilliant at school, but they couldn't go to university because of Laoye. We all hated him, I hated him, and he died because of our hatred.'

Without turning I put one hand on hers, still on my shoulder. Her other covered mine tightly. 'Can you understand? Do you forgive me?' she asked. 'We were so worried that if we told you anything, you'd blurt it all out, and then it would not just have been our future but your own future that would have been ruined.'

From the open window, I could smell cooking from family kitchens all around us. The orchestra of wok cooking echoed throughout the residence complex. The sun threw out a last ray of warmth and sank behind the distant hills, its beauty wasted on the bleak, uniform suburban block where there were more pressing affairs to attend to. Laoye's favourite line leapt into my head: 'However beautiful the sunset is, it is still near the dusk.' Then, he had told me I was too young to understand it. But I understood it now.

It was hard to know what to say to Ma, but next door, I heard the sound of Uncle Thunder's wife's pans sizzling. An idea came to me. I dragged Ma to her feet. 'Let's start cooking.'

We left a little for Ba. After dinner I helped her with the washing-up. The electricity went off and we sat in the soft glow of a candle. I imagined her as a little girl – I knew she had been Laoye's favourite daughter because she had told me so herself. I asked her what exactly Laoye had done to be labelled a counter-revolutionary.

He had come from a rich merchant's family in the South. He had been sent to study in Beijing where he fell in love with a fellow girl student, although his parents had found him a wife at home. He ran away with the girl student – Laolao. They settled in the North, where life was hard, and soon he had a family to support. He joined the Nationalist army, where he progressed well – his beautiful calligraphy stood him in good stead: he worked in the propaganda department, writing articles against the Communists.

When the Communists liberated China, Laoye went into hiding and was safe for a while. Then there was a movement in which everyone was encouraged to confess. Laoye thought that if he did so, he would be pardoned – after all, he had only written propaganda and had never killed anyone. Also, he knew he couldn't hide for ever.

However, in movement after movement, he was criticised in mass rallies. When people ran out of bad elements to criticise, they attacked him again. He was confused: he had genuinely repented and had worked hard to try to 'correct' himself. He had cleaned public toilets, and swept the street in which they lived every day for five years. Still his repentance was not accepted. 'You must be honest to the Party and to the people,' he was told. So against the better judgement of Laolao and the rest of the family, he confessed things he had not done to satisfy his persecutors.

He wrote petition after petition to Chairman Mao, believing that the man he revered as a god would see how he had been wronged and pardon him. 'He wrote beautifully . . .' Ma said.

'Don't say any more, Ma. I know.' I had read his confession a long time ago.

'What was I like when I was little?' This evening I felt closer to her than ever before: mourning Laoye had united us.

'I walked about with you night after night to stop you crying, but I couldn't. At last Nainai made a suggestion. I wrote a poem which went, "Heaven above, earth below, we have a crying baby at home; whoever walks by must read this poem, then my baby will sleep through the night." It was a kind of prayer, so the more people who read it, the more effective it would be. I wrote it on coloured papers and pasted them in all the usual – and some unusual – places, telegraph poles, shop windows, public toilets . . . I put them up high deliberately so that people would be curious and crane their necks to read them.'

All the mothers in China wrote and displayed these poems, and all the non-mothers peered up to read them, then spat on the floor and said, 'Damn it, it's another one of those.' But by that time it was too late – the poems had taken effect. 'Anyway, it did the trick, and you slept peacefully.'

Later, I lay in bed watching Ma's shadow as she sat alone in the candlelight, waiting for Ba. Again I thought of Laoye, and my discovery of his letters, how unkind I had been to him. I found the darkness comforting. I woke to hear the soft murmurs of my parents – Ba had come home at last and was making up with Ma. For a brief second, I felt myself transported back to my childhood, to the days before Ma made the decision to send me to Nainai's. I had not understood her then, and even now, I could not imagine what she must have gone through. I had been blind to her love, the sacrifice she had made for my sake – that was how much she loved me.

Before I left for Pleasant City, I went to see Nainai. She had adapted well to life in her high-rise flat. She liked her new neighbours and her home was always full of visitors. Shushu was planning to quit work and set up a small shop selling groceries. Yeye supported the idea, but Nainai was against it. They asked me to be the arbitrator. I told him to forget it because it would never be successful and profitable, but secretly I would have been ashamed to have a trader in the family.

I got through most of the Bible on the journey back to college. My notebook was full of quotations and questions I wanted to ask Lucy, but when I arrived in Pleasant City, I learned that she had left for England. Red announced the news to us in the dormitory. The way she talked about Lucy, the way Hair and Willow received the news, carrying on with their hair-brushing and admiring themselves in the mirror, made me realise how different I was from the others. 'She was considered unsuitable and a bad influence,' Red said. Willow and Hair kept on brushing without a word. Their backs were towards me, but their silence said, Who cares? She is just a foreigner, she is not one of us.

I stepped outside. It was drizzling – I had forgotten how cold it could get in the South in the autumn – but I walked towards the West Lake. I was getting wet but I did not mind. As I walked past the Foreign Experts' Building I glanced inside. The door was wide open, and the fat receptionist stared straight at me: Her eyes shone through the thick pair of glasses and I shuddered and hurried on. Had she reported me to Teacher Yan or had Red? I might never know.

I turned to the lake. The rain had created a curtain of grey, which hung heavy above the water. The pitter-patter on the wide green leaves of the lotuses sang in my ears like a soothing melody. Who was I? Why was I different from Hair, from Willow, and even from Steel, although we had so much in common? Who was Lucy, and what had I meant to her? I had wanted to talk with her about the Bible, I had wanted to show her how it had moved me and challenged my views.

I had wanted her to be my friend, but now there was no chance of that.

'Taotao.' It was Steel's voice. I turned and saw him putting up an umbrella. 'Taotao,' he said again, 'I just heard about your grandfather from Willow. I hope you are not too upset.'

I touched his hand, which was cold and wet. I had lost Laoye, I had lost Lucy, but perhaps Steel had come back to be a friend. Our eyes met. Yes – we were friends again. Sharing the umbrella, we walked back slowly. When we passed Lucy's old flat I stopped. 'You know Lucy's gone, don't you?' He nodded. 'She recommended a book to me before she left – the Bible.' Steel was the only person with whom I could discuss it.

'I know,' he said. 'I saw you taking it out of the library when . . .' It had been the same day on which he had given me the love letter. A spasm of guilt ran through me, and I searched his eyes for forgiveness but found only concern. 'Is it full of religious doctrine?'

'No – well, not only that. You'd be surprised by how enjoyable it is. It's all about life and the history of a nation, really, like an epic.'

He smiled. His face was thinner than I remembered it. That silence which I had taken for shyness when I first knew him I recognised now as strength. 'I am reading Karl Marx, but I wouldn't recommend it to you. I am sure you would think it's too political and boring.'

I stuck out my tongue. 'I've read enough Chairman Mao never to want to touch Marx.'

'So, you won't force me to read the Bible, and I won't force you to read Marx.'

We laughed. 'But, Steel, why should you want to read Marx? Isn't political lesson enough theory for you?'

'I want to find out things for myself, not through Teacher Yan, who probably hasn't read the originals.'

Our classrooms were in view now. The rain had stopped, and Steel closed the umbrella. 'Have a look at this and tell me what you think,' he said gently, took something out of his pocket and put it into my hand. I was about to look at it when he stopped me: 'Don't take it out in front of others. Read it when you are alone.' He laughed when he saw me hesitate. 'Don't worry, it's not another love letter.'

162

I went in, dried myself, climbed under my mosquito net and pulled out what Steel had given me. It was a hand-copied booklet by Square Field, on the subject of true democracy and Marxist theory. I knew who Square Field was, and I knew why he had to use a pseudonym. My political consciousness amounted only to a firm belief in the abolition of political teachers, but I was touched by Steel's trust.

Chapter 6:

Graduation

There was a new understanding between Steel and me, and our friendship resumed on a deeper and, for me, more satisfying level. We picked each other's brains, but kept our hearts separate. We still saw little of each other, though. As time went by we were drawn into our studies and before long had to start working in earnest for the final academic threshold we had to cross: graduation. Afterwards, we would be guaranteed a job by the government and all the status symbols that went with it: housing, permanent employment, pension, free medical insurance and so on. I would not fully have appreciated this but for Hair, who had been born into a peasant family and had craved a city residence permit since she passed the university entrance exam. This, after all, was what most of my classmates had set their sights on.

In our last term we learned that Willow and Steel were now a couple. Hair told me that they had spent the last holiday travelling to the Three Gorges along the Yangtze and 'Things developed from there,' she said knowingly. They were from the same county, and I knew they always went home together on the train. They had had plenty of time and opportunity to develop their relationship, away from the prying eyes of fellow students. No boy, not even Steel, could resist a pretty girl like Willow, I supposed. I sat at my small desk looking at myself in the mirror. Although I had rejected Steel I loved him as a friend, and I feared losing him as a confidant. Willow looked radiant, but Steel had not changed, except that he came to our dormitory more often and Willow made him tea.

Suddenly Red was no longer willing to do good deeds. Instead, she lectured us: 'You should really do more exercise. A period is not an illness, try to be braver.' We soon learned why. She had become a Party Member, so there was no longer any need to do good deeds. Teacher Yan announced the news at the political lesson, and Red bought sweets for us all. After graduation, we would all be assigned to jobs; and as a Party Member she would be sought after by future employers.

Teacher Yan said we should trust the leaders to give us a fair assignment according to our ability, our ideological consciousness and academic record, but mainly our ideological consciousness, she emphasised. Nobody believed her, and some of us began our own back-door networking – Hair found a distant relative in Pleasant City who was willing to help her, so she put on her thickest face cream, and disappeared at weekends to see him.

As graduation loomed ever closer, I realised I was not looking forward to it. Away from home, from responsibility, and just getting used to the good things of the South – the food, the weather, the summer flowers, the siestas and, above all, my new friends – I didn't want to leave.

The university arranged many extra lectures from outsiders. In one a previous graduate who had volunteered for a job in Inner Mongolia talked about his fantastic life there. He had ridden on horseback to teach the nomads. I was going to talk to him after the lecture, but Teacher Yan grabbed him. Pity. Then an ex-Red Army man talked about his experiences during the days of fighting the Nationalists. I hated that grin on Teacher Yan's face when she announced his arrival and the patronising way in which she escorted him. But the old man was sincere enough, even though he must have told his stories hundreds of times. When Teacher Yan asked if we had any questions, Steel raised his hand. She frowned but let him stand up to speak. 'When do you think we will realise Communism?' he asked.

The old man laughed. 'In those days when we were fighting so hard, we thought that once we had defeated the Nationalists, who exploited the poor and worshipped the rich, we would be in heaven. Now we are liberated, we see we still have a long way to go. We'll get there in the end. Our hope is in you – the generation who will carry forward our dream.'

'But it's been so long. Perhaps we should be more realistic about . . .'

Teacher Yan interrupted. 'We are running out of time, Steel. You can ask more questions in private.'

The weather grew hot. Our lessons ceased and we began our revision. Hair and I sat underneath a willow tree with the view over the West Lake to recite and revise. Lots of our time was spent in memorising facts, which I was good at, and Hair wasn't, dates, numbers and theories for the political class, which we doubted we would ever need once we had passed the exam, and which bored us to death. 'Define the significance of the Gutian meeting in the development of the Communist Party of China,' I asked Hair wearily for the third time.

She stared at me, as if it was my fault she could not remember, and moaned. A bell rang, and her eyes shone. 'Lunch, thank goodness.'

I put down my book, truly hoping she would get through the exam.

In the dining hall, a notice was pinned on the board next to the menu and prices. It called on us to go on a demonstration with students from the university on the other side of the lake, our traditional rival – the Central China Technology University. 'Join the anti-corruption pan-university alliance demonstration, which also calls for democracy and freedom of speech.' It was signed Square Field. My heart leaped into my throat. So that was what Steel had been up to. Lots of people were reading it, and I half expected them to say something, but they continued to put food into their mouths. I felt almost sorry for Steel. The proposed demonstration day was 4 May, the Youth Day.

We were all in class on that day except Steel. Red and Teacher Yan stood at the foot of the stairs deep in discussion. My concern increased.

Before lunch, Red cleared her desk. 'Do you know what happened to Steel today?' I asked casually.

'Poor Steel had to go off to see his aunt in town. Apparently she is very ill.'

I couldn't tell whether she believed it or not. We were alone in the dormitory and I felt a sudden urge to get behind her façade, to know her better. After all, we had lived together for nearly four years, and I didn't want to leave without trying to reach her human side. 'What do you like? Who do you really feel close to?' I wanted to ask. But as if she could read my thoughts, she put on that clinical smile again and said she had always admired my academic record and would like to learn from me. As I stood up in frustration to leave her, she asked me whether I had thought of a job I wanted to do yet. I said I hadn't.

A lie, of course. I had received a letter from Ba about my assignment. He could get me a job in Beijing. A friend's friend worked in the personnel department at the Ministry of Defence, and knew of a vacancy for an English translator at the Number 7 Science Institute. I had never thought of working in Beijing, or for that matter in an institute. I wanted to go to Tibet or Inner Mongolia, anywhere that was remote and beautiful. The idea of becoming a technical translator in the Science Institute did not appeal to me. But I wrote and accepted his offer. I had to live in the real world, like everyone else. All around me people were desperately trying to get jobs in the cities and in big state-run organisations. Saying no to an opportunity in

Beijing would have been foolish.

I did badly in the exam, but not badly enough to fail. Despite my good memory, I got the date of the Gutian meeting wrong. Hair got it right. When we checked, she grinned, and I had to congratulate her. Hair was a lucky girl. She never seemed to worry. She slept and ate well, and in the end things usually worked out for her. Good fate, Tainainai would have said. Was that because she was a horse? Willow was a sheep, not such a lucky sign.

On a hot, sticky afternoon after lunch, the dining-room tables were cleared, and we sat in the huge hall waiting for the official announcement of the job assignments. Teacher Yan, in her trademark white shirt, gave a lecture first: 'I cannot stress enough the importance of being red in terms of one's career prospects. Those whose behaviour has been "anti-government" need to examine themselves hard.' At this her expression hardened. I looked away, and spotted Steel. He sat with his back erect, gazing out of the window. I thought of how much I would miss him, and our talk of Tang poems.

Then we learned the details. I knew that the Science Institute awaited me. Hair was to work at the Pleasant City steel factory as a translator; her distant relative worked there, too, in the administration department. Steel was to teach at the foreign-language department of our university, and Willow was to return to the village she had come from to teach in the local middle school. Red was to work at the municipal government foreign-affairs office.

Hair's distant relative turned out to be no more than an acquaintance from the same part of the country whom she had managed to charm into offering her a job. When Red's boyfriend came to see her, Red introduced him proudly as Big Enlightenment, assistant director of the policy unit of the municipal government, which was how she had ended up with such a high-profile, lucrative assignment that offered trips abroad. As Willow had made no attempt to curry favour with anyone, she had been sent back to the countryside, to which her parents had hoped she would never return.

I couldn't understand how Steel had come by his job: not everyone knew about the demonstration but his political views were no secret. I couldn't see him begging for a job about which he felt, at best, indifferent. There had to be a story behind it.

In the evening a big graduation party was held and the college principal came to congratulate us. I had never seen him before and confused him with the accountant who had issued us with our textbooks, and with whom I had once quarrelled.

Willow cried throughout the meal. We tried to comfort her, but didn't know what to say: it was as if we had betrayed her somehow when really we had just made the most of our resources. She had only herself to blame. I supposed that if Steel really loved her he could ask to be transferred to work in her county, but I knew it would be a hard choice.

It was hot, and we moved up to the physics block where there was a big flat roof from which we had a view of the whole city. It was our last night together. I felt closer to Hair, Steel and Willow than I had ever felt. They were the brothers and sisters I had never had. As I was about to leave, I knew that something of the South had seeped into me and become part of me. Somebody had brought a cassette player and we danced. The warm summer breeze was like water, caressing my bare arms and legs. Hair was drunk. She slung one arm around me, and we danced like two chopsticks. Behind us sat Steel, alone, upright and annoyingly sober, watching us like a hawk.

At midnight none of us stirred to go back to the dormitory. The door would be locked, but who cared? The night was warm. We wandered out of the college through the back gate, which led to a railway station. We climbed over it one after the other, trying not to wake the gatekeeper. I was the last over as my friends waited silently on the other side. In the distance I could hear a train coming, the sound so loud I thought the gatekeeper must wake up now. As soon as I was safely over, the train passed with a mighty roar. The lights were on and we saw the people inside. I imagined myself on it, as I would be tomorrow.

We followed the railway line, which ran parallel for a while with the West Lake. Where the trains forked off, we walked by the edge of the lake and were soon on the side open to the public, beyond the college grounds. Again we had to climb over a locked gate, softly, without waking the guard. This was the second rule we had broken. Two in one night. How exciting it was to break rules, and to do it in a gang, Hair on my left, Steel on my right, like quotation marks, Willow clinging to Steel's shoulder. Our steps in silent unison, we marched. Our feet fell gently on the grass and our only observer was the moon. It was clear and vigilant, following our steps, guiding us.

The scent of the late-night flowers blossoming in the park hit us like a drug. 'The breath of the flowers ambushes us so we know the day and night' – the line echoed inside me. I exchanged a glance with Steel and knew from his twinkling eyes that he was thinking of the same line. Hanging onto his shoulder, Willow smelt and floated like a flower. Her eyes were twin lakes, full of autumn ripples. We drifted. Hair and I walked towards the lake, while Willow and Steel headed to a bush.

I had been here several times during the day when it had been crowded with swimmers and children playing around the flower-beds, but now it was perfectly calm, still with expectation. I heard a splash and the next minute saw Hair break the surface, shaking the water from her hair like a dog. 'Come on in,' she whispered. 'I will be here, don't be afraid.' I had never swum, and was terrified of water.

I took off my dress, closed my eyes and slipped into the darkness beneath me. A feeling of peace – it felt like a second and like an eternity – until I felt Hair holding me up.

I was soon freezing, and climbed out of the water. We sat on the bank and dressed. A blindingly bright light pierced the darkness and an engine broke the silence. It was the night patrol vehicle. Wet, with our dresses clinging to our bodies, we ran and crouched under a tree, like some hunted night creature, watching the light move slowly away. Before it turned the corner, it shone on the bush where Steel and Willow hid, and cast a shadow of the two embraced figures on the concrete bank of the lake. I shuddered. Something silent and powerful had crept out of the night into me and I absorbed it greedily.

We walked back towards the college together. Passing the railway line, we lingered: it was the route to freedom for us, and we were reluctant to go back into the restraint of the college where we had spent our youth. I lay down in the sand, and reached out my arms. They all came to me, Willow, Hair and Steel.

Chapter 7:

In Transition

Steel came to see me off at the station. Our conversation was limited to my journey and my luggage. I smelt his sweat as I wiped off mine with the back of my hand. All around us was noise and heat and I felt irritable. Instead of being grateful for his help I was snappy and rude. He got on to the train with me and busied himself arranging and rearranging my luggage. I knew he was avoiding talking to me. When the whistle blew, he rushed off and stood waving at me on the platform, his face red and wet from the heat. 'Where is Willow?' I shouted.

He looked around as if to make sure nobody could hear us, and muttered, 'I don't know.'

'How come they want you at the foreign-language department?' I shouted again, not wanting him to escape.

Again he glanced around quickly and answered, as if I had embarrassed him, 'The head of the department was my Ba's student, but I never asked him for any favours.' He blushed. 'I will see you again,' he called, as the train moved.

I slumped into my seat and did not look back. I knew we would meet again: he would come to see me in Beijing. The thought was a great comfort. I was apprehensive about Beijing and I was not looking forward to the Number 7 Science Institute of the Ministry of Defence. I expected it to be rigid, military, secretive and suffocating. I imagined a comfortable but dull life. I knew my parents would expect me to marry a nice young man from Beijing and settle down. I would have a Beijing resident's paper, a great privilege. People went to desperate lengths to get them – marriages of convenience, bribing municipal officials in charge of issuing papers – and I had it on a plate. The resident's paper guaranteed abundant food rations, and a better quality of life. Yet I knew it wasn't for me. I wanted adventure, not routine.

Opposite me, three travelling salesmen set up a card table and started to play, spitting out the shells of watermelon seeds. They did it without thinking. A mother sat shielding her baby's ears with her hand, as if to keep the shouts of the card-players from disturbing the child. A middle-aged couple from the countryside sat next to each other, looking down at their shoes timidly.

The time had come for me to join the real world and I was afraid, but there was no looking back. The ticket collector came along and I gave her mine mechanically. I glanced outside the window. We were leaving the city centre. It was an ugly scene, emphasised by the contrasts. The tall pagoda I had climbed with Hair and Willow glistened in the distance, but immediately before my eyes, close to the railway lines, were rubbish heaps with shabby run-down houses emerging from them like mushrooms in decaying wood. Dirty-looking children played in the yards dangerously close to the train, looking up at us as if we were from another world. A lake appeared, soothing my eyes. After we had passed it I realised it was the West Lake. Like my four years in Pleasant City it was left behind unexpectedly, suddenly.

Night fell. The peasant couple opposite leaned against each other. I thought of Willow and her destination in the country-side. Once in the country, always in the country. How disappointed her family would be. I thought of Hair: I knew she was pleased with herself – she was probably humming along a street in Pleasant City enjoying her new-found freedom, with her 'cousin'. I imagined Red cuddling with her boyfriend. We had been like a family – albeit an odd one, Steel, Hair, Willow and I.

At the farewell party, my classmates had congratulated me on going 'back North'. Despite my protest that my home town was a night's train journey from Beijing, I had always been known in this southern university as 'the Beijing Girl'. I didn't feel as if I was going back to Beijing, I was entering it for the first time. Passing through or spending a holiday there was one thing; working and living in the great city was a different proposition altogether. Beijing was the capital, where things really happened and were decided. I would cycle in the city where Chairman Mao had lived, where all my childhood dreams had been centred. I thought of the bright lights of Pleasant City, and realised with a thrill that the lights in Beijing were bound to be even brighter.

I looked at the scrap of paper I had been given. It was the address of Building the Country, an acquaintance of Ba's, the son of an old colleague who had gone to work in Beijing for a film company. My official start date at the Institute was in three months' time. Ba had given me Building the Country's address and arranged for me to stay there while I waited to register at the Institute.

I spent a sleepless and exhausting night on the train, uncertain of my future, not knowing where I wanted to be. In the early morning the peasant couple got off at a small station. I envied the contented look on their face – they knew their destination and were happy with it. Impatiently I waited for the train to arrive in Beijing. I wondered about Building the Country, and hoped I would like him.

Stepping out of the station in Beijing was like bumping straight into a colour TV screen. Compared with my last trip here, everything was as vivid as if it was a funfair. It was 1988: China's door was wide open to the outside world, or so the radio kept telling us. In Beijing, the signs of change were more dramatic than they had been in the provincial southern city where I had spent my student years. The Cultural Revolution had been officially condemned, private businesses had sprouted like bamboo shoots after the rain, and women had started to wear makeup. Large billboards flashed advertisements for everything from cigarettes to underwear, and posters of large-bosomed western women stared straight at the crowds who thronged out of the station like ants. I felt like a tiny drop in a vast ocean.

Building the Country was instantly recognisable: he was unusually tall, standing like a crane among crowds of chickens outside the station. Ba had told me that his nickname was 'the Stick'. He walked swiftly ahead, slinging my heavy luggage across his shoulder as if it were a school satchel. He drove a small van with the company's name, Window to the Outside World Film Company, written on its side. He chatted quietly with me while we sailed smoothly into the streams of Beijing traffic. I hesitated to call him Uncle Building the Country, as Ba had instructed. He seemed young and it would make me appear childish. 'Call me anything you like,' he said, sensing my hesitation. I liked his casual air.

It was dark by the time we stopped in front of a five-storey building, and climbed the stairs, passing double-locked metal doors. On the second floor, a man opened his door an inch and peered suspiciously at us, then clanged it shut. The concrete stairs were barren, cold and dusty, and our steps echoed heavily. I was cheered by the sight of potted flowers leading to the fifth floor and Building the Country's flat. This also had a metal door, but it was painted a pleasant green. The stairs were swept clean.

Forever Green, Building the Country's wife, opened the door with a finger to her mouth. 'Small Wave is asleep,' she said. 'Come in, Taotao.' She extended a hand and I gave her mine. She was of medium height, her long hair swirled up on her head, and her face shone, with fine wrinkle lines concentrated at the corners of her mouth and around her eyes – clearly a woman who smiled a lot. She gave me a warm smile now. She wore an apron, and the smell of crispy chicken came from behind her. I guessed it was she who had put out the flower-pots and painted the door.

We had a delicious dinner, and talked in hushed whispers so as not to wake their six-year-old son. After dinner Forever Green showed me where I would sleep in a tiny space between the kitchen and the bathroom. Like most Beijing dwellers, they had only one bedroom. A makeshift curtain gave me some privacy, and a small vase with a few jasmine twigs had been placed on a window-sill by the little bed.

I lay in bed and listened to the sounds of the city outside. It was new to me, the endless traffic that seemed to go on all night. Downstairs I heard heavy footsteps on the staircase, and doors banging. At midnight I was woken by the sound of water taps, pulled aside the curtain and saw a small boy rubbing his eyes and peering, bewildered, at me. Then he retreated murmuring, 'Mama, Mama,' and staggered into the bedroom.

I heard Forever Green's voice: 'Here, Small Wave, here.'

The next morning I was woken again by Small Wave, who was standing in front of me and tickling my foot. I giggled and jumped up to catch him. He ran away, shouting, 'Sister Taotao, Sister Taotao, it's time for breakfast.'

We had breakfast with the window wide open. The noise of bicycle bells flooded in. Small Wave studied me while he played with his chopsticks. Suddenly he asked, 'Which one do you like best? Helicopter or submarine?'

I gambled: 'Submarine.'

'Yes!' he shouted. I had given the right answer. 'Look, this is my latest model.' He rushed to collect up all his submarine toys and scattered them on the table.

Forever Green smiled indulgently. 'He wants to sail a submarine when he grows up.'

'One I've designed myself,' he added.

After breakfast Building the Country drove off to work and Forever Green took Small Wave to school on her bicycle and herself to work on a women's magazine.

I did the washing up, unpacked, and sat for a while. This couple intrigued me: they were half-way between my father's generation and mine. In his usual modest way, Ba had asked me to call them Uncle and Aunt, but I could not. Building the Country did not want to be an uncle, nor Forever Green an aunt: 'I am not as old as that,' she said cheerfully. 'Call me Sister Green.'

I went out. There was a grocery shop on the corner and the old man in it looked me up and down suspiciously as I walked past. At the bicycle shed, two nannies from the province of Anhui, both holding babies, were chatting in accents I did not understand. They wore colourful dresses, and bright red lipstick – Beijing was full of red lipstick. At the entrance to the building stood a makeshift shed that housed construction workers, young peasants from Hebei province, near Beijing. Bare-chested, they called to each other in loud voices. The whole of Beijing was being rebuilt – the city was one gigantic construction site.

I walked around the rubble surrounding the bright, new-looking estate where Building the Country's flat was. I turned by the canal, which was dirty, the water still, but compared with the roads, it was peaceful. The canal was a vestige of an older Beijing among all the modern construction. An emperor had commissioned it to be built to link North and South China by water. It featured in Laolao's story, the one about a young scholar in the South who fell in love with a girl in the North. The world had been much bigger then.

A handful of old men and women were stretching and singing softly to themselves after the morning's session of *T'ai chi* and Peking Opera singing. I felt like a truant, but I wanted to wander, and dreaded joining the work routine. The prospect of doing the same thing, in the same place, with the same people, day in, day out, horrified me. We had no choice over where we worked: our work units were assigned to us and we stayed there for life. There was no way out. All these

people, the cyclists streaming on the road, the old men doing
T'ai chi, even Building the Country and Forever Green were
resigned to their fate. Why should I be any different?

In the afternoon I slept, then got up and wrote some letters.
Ba rang and asked me how I was. 'They treat me very well,' I
said.

'Come home, if you like,' he said. 'It's only an overnight
train from there, and Nainai wants to see you.'

I was tempted – I could spend some time with my parents
and Nainai. 'No,' I said. I wanted to drift a bit, and enjoy my
freedom before joining the Institute.

Forever Green came back with Small Wave earlier than I
had expected. They caught me examining a photograph in
their bedroom, a studio shot of Building the Country and
Forever Green in their youth. They wore green army jackets
and leaned on each other. Their faces had been coloured and
their lips touched up with red.

Small Wave was tired, and went to bed early. Building the
Country did not come home until late. He went first to check
on his son, then sank down on the sofa and sighed. It had
been a tiring day. Negotiations with a foreign film group had
been tough. Just before a final agreement was reached, the
foreigners had changed their minds about some critical detail.
To top it all, the manager of his company was corrupt. 'Some
people should not be in positions of power if they abuse
them,' he said. The more I listened, the less keen I was on
joining working life. 'That's nothing compared to my boss,'
Forever Green cut in.

'How did you two meet?' I asked.

They exchanged a smile, and Forever Green tapped
Building the Country's hand playfully. 'We met when we
were members of two opposing factions of Red Guards, both
avowing that we were the most earnest defenders of
Chairman Mao,' she said.

'The head of your faction was very keen on you, wasn't
he?' Building the Country winked at Forever Green.

Their intimate jokes and their open affection embarrassed me. My parents never showed affection in front of others, not even me. I looked away.

It was Sunday. Building the Country had to go to a business banquet. Forever Green and I went swimming with Small Wave. It was a long bus ride into the city centre to the open-air swimming-pool – the Beihai Lake. Small Wave jumped on the bus ahead of us and called triumphantly, 'Ma, Sister Taotao, I've got us seats at the front.' He chatted away, drawing my attention to the buildings and people we passed, looking around to see if anybody else on the bus was watching him. He was an engaging little boy. I was shy because of my north-eastern accent and answered him in monosyllabic murmurs. We passed the busiest shopping street, and the bus was caught in the traffic. The ticket collector, a girl in a pony-tail, had gone over to sit with the driver and together they sneered at the crowds outside: 'These provincial people, when will they ever stop coming to Beijing? Look at that funny old man.' She laughed, pointing to a stooped figure wearing a traditional blue jacket and a pair of brand new cloth shoes. 'Peasant,' she concluded. The old man reminded me of Laoye. I was seized suddenly with longing for home and a familiar face.

In Beihai Park, Forever Green and I sat on the bench watching the children splash in the lake. Small Wave dived in and out of the water like a duck. Once in a while he swam near us to check we were still watching him.

'Don't take any notice of the bus driver,' Forever Green said suddenly. 'I'm not from Beijing myself. Not many of us are.' She waved at Small Wave reassuringly. 'You asked how Building the Country and I met. We were both Red Guards. I was keen, going about the neighbourhood rooting out the rightists, the devils, and the snakes, exposing them, looting their goods and pushing their heads down at public rallies . . . until the opposing faction exposed my own uncle to be a rightist – my favourite uncle.' She took out a cigarette case, lit one elegantly. The green shirt she wore blended in with the shady tree behind her, but the wrinkles on her face deepened. 'I was dating Building the Country then, and I said to him, "I am from a disgraced family now. You can leave me, I will understand. I don't want your pity, just go." ' She stared at the lake. I could imagine the spiky, haughty look she would have worn when she was young. Then her eyes softened. 'He said, "I am with you, whatever you are."

'You soon realise those ideologies are worth nothing, all the silliness and slogans. We fought our opposing factions to death – there was blood on each side – and for what? I am glad I got out as early as I did. But I still saw my uncle die – after a public-humiliation rally. He threw himself from the roof of the school where he used to work. That did it for me. "No more," I said to myself. I resigned from my post in the Red Guards, and Building the Country resigned with me. We were both labelled black elements. You could say I married him out of gratitude.

'People say our youth was misspent but, looking back on it, I don't think so. It was exciting at first. We defied all convention. We were the future, and the new masters. There was such a feeling of confidence and of trust. We really believed we could make a difference. We travelled every-where, all over the country. I don't regret it at all.'

Small Wave, slippery as a seal, dived into her arms and she held him tightly, not minding the wet. 'Having a child makes you think. You will know this one day – it makes you realise what is important in life.'

On the way back I thought of Uncle Thunder, my parents' neighbour and friend. He had been an activist during the Cultural Revolution and would not have hesitated to criticise or even beat up class enemies like Forever Green's uncle and Laoye. But Uncle Thunder had also been a warm, devoted friend to my parents, and a playful, doting uncle to me when I was a child. I could not hate him, despite what had happened to Laoye. Life puzzled me.

When we got home Building the Country was cooking. The negotiations had gone better today. In fact, everything was almost finalised for the film to start. 'I am going to Inner Mongolia in two weeks' time.' He stole a glance at Forever Green.

Small Wave's mouth turned down. 'You're not going away again, Ba, are you?'

'Yes, but I will bring you presents.'

'I'd rather you didn't go away.'

After dinner we had dates, which Building the Country munched heartily. Forever Green picked one up and put it into his mouth. I asked Small Wave to show me his models.

We all went to bed early, and I dreamed of Forever Green's uncle and Laoye. They looked so similar they might have been brothers. They were in a beautiful garden where they were at their ease. I had an ache in my heart that stayed with me when I woke. I smelt Forever Green's perfume, and felt homesick. The affection among the family I was lodged with highlighted my loneliness. I decided to ring Ba in the morning to tell him I was coming back.

He sounded pleased on the phone, but he also wanted to be sure I was making a good impression in Beijing. 'Are you helping with the housework there? Make sure you behave well and be polite and helpful to Uncle and Auntie.' Did he think I was a child who needed reminding of all the basic things? Suddenly I was less sure about going home.

For the next few days I wavered over whether to buy tickets or stay on. I clung to the idea of remaining in Beijing, as if there was something I had to achieve there. Surely this was where life was to be found, if anywhere, in China. I feared missing out on some calling or vocation.

On one especially hot night, we had dinner early. Both Forever Green and Building the Country were absorbed in playing with Small Wave. It was a cosy picture, but I felt closed in, restless. I was filled with an impulse to get away. I stood up. 'I'm going out for a little walk,' I said. They turned briefly to wave, and returned to their game. I was glad they did not make a fuss.

The street was full of people fanning themselves as they walked towards the canal to cool off, and of bicycles carrying families and lovers towards the park, which was free of charge at this time of the day. I felt a little conspicuous walking on my own, and craved crowds and bright lights. I boarded a bus to the city centre. I got off at Xidan and sauntered along the Avenue of Eternal Peace towards Tiananmen Square. Streams of traffic flowed past me. I thought of the sleepy, comfortable family picture I had left behind: it was both attractive and suffocating. Now, with my hands in my pockets I felt carefree and my steps were light. The street was a place where I could hide, be part of the crowd. It had a rhythm, and I was alive with it. I could sing in it, I could live in it. I knew that this was something I could be part of.

The brightly lit shop signs at the sides of the streets flashed excitingly, and I was drawn towards a clothes shop. The clothes lay on open shelves, where I could browse and touch them. In Pleasant City the shops were still old-fashioned, staffed with grumpy assistants who guarded their goods behind long counters. Hair and I used to annoy them by asking constantly to see clothes that we did not buy. They passed them to us as reluctantly as if we were asking to see their own wardrobes. When we returned the clothes, they'd dust them with their hands and turn their backs on us.

Here, when I saw the prices I sneaked out quickly. Outside, I comforted myself: it was nice to fantasise, to have felt those beautiful garments. I could not imagine how anybody could afford them, but maybe this was naïve of me – there were certainly many fashionable-looking people around, young couples who walked hand in hand, another sight I had seen rarely in Pleasant City.

I stopped at the neon lights of the Eternal Peace Theatre. There were two queues for the performances tonight. The long one was for the 'World Famous Hong Kong Pop Singer

Shen Qi' and the shorter for *Attracting Arrows Through Straw Boats* – a traditional Peking Opera, one of a few that had been revived now the Cultural Revolution was over. I studied the poster for the opera and I recognised the character, with long fake beard, colourful robe and high platform shoes. His face was painted dramatically: the eyebrows slanted upwards towards the forehead as if they were two arrows. He held a fan and smiled confidently. Behind him was a turbulent river. I joined the short queue, with only three people ahead of me: an old man and two foreigners. The eyes of the well-dressed young people on the opposite queue rested on the two westerners.

The small theatre was so empty that I could choose where to sit. I took a seat in the front row. I had never sat so close to actors before. It was only the fourth time in my life that I had been to a theatre: once with Yeye to watch the Korean delegation singing Chinese songs, once with Ma and Laolao to see a Revolutionary Peking Opera, and once to perform in the People's Palace in my home town. I sat in my seat like a real VIP and felt a sense of adventure. I glanced back. Small clusters of people were scattered in rows behind me, whispering to each other. The old man standing ahead of me in the queue came to the front row and sat two seats away from me, silent, motionless.

The instruments started. Like heavy rain, like soft rain, like pearls dropping into a jade plate. I knew the plot of this particular play – it was taken from the classic book *The Three Kingdoms*. The story was of the clever strategist Zhu Geliang, who outwitted another equally sharp politician in the fight to rule central China. Laoye's words echoed: 'When you are old, you don't read *The Three Kingdoms* because you are already shrewd enough.' I peered at the old man sitting beside me. His body swayed and he nodded in time to the rhythm.

The protagonist appeared. He sang, and I felt my body start to sway and my head to nod. I knew the story already, so why was I here? My eyes closed, I followed the sinuous bends and twists of the singing, expecting the turning, reaching it, relishing it. Appreciation of Peking Opera – Laoye had taught me this, and this decadent, indulgent, most bourgeois pastime had entered my life like a refreshing stream. I came alive.

I glanced back; the audience also seemed alive. The reserved-looking old people had become noisy, cries of '*Hao* – good' echoed in the auditorium. They clapped and beat their thighs. Some sang gently. They were enchanted and I felt Laoye beside me, clapping, happy.

Outside soft warm rain was falling. The music of the opera still rang in my ears, and I sang to the accompaniment of the raindrops. It was late, but instead of heading for the bus home, I strode in the opposite direction towards Tiananmen Square. I still felt Laoye's presence – he could not resist coming. I sat down alone in the square opposite the huge portrait of Chairman Mao. It looked faded, dated. Surrounded by colourful flags and brightly dressed crowds, it had lost its air of solemnity. Curiously it reminded me of the old Kitchen God poster I had discovered, hidden by Tainainai behind Chairman Mao's portrait. An era had passed, and now its god was fading. Who would he hide behind in a few years' time, I wondered.

I caught the last bus back to the suburb. I was full of a new courage. Tonight I had walked with Laoye by my side.

When I knocked on the door Forever Green was still up. She did not seem at all surprised to see me so wet. 'Go and get changed,' she said, and brought me a glass of hot water when I lay in bed. 'We must make you a spare key,' she said, and bade me good night.

Somehow, I thought she approved of my wanderings.

Two days later, Building the Country came home smelling of alcohol. He had just been to a business dinner where they had finalised arrangements for shooting the film. 'How do you feel about going to Inner Mongolia for two months as interpreter for our company?' he said.

'*Where?*' At first I thought he was actually drunk. I was

helping Small Wave cut out a submarine from the pages of a foreign magazine. Inner Mongolia sounded as though it was outer space.

'Inner Mongolia. Our own interpreter has decided to study in America, and we need someone urgently. I am leaving in two days' time by train, and if you are coming, you need to be ready to be picked up by a jeep next week. We will pay you,' he said.

'Me?' I stared at him in disbelief. Was this what I had been waiting for? 'Let me think about it,' I said slowly, getting up from the table.

'Where is Inner Mongolia?' Small Wave asked.

'It's in the North,' Building the Country replied.

'Does it have submarines?'

'No, it has a sea of grassland.'

I saw a vision of greenness, then thought of the concrete buildings, the dust rising from the construction sites and the rude ticket collector. Next to me Forever Green spoke: 'We went there once, on our honeymoon, when we were travelling up and down the country. We kept our Red Guards badges and used them to travel free on the trains. We rode horses there. Do you remember, Building the Country?'

'I will go,' I said.

FOUR

Butterfly Dreams: Inner Mongolia

One day Zhuang Zi woke up from a dream. He had dreamed he was a butterfly, flying among the flowers, dancing in the wind. He was so happy being a butterfly that when he woke up he didn't know whether he was Zhuang Zi the human or the butterfly. Was he actually a butterfly dreaming of being Zhuang Zi the human?

From *The Book of Zhuang Zi*

Chapter 1:

'Three Trees'

———✦———

W e had been driving for nearly an hour, and the driver hadn't addressed a word to me. Was it my clothes that put him off? I wore a white shirt, high-heeled shoes and red lipstick – my idea of a working woman's outfit. Perfect for the office, of course, but for a bumpy dusty journey like this? I should have known better. I had borrowed the lipstick from Forever Green. It was the first time I had worn makeup. As everyone in Beijing wore lipstick, I felt I should, off to work in a film, on my first assignment as interpreter. I would be treated seriously, I hoped. The red lipstick was a statement.

The hot afternoon sun licked my skin mercilessly through the car window. Each time I wiped the sweat off my face, a smear of lipstick came with it. We were in a queue of cars and coaches, crawling along the spiralling mountain road on the hills north of Beijing. The tourist coaches were heading for the Great Wall, and we into the grassland where barbarians had lived, those whom the Great Wall had been built to keep out.

At Ju Yong Guan, one of the major passes through the Great Wall, the traffic came to a halt. All the coaches stopped as the tourists struggled out and took snapshots of each other. Driver Zhang stopped and got out of the jeep, ignoring the cars behind him hooting loudly, and asked me to take a souvenir picture of him. His cigarette hand pointed significantly to the Great Wall behind him as he smiled for the camera. I was offended when that smile disappeared as soon as the shutter clicked.

As we drove slowly under the gate, I was full of trepidation and excitement: no tourists went beyond this point. On this side, nobody bothered to maintain the Wall and its battered carcass was in plain view – ruined by the years of rain and wind from the Gobi Desert. When the Wall had disappeared into the distance, I decided we had been silent for long enough. 'Do you know what this film is about?' I asked, trying to be friendly.

'No. It's got a lot of Mongolians and some westerners in it. Ask Building the Country when we get there. He's the co-producer, he should know,' the driver said, sounding as if he didn't much care.

The landscape started to change. The hills became gentler, giving way to open spaces, and a refreshing breeze blew, created by the change in height from the high hills to the plains. We were near the Hebei-Mongolia border. Far ahead, a sign in the middle of the road, supported by two wooden poles like a huge curtain, welcomed us to Inner Mongolia. The car swerved to avoid a big stone and hit a pothole. I looked back as the car bumped and lurched under the sign and saw the reverse. 'Do come again. Your families are awaiting your safe return, please drive carefully.' At either end of the sign were pictures of Han and Mongolian-dressed women, each with a baby in their arms.

The car stopped. Driver Zhang got out, threw away his cigarette end and cursed. 'Lazy Mongolians – they never maintain the road properly.' He wiped a mud stain off the car with a piece of cloth.

I waited in the quiet. Apart from the condition of the roads, it didn't look much different from the Hebei Province of Han China. 'Are we really in Inner Mongolia?' I asked doubtfully.

'Of course.' He pointed to a road sign that read, 'Three Trees'. He was getting a bit impatient. A tyre had burst in the pothole, and the jack was nowhere to be found.

'Three Trees!' I exclaimed. 'But that's where my grand-parents were sent.'

'Oh, yeah?' The driver showed little interest. I thought of Laolao and Laoye's ten years of exile. In their letters to us they had described fruit trees, dogs and cats, a paradise. I found it hard to match the lush, colourful picture I had imagined with the bleak scene before my eyes.

I spotted a low brick house hidden behind a clump of bushes set back from the road, got out of the car, ran ahead, followed by Zhang, and saw a discoloured sign, 'Oil', sticking out from behind a branch. I peered through the dusty window. A man was lying in a makeshift bed. We knocked hard and he woke, saw us and jumped up. He was a big, burly man, and he walked unsteadily towards the window. 'What do you want?' he shouted.

The driver spoke behind me: 'Brother, my tyre's burst. Can I borrow your jack?'

The man opened the door, and yawned. 'Where did you come from?'

'Beijing.'

He looked at our new jeep. 'I have an old jack, but it will cost you thirty yuan.'

'What?' The driver was shocked. 'Brother, come on, this is too much. We are not rich.' He offered a cigarette. The man shook his head. 'I don't smoke.' His hands were still on the doorknob and I thought he was about to shut us out.

Driver Zhang gave up. He could not see any cars coming and it was getting late. 'All right,' he said. They talked as if I wasn't there.

I sat in the shadows and watched the driver change the tyre. The petrol man squatted against the wall and studied me curiously. 'Are you from Three Trees?' I asked. The man nodded slowly. 'My grandparents lived here, back in the nineteen seventies,' I said tentatively.

The man narrowed his eyes. 'What were their names?'

'Field of Jade and Smart Scholar,' I murmured, somehow uneasy about saying their names to this stranger.

The man's eyes opened wide. 'The people from Sunny City?'

'Yes.'

He stood up abruptly. 'I know them. Uncle Smart Scholar wrote Spring Festival couplets for us. How are they? I heard he was rehabilitated.'

'He died of a stroke a year ago.'

The man opened his mouth then shut it. He was quiet for a while. 'He had a heart problem, didn't he? Funny, when he was here he told us the countryside was good for his heart and he didn't get ill at all. There were no movements here, no politics. We were just poor peasants and there were too many Mongolians around.'

At dusk, we approached a small town. With our business letter of introduction, we checked into the town-centre hotel appropriately named The Border. The girl at the counter, a Han Chinese with dark skin, smiled cheerfully at us, but the driver dived immediately into his room and switched on the TV, leaving me with my luggage to follow her to my room at the end of the corridor.

We were on the edge of the grassland. Dark-skinned weatherbeaten Mongolians and Han Chinese were more common than the pale-skinned Han Chinese from the central regions. I saw more people here in the hotel than I had during the entire journey. As I walked past each room, I caught glimpses of them, feet on beds, chain-smoking in front of a TV, or chatting in groups.

When we were alone, the receptionist lowered her voice. I seemed not much older than her, so she talked to me with a mixture of jealousy and curiosity, wanting to know what I did and where I was going. 'Who is that man?' she asked, with a dry smile. I pushed her out of my room and slammed the door.

I went to the window and stared into the distance, beyond the edge of the town. I could see the grassland beckoning to me. Below my window, in the fast fading light, the local market traders were packing away their fruit and vegetables, their voices weary from days of shouting and sitting in the dust. I kicked off my high-heeled shoes, and took off my white shirt, now yellow with dust. In the small mirror I had brought with me, I examined my face: my lips were cracked from the wind and dust, and the lipstick had almost worn off, leaving thin red lines like streams running through a drought-stricken land. I went to wash my face.

I started a letter to Laolao. I must tell her about my encounter at Three Trees. The man I had met there had offered to take us home for a meal and refused any payment from Zhang – the incident had raised my status dramatically in his eyes. But I could not go on with the letter. I wanted to exchange memories with Laolao, but I was facing the excitement of the unknown. The wind from the grassland swept in through the open window and I felt restless.

I thought of Laoye. I wanted his soul back. The man had said Laoye wrote Spring Festival couplets for him. I remembered Laoye's delicate hands, which years of calligraphy had made so graceful, and imagined them ploughing the field, holding the spade. When he straightened his aching back to look around, sweating beneath the merciless scorching sun, had he recited, 'Out of West of Yang Guan one never sees a familiar face?' Had he resigned himself to his fate and been content to live the rest of his life in exile on the border? On our way we had seen low houses brightened by faded Spring Festival couplets, which seemed to have been there for ever. Had he written them? Had it given him some pleasure to leave trails of beautiful script in a bleak, hostile landscape? At least, as the garage man had said, he had been sheltered here from the political storm that had swept other parts of the country and would surely have killed him.

I turned off the light and lay down, leaving the window

open. It was the start of a restless night. My mind turned alternately between memories of Laoye and the beckoning grassland on the other side of the town. I was disturbed occasionally by other guests talking loudly in the corridor in a mixture of Chinese and Mongolian. Next door, the driver had the TV on at full blast. I was woken several times by the noise, which wove itself into my dream of Laoye's past.

Chapter 2:

The Grassland

$$\text{———}\bullet\text{———}$$

Outside the small town, we reached an expanse of bare earth, a passage leading to the vast grassland. As we drove towards it, I felt it turn into a green sea; the car was a small boat among the waves.

The grassland hit me like nothing ever had before. It enfolded me, soothed and relaxed me. There was no choice but to surrender to its power and magic. The green was mesmerising, the space awe-inspiring.

We were free, Driver Zhang and I. We smiled at each other; his eyes, black and clear, gazed into the distance. Most of the time, we drove in silence, surrendering ourselves to the grassland's magic. There was no sign of life, so it was quite a shock to see birds of prey flying low to check the car. There were no roads, and we followed the tracks made by other vehicles, stretching in a straight line as far as the eye could see. Sometimes he left the track and did a detour before rejoining the straight lines. The beauty of the grassland made us both childlike.

At dusk we arrived in a small village, passing low mud houses along a quiet street, whose layout I could just distinguish in the fading light. We stopped in a courtyard surrounded by red-brick bungalows. In the middle, there was a well where two western-looking women were trying to pump water. They giggled as they struggled and the sound echoed like raindrops on a dry dusty road. Not far away, a Mongolian man stood silently with a black horse, looking on, bemused.

A voice called to us in an elegant, Beijing accent, 'Come in, I am here, room eight.'

In his Spartan room, Building the Country, tanned, was soaking his feet in hot water. The room smelt of sweat and smelly feet. 'We haven't had a bath for days,' he said. 'This place is so primitive, all we've eaten is sheep meat.' His eyes twinkled and I knew he was showing off. He told me that the main party had gone to the grassland to shoot on location. He and a few of the crew had been left at the base here to collect me and bring more equipment. 'We'll set off tomorrow morning first thing. The journey will take most of the day.'

I was taken through dark corridors smelling of animal fat to a room with two beds and a bare, high-hanging lightbulb. The floor had just been washed and was wet, and a thin pale young woman was inside brushing her hair. She put down her brush and stretched out a slender hand. 'You must be our new interpreter. I am Jade, the company secretary.' She started to complain of the harshness of the life she had experienced this last week since they had arrived in the grassland. There was no running water, they ate nothing but mutton, and the Mongolians smelt. 'Worst thing is, I have started to smell too, might even have fleas.' Her voice rose in indignation. 'I am counting the days until this ends.'

The next morning, we climbed into a coach and drove through the village and further into the grassland. The driver and Jade joked along the way, and I sat next to Building the Country, who dozed. The two western women I had seen the night before sat at the back. The tall blonde one noticed me first and nodded; the smaller, dark one giggled and ignored me.

As the houses became scarce, the telegraph poles appeared more prominent. They connected with each other in a straight line down to the horizon and looked ill-placed and awkward in the surroundings. In the afternoon even these disappeared and the grassland unfolded before our eyes. Houses and telegraph poles were mere commas in its long, continuous narrative.

When we paused for lunch, the blonde woman stopped beside where I was sitting. 'Renee, Marie.' She pointed at herself and at the woman behind her. 'Nice to meet you.'

'I hope you will understand my English,' I said.

'Oh, no problem.' Marie giggled, and the huge earrings beneath her masses of black hair rattled. 'It's *our* English you've got to worry about. Renee's German and I'm Mexican. The director is from Argentina, the leading actress from Italy.' She turned to Renee. 'Do you know anyone who is English?'

Renee laughed. 'I think David might be, or is he a Scot?'

The atmosphere in the coach relaxed. The men – the driver, Building the Country and a silent Mongolian – must have assumed we were laughing at some private female joke. Jade felt left out: she tugged at my elbow and demanded a translation of what had been said.

In the darkness, the headlights illuminated a cluster of yurts – the Mongolian tents. Building the Country turned to me: 'There they are.'

The coach drew to a standstill, we got out and walked towards the yurts. As we approached the first, I saw a point of red light. At first I thought it was a night bug but as we got closer I realised it was a man smoking a cigarette. As we drew near to him, he stood up. He said, 'Hello,' to Building the Country, then nodded silently at the rest of us. He did not seem surprised to see us. His face was pale and thin and there was something unfamiliar about him. I assumed he was Mongolian.

'Hello.' Building the Country waved his hand. 'Are they all in there?' The man stepped aside to lift the thick curtain. As we walked past him, he turned away his face to inhale more smoke, then breathed out with a deep sigh. I was alarmed and glanced back at him. I thought I caught a glimpse of anger and frustration on his face.

A woman stood next to a gas-light in the middle of the yurt with her back to us. She turned sharply at our footsteps and I was startled by her beauty and by the look of anger on her face, echoing that of the young man outside. She was obviously Mongolian, with wide high cheekbones. Her black hair was swept into a knot at the back of her head and her jet-black eyes radiated power and vitality. She looked like some animal lurking in the dark. But her eyes softened as Building the Country said, 'Saraa.'

Her brows arched and her mouth twisted into a smile. 'Building the Country, I thought you were somebody else. So this must be . . .'

'Yes, Taotao, our new interpreter.' Building the Country turned to me. 'This is Saraa, our leading Mongolian actress.'

Saraa took my outstretched hand in both of hers. 'Oh, it's so cold – you poor thing!' she exclaimed, rubbing it. Her palms were warm and transmitted to me her friendliness and charm.

Then she embraced Renee and Marie and greeted them. 'Hello.'

'Hello,' they responded, and smiled. More hellos came from elsewhere in the yurt. I looked round and saw a dozen other girls lying in the dark corners, wrapped in blankets. Other lumpy forms were motionless, asleep.

I yawned, and so did Building the Country. 'You have all the time in the world to talk tomorrow, but now we should get some rest.' He moved towards the door, followed by Renee and Marie.

Saraa crossed to the far corner of the yurt and pulled some blankets from underneath one of the girls, prompting protests and groans. 'Let's set up your bed,' she said to me. As she laid out the blankets, there was silence, until one of the girls started to sing softly. It was a song I did not know, in a language I did not understand, but it moved me. I lay down next to Saraa, who joined in the singing. A figure hovered at the door. It was the young Mongolian man. Saraa carried on singing. I was not sure if she had seen him.

It was a strange sensation to sleep among new people so close to the earth. I woke in the early hours of the morning, got up and moved forward gingerly. I stepped on one of the Mongolian girls, who woke, realised what I needed and pointed to the door.

It had been a starry night, with quite a cool breeze. Now day was breaking. I gazed at the contours of the hills beside which the yurts were pitched. Against the velvety sky, the line was as clear as if it had been painted, the edge a mixture of blue and purple. I walked on fresh-smelling grass wet from dew, and the ground steamed beneath my feet.

Mysterious lumps were scattered some distance away from the main cluster of yurts. Curious, I went closer. They were sleeping-bags. Inside the first I saw two heads, a man's and a woman's. They were fast asleep and I walked past them, my heart pounding. Soon I saw another pair, westerners, sleeping next to each other this time, in separate sleeping-bags. The man had a suntanned face and the woman's hands reached out towards him. I quickened my step and walked to the end of the sleeping-bags. One couple was wrapped in a big green military blanket, the woman's thick black hair spreading out of it on to the dew-soaked grass, the man's face snuggled into her shoulder. It was Saraa and the man was the Mongolian who had been smoking outside the yurt.

My face burned. I stumbled back into the warmth of the yurt and tried to sleep, but the vision of those entwined couples replayed in my head like scenes in a film.

This was no place for the past, for history, for Tang poems. The weight of Laoye's suffering had been lifted and memories of him faded away like a previous life. I lived for the moment. And now I was a butterfly.

Chapter 3:

Pride and Prejudice

When I woke up again, the sun was streaming down the valley. I washed quickly and ran outside. The sleeping-bags had vanished, and my night-time wander seemed no more than a dream. Following the gentle slope, I climbed to the top and sat down, almost breathless. A slim figure came out of one of the yurts, and went towards a wooden frame in the middle of the camping ground. His eyes passed over me, then moved on. I recognised him as the suntanned westerner whose face I had seen during my night walk. I felt like hiding, as though I had seen something I shouldn't.

He got to the middle of the wooden skeleton he was constructing, picked up a chisel and bent down to chip at a piece of wood. Occasionally he straightened his back. I was transfixed by the intensity of his movements. The air was full of the sweet smell of grass and the buzz of low-flying dragonflies. I turned to lie flat on my back on the grass. The sky was cloudless and seemed so close. I felt light as a feather, the breeze could have carried me away.

My peace was disturbed by Jade, who had run up the hill to me. 'Come on, I want to chat with that carpenter. You can translate for me.' She grabbed my arms, pulled me to my feet, then rushed down the hill. She smelt of perfume and was dressed as if she was on holiday. We ran down so fast that before I knew where I was we were in front of the carpenter, who stopped work with a sigh. He looked up with annoyance at our approach.

I was embarrassed and stared at his hands. One held the chisel, the other hung down loosely, touching his jeans. They were big hands, almost disproportionate to his height, and the one that held the chisel was brown, strong, with white knuckles, like the paw of an animal.

Jade giggled. 'Ask him what he's doing.'

'What are you doing?' I asked mechanically, playing the role of interpreter, but feeling silly.

His eyes rested on Jade's white shoes and his mouth twisted into an ironic smile, then he returned to his work as though we were not there.

'Go on, ask him again what he is doing,' Jade said.

I was angry with her for embarrassing me like this, and with him too, for ignoring me. I spoke to him coldly: 'I'm only translating for her, I'm not interested in what you're doing.' Then I turned abruptly to Jade. 'Breakfast is ready, let's go.' Without waiting for her, I headed for the main yurt.

'Arrogant, isn't he?' I said to Jade, when she caught up.

'They all are, these foreigners,' she agreed. 'Actually, that carpenter isn't too bad. The worst one is the director. He has got a *temper*.'

Breakfast was being cooked in the open air, and people were emerging from their yurts, drawn by the smell. The coach driver, looking refreshed and relaxed, winked at me as he swallowed a bowl of hot meat juice. Jade ran up to him and they engaged in eager conversation. From her expression, I guessed they were swapping complaints about the food.

I glanced back at the carpenter, still bent down working, alone. His body moved rhythmically. Maybe he was a born loner and did not like company. I went towards the breakfast queue. Everyone was clutching a bowl or a mug, but I had nothing. I joined the end of the queue anyway and stood behind a tall, thin Mongolian-looking man. His trousers were dirty and he smelt. The queue moved slowly.

'Hi there,' someone called from behind. It was Saraa. The young man before me half turned, and I recognised him as Saraa's sleeping partner in the army blanket. As Saraa approached, he turned his back to me again and moved forward a few steps in the queue. Saraa came running, a bowl in her hand. 'How did you sleep?' she asked me, ignoring the young man in front of us.

'Very well,' I answered. She looked beautiful, radiant, but tired; there were black shadows beneath her eyes. 'I haven't got a bowl for breakfast, so I don't know why I'm standing here,' I remarked.

'Have mine.'

Two bowls were presented to me: the young man had turned to face us and his bowl collided with Saraa's, *ping*. 'Use mine,' Saraa decided for me. 'I'll share his. You don't mind, do you?' she asked him.

'Of course not,' he replied, and turned his back again. Saraa thrust her bowl, a pretty enamel one with a picture of two Mandarin ducks, into my hand. 'There you go. Give it back to me when you've finished.'

When I had been given my share of the meat juice, I retreated to the front of my yurt and sat with the others. It was hard to digest something so oily first thing in the morning and I put the bowl down. I saw Saraa and the young man standing next to each other, in a corner of a yurt. Saraa, her head tilted, was drinking from the bowl. I averted my eyes and examined the bowl Saraa had given me: the Mandarin ducks were a symbol of love in Chinese culture. Was it the same for the Mongolians? Had the young man given it to her as a love token?

While we were having breakfast, a truckload of brightly costumed Mongolians arrived from a nearby village. Soon another truckload of handsome Mongolian horses and camels arrived. The Mongolians stood together rigidly, examining the westerners and the Chinese with equal curiosity. The director, a tall thin man with wavy blond hair, gave them a big smile to try to win them over, only to find that he had startled them. He shrugged his shoulders and retreated towards Building the Country, who waved at me. I put my bowl down and thought: Here we go! Work has started.

The director spoke with a strong accent and it took me a little time to understand him. He walked away from me, looking worried and, I suspected, a little contemptuous. 'Can you move to the other side of the tent?' I shouted, but my voice sounded thin and unconvincing – I wasn't sure whether to sound authoritative or polite and added, 'Please,' when nobody moved. Then it dawned on me that the Mongolians might not understand much Chinese. They did not.

Saraa came to my rescue. She asked me what the director wanted, then turned and spoke to the Mongolians. They smiled and gathered around her, chatting in their own language. I felt ashamed: my first translation task and I had had to stand by and watch. A little girl, wearing a pink dress, her hair in a thick black plait, touched Saraa's hand and smiled up at her. Saraa was talking to an earnest-looking old man and did not notice her. The little girl looked around shyly, caught my eye and smiled. It was as if a flower on the pasture had opened especially for me. I felt honoured. I took her hand, and she trailed along behind me like a dog. She had come with her father, who was now changing into an even more colourful costume than the one in which he had arrived.

I took the little girl to the dressing tent, where Renee and Marie were putting on lipstick, both wearing long gowns that made Renee look even taller. 'Is this your little sister?' she asked, her eyes twinkling. I recognised her as the woman who had slept next to the carpenter last night, and I wondered about their relationship: she was very tall, the carpenter comparatively short – they would be an odd pair.

'Were you singing in your tent last night?' Marie asked. 'What was it? It was beautiful.' She rolled her big black eyes.

'I wish I knew,' I confessed. 'It was a Mongolian folk song. You have to ask Saraa what it's about.'

'I remember a little bit. It went like this.' Marie began to sing then stopped. Then the little girl, who had been looking alternately at Renee and Marie, picked up the song where Marie had stopped.

'She knows it,' Marie exclaimed. We listened as the child carried on, pleased with the attention she was getting. Marie soon caught up with her and before long I was singing along too.

None of us noticed the director storm in. The little girl was on Marie's lap, playing with her plait. 'Stop it! What do you think you're doing?' The director waved his fists at us menacingly. 'We've worked the whole morning on this shot and now you've ruined it.'

He stood where the light streamed in, his back towards the door. We stopped dead and the tent was silent. After a few seconds, Marie stood up. The little girl hid behind me and held on to my shirt, trembling like a leaf in the wind. 'Sorry, we weren't thinking,' I murmured.

The director came a step nearer to me, so close that I could see the pale colour of his eyelashes and the anger in his eyes. 'You are supposed to be helping me to translate. Go back to your place instead of idling here,' he shouted, then stalked out.

I was not too upset by his outburst – I had found the way he had erupted quite comic. I supposed he was entitled to feel angry: it was his film. But the little girl was very upset. When I handed her back to her father, she grabbed his hand and began to sob. I felt helpless, as the young man's face darkened, and he glared at the director. His friends gathered around him.

I ran to Building the Country and told him the whole story. 'Come with me. We must find the director and apologise to the Mongolians,' he said decisively.

We found him sitting in the technicians' tent, having an

earnest discussion with the carpenter, who was making notes. They looked up as we approached, and I saw pride again in the carpenter's face. My back stiffened.

The director greeted us coldly, still angry with me for spoiling his shot. He was unable to see what the fuss was about. Hadn't he had to scrap a morning's work? Surely he was the one to whom an apology was owed.

'But the Mongolians wouldn't have seen it that way, especially not the little girl,' I said, conscious of the carpenter's eyes on me. I noticed his hands again, which rested on his knees. The director looked surprised. 'A little girl? I never saw her.' There was a moment's silence as he stared at the ground, then at the carpenter. He shrugged his shoulders and walked towards the Mongolians, who had gathered in a semi-circle around the young father and stood in silence. We stayed and watched from inside the tent. The director went straight to the little girl and stooped down to touch her head. She shied away from him, and clung tightly to her father. The director fumbled in his pockets, then surprised everyone with a deep bow. 'Sorry,' he said.

In the next few days, I learned some Mongolian words from the extras and the little girl. Luckily most of the girls came from the same part of Mongolia as Saraa and were bilingual in Mongolian and Chinese so they could understand my instructions. As I ran back and forth with messages from the director to the extras and Building the Country, my Mongolian vocabulary built up, but it took them a long time to acknowledge it.

Every day we filmed separate scenes; some made sense to me, some did not. They were so disjointed that I could not pin them together to form a picture of what the film was about, but I settled in and enjoyed the filming.

We moved in three coaches and one truck to the next location. I followed Marie and Renee on to the second coach. Renee stopped at a seat next to the carpenter, who was listening to music through earphones with his eyes closed.

She pinched his shoulder and he opened his eyes, smiled and moved to give her space. Marie and I sat down in the row behind them.

I started to sing to myself, the song that had got me into trouble. The carpenter looked back. His eyes met mine and he smiled, his white teeth showing. His face transformed and became handsome. But I didn't smile back: he had slighted me and I was not ready to be friendly.

He whispered something to Renee, who giggled and turned to me. 'Taotao, you've an admirer here. David said you taught the director a good lesson.' She winked at me, and despite myself I smiled, surprised and pleased that he had been on my side. He stretched out a hand. 'Hello, Taotao.' His voice was soft, almost like a whisper. I took his hand, which felt rough – I could feel the lines engraved on the palm.

They resumed their conversation and I fell asleep. When I woke, Renee's head was on David's shoulder, and she was fast asleep. He was sitting upright to support her. How considerate, I thought.

We arrived in a schoolyard under moonlight. A tired-looking man, the caretaker, led us to our rooms, which were the classrooms. We made beds by pushing several desks together with a quilt on top. I climbed on to one and immediately fell asleep.

The next morning, on the coach I walked automatically to the last seat but one. Until we moved off, I did not realise that the shoulder I had spent our journey yesterday watching had gone. Instead I saw in front of me a Mongolian girl. Why should I feel a pang of disappointment? Nobody had dictated where we should sit.

Chapter 4:

Startling Moon

~~~~~~~~~~~~~~~~

We left the grassland and headed towards brown hills. They were barren, covered with sand and rocks, as if they hadn't changed since the beginning of the world.

We parked in the middle of a wide valley surrounded on both sides by hills. It was the Mongolian girls' turn to perform. They followed Saraa noisily into the tent to get changed while the technicians set up the recording equipment. The hills looked paler against the brightness of the sun. The director, in a white shirt, strode over to me and asked me to tell the Chinese driver to move the truck out of the way.

I did as he asked, then sat next to the driver in the shade of the parked truck. The afternoon spread before us, and everybody was waiting for the Mongolian girls to be ready. I watched the driver rolling a cigarette and for the first time I felt a craving for tobacco. 'Can I make one?' I begged.

He laughed, pretended to be shocked, then handed me the cigarette he had rolled for himself. 'Here, have this.'

'No, I want to make my own.' He shrugged his shoulders and passed me his packet.

I heard a laugh and looked up. David was sitting not far from us also rolling a cigarette. 'I didn't know that nice Chinese girls smoked.'

His smile was infectious and I felt light-headed. 'They don't.' I laughed. 'But I do.'

All the westerners sat under the direct sun, while the Chinese and Mongolians sat in the shade and laughed at the foreigners, who turned their bodies to face the heat, like sunflowers. The aroma of tobacco hung in the dry air and merged with the landscape. I felt a sense of completeness, and wished time would stop. I rolled my cigarette and smoked it as I sat and watched the girls on camels disappear into the mouth of the wide valley again and again. The sun was hot, the girls even hotter in tight armour, their faces red. The director was not satisfied: he looked more and more impatient. At the fifth attempt, Saraa's camel ran berserk, causing two girls to fall off.

I had been halfway up a sand hill when I heard the screams. From the top, I saw a thin figure running towards the girls on the ground. His movements were familiar to me now, like a leopard's, powerful and fast. I felt a small creature fall into my hands, a lizard. It took one look at me, closed its eyes and played dead. I held it in my hands awhile before putting it back onto the sand where it whisked into a hole.

What was this new feeling of affection in me? I could love all the creatures in the world, I thought. I got up and slid down the hill, then ran towards the mouth of the valley where I collided with David. 'He shouldn't have pressed these girls so hard,' he said. 'It was too much, even for the camels.' He stomped past me, took off his shirt, sat down and lit a cigarette. A book lay at his side.

I warmed to his concern for the Mongolian girls and when I glanced back, he was lying flat on his back. A thought occurred to me, which made me blush. If I were one of the Mongolian girls he would have carried me in his strong arms.

The shooting came to a temporary halt while the girls were treated. The director sat with his face in his hands, a forlorn figure in the late-afternoon sun. I continued walking through the valley. The Mongolian girls must have ridden as far as this, I thought: the tracks left by the camels were still visible. The valley narrowed between the mountains on either side. I stared in awe at them and reached out to touch the rockface. It was magical: I knew it had not been touched by humans for centuries. On the rough surface, as high as my arms could reach, carved lines made a darker pattern. I leaned close to study them, and discerned something that man had made: there was an engraving of a person with an arrow-like object, and an animal, like a sheep with horns. I stepped back to scan further and beyond; the whole of this side of the hill was covered with pictures, a giant mural.

I touched the image of the man. Close up, I could see finer lines radiating from the thick ones – it was like looking closely at the tip of a paintbrush as it moved. I remembered watching as Laoye taught me calligraphy. Thousands of years earlier someone had held his knife and carved this. I could almost feel the knife moving now.

I stumbled back slowly, dancing backwards and forwards, feeling like a feather. I found David still sunning himself where I had left him. His whisper made me jump: 'Did you see it?'

'Yes,' I whispered back. Our eyes met, and we recognised something in each other that united us. We were strangers no more. We had communicated in a language only we understood.

Building the Country grabbed me and took me to the director. He told him that the local herdsmen had said heavy rain was on its way and we should leave early. The director insisted that we stick to his schedule, and carry on until the last minute. Building the Country kept looking at his watch and the Mongolians were visibly agitated.

It got dark very quickly. When at last the director agreed that it was time to go, we were told that the actresses' coach had broken down so we all packed ourselves on to the back of the truck with the extras and other supporting staff. We drove through the valley where we had walked and worked in the daytime, pressed tightly against each other for warmth as the chill of the evening sank in. I sat next to an old Mongolian woman. David stood at the front of the truck, his hair blowing in the wind.

The hills were dark and so high that they blocked out the moonlight. A silent storm brewed in me and I felt intoxicated. We were so far away from anywhere; I felt alone, despite the press of people. The only other person who existed for me here was David.

When the truck sailed out of the narrow valley the full moon appeared. A collective murmur of joy erupted. 'The moon emerges, startling the mountain birds' – the line flashed through my mind. Tonight the moon had startled us all, and now I understood.

'What did you say?' David intruded on my reverie.

' "The moon emerges, startling the mountain birds . . ." ' I stopped. The English translation did not do justice to the poem. The way a character was constructed and placed to convey so many contrasts and associations could never be expressed in translation, which limited the meaning and rendered the poem one-dimensional. What could I say to this foreigner who did not speak my language?

But David was waiting, his face glistening in the moonlight. It showed off his angular features, strong, yet gentle. I wanted to stroke his cheek. 'How could the moon startle?' I asked.

He looked up at it. 'It can, just like that. I would say it's startlingly beautiful.'

Again, we had communicated, as we had in the valley earlier. We had discovered the sacred kingdom of beauty. He was more to me than a stranger who had understood my Tang poem: although he was a foreigner with no background in classical Chinese literature, he was a soulmate.

I shivered in the cold. David took off his jumper and handed it to me. I wrapped it around my head to stop my hair blowing loose. It smelt of him, of wood and wind. My teeth chattered with cold and excitement.

I gazed at him. A few days ago he had annoyed and humiliated me: now we had shared a secret. It all seemed quite natural, as if this change had been meant to happen. I had so much to say to him that I didn't know where to begin. 'How are you getting on with your novel?' I shouted. Seeing his face, I added, '*Catch 22*, the book you are reading. I have read it, too, in Chinese.'

'It's a great book,' he said, surprised. 'But how come you've read it?'

'It's a world classic, isn't it?' I said, and wondered if, after all, we really had anything in common. But there he stood, so close and yet so distant. 'Do you travel a lot?' I asked.

A strange look flitted across his face. 'A great deal. I've worked on all sorts of projects with different film crews, and have been to many places. I make many friends but then I lose them.' He paused, and stared at me sadly.

Was he trying to tell me something? I chose not to look for his meaning.

Black clouds gathered around the moon. We heard thunder, and then, suddenly, it poured. The raindrops were heavy and cold. There was chaos and we tried to find shelter, but there was none on the truck. A Mongolian pointed towards the top of the mountain: there was a monastery half-way up. The truck stopped and we abandoned it and started to climb. I soon lost David.

Climbing the hill in the darkness with many others was different from my solitary daytime wander. The hills then had been distant, remote: now they were so close that I felt they were breathing with me. The crowd moved uncertainly and a hushed silence fell. I was looking for David. I couldn't bear to be separated from him just yet, or for the bond between us to break. I saw a figure in front of me stoop down and put something on a pile of stones, then walk on. I caught up and found many more piles of stones leading to the monastery, where a spectacular hut stood outside the gate. I caught sight of Saraa adding her own stone to a small pile. Her wet hair clung to her face, making her cheekbones seem even more prominent. 'What's this?' I pointed to the little heap.

'Our custom.'

'Religious?'

'No, well, sort of. I do it for good luck.' She hurried off.

I lingered by the small stone structure. I wanted to see David. People rushed past me to get out of the rain, but I did not mind it – I wanted to get soaked. I saw no sign of him, though, and eventually, dripping wet, I reluctantly decided to go in. I felt about on the wet ground until I found a small stone, which I placed on top of Saraa's. 'Good luck to me,' I murmured in the darkness, to whomever Saraa and the Mongolians had dedicated their stones.

The air smelt of burning candles as a procession of purple-gowned monks, holding red lanterns, silently directed us to sleeping places. After the rain and wind outside, their orderly appearance brought comfort. We lowered our voices and obeyed the monks, who used gestures rather than words. Even the director followed like a lamb to his quarters. We slept in a big open hall where the monks usually stored their groceries. It was filled with big cushions and we were given blankets to wrap round ourselves. Before I took off my wet jacket to get into bed – which consisted of two layers of blankets – I looked round the roomful of Chinese, Mongolian and foreigners, and saw David several spaces away, his back towards me, his body bent, looking vulnerable.

Amid a strong smell of candlewax, I tossed and turned, listening to the rain outside, and to the breathing of people around me. The knowledge that I was sleeping in the same room as David excited me, and it was hard to sleep. In the next room, the monks chanted in a low murmur, the sound mingling with the rain. For the first time in my life I thought about religion. I did not care about the film we were making, did not mind being stranded. I wished we could stop time now for ever. I had found something I wanted to hold on to, that I feared losing. Was this why I had made my first act of worship in adding my stone to that pile? Was that why people became religious? Through fear rather than faith?

In the morning, we woke up to the news that the truck was gone, washed away by a torrent. I ran outside to see. It lay half buried in the mud that had built up during the night, and looked so small. I was surprised to see what a steep hill we had climbed in the darkness.

I brushed my teeth, and peered down the side of the hill. Many of the piles of stones had been washed away by the water. I tried to locate the pile to which I had added my own small stone, but failed. When I turned to go back inside, I met David on the way out with his toothbrush. Looking tired and withdrawn, he returned my greeting with a weak smile. We both acted as if the previous night was just a memory.

There was something sweet about comradeship built up in conditions like this. Already I felt as close to Renee, Marie and Saraa as I had to Hair and Willow. With David it was different: the closeness had a forbidden air. The mural and the moon poem had brought him into my heart, which had never before been opened to a man. And although I had only just begun to get to know him, I felt a twinge of pain at the prospect of saying goodbye.

Chapter 5:

A Beast

An emergency meeting was held and we split into two groups. Someone called the county government for a coach to transport the actresses to the next location. The men and other production staff would stay behind until the truck had been retrieved and mended. This small goodbye was a rehearsal for the big one to come, and somewhere in my heart a warning bell rang. I joined the actresses and the director on the coach, and we left the brown hills behind us.

I sat at the back of the coach, alone. I wondered what David was doing. Was this how Steel had felt about me? That the past had ceased to matter, that only the present existed, that the world was big enough only for the two of us? When I was near David, everything else disappeared.

We approached some houses. 'This is a very big town – what is it called?' the director asked.

'Huhehot,' Saraa said enthusiastically, 'the capital of the Mongolian region.'

'Ah.' He nodded, and stared at the dust-covered streets without interest, slumped back in his seat.

Saraa turned to me. 'I'll show you around tomorrow.'

That night we stayed at a local hotel. In the lift the attendant recognised Saraa and asked to have a photo taken with her. I stepped aside, but she drew me in, holding me in front of her with both arms.

We waited at the hotel for the other half of the party to join us from the mountains. Saraa and I borrowed bicycles and cycled around the city all day. We went to the antique markets, which were full of Chinese and Mongolian relics. Longing and impatience built within me.

The bikes and the dust reminded me of my life before Mongolia. It seemed so shadowy against the vivid present. I remembered my dread of joining in the bicycle streams in Beijing – the routine that awaited me. I had avoided doing so, in the short term, and I did not want to think of the future.

We cycled against the wave of bicycles towards our hotel. Saraa was in front: she rode the bike as if it was a horse, her bottom and hips high, her back straight. I pedalled up to join her. She heard me and slowed down. 'I went to school here, you know,' she said calmly, her head erect. 'My family is from the countryside, and they sent me to school here, in the capital, to better myself. I hated it.'

'Why?'

'I was the youngest. They were all much bigger, tougher girls.'

I seized the opportunity: 'Did . . . whatshisname go there with you?' I asked cautiously.

'Yes.' She smiled, knowing who I meant. 'But he was in a different year, and his family was from Huhehot.' She paused, lost in thought. 'He plays the violin very well. We met in the school entertainment troupe.'

It was nearly dark when we got back to the hotel. The barbers by the roadside were packing up. At the gate, the familiar sight of the green truck greeted us. The men were getting off, looking tired and ragged. My heart beat fast, as my eyes searched for David. Beside me, Saraa had already parked her bicycle and walked steadily but swiftly to the thin young man. Then I saw David, his hands on the door of the truck, talking to the driver, who laughed.

I parked my bicycle, and ran towards him. He didn't see me

coming until I tapped his shoulder. Then he turned, his arms shot out and he held me tightly. I closed my eyes and breathed in his smell, which brought back the brown hills. I could not say a word. The driver was peering at us curiously. I untangled myself from David's embrace and struggled for words. 'Hey, you're so dirty,' I managed. He held my hands in both of his, then brought them to his mouth and kissed them. Then he smiled at the driver. 'You're right, I need a wash.' He let go of my hands and went into the hotel.

In the evening, we held a reunion party at the hotel bar. I felt shy and tried to avoid David. My outburst of emotion at the hotel gate had alarmed me so I compensated for it by holding back. David pursued me in a silent way, hovering on the fringes of whichever group I was with. Later that night, when we had all drunk a lot, we danced. I danced as I never had before, with everyone, and once with David.

The next day, we didn't set off until late. I found my seat on the coach and waited expectantly. David got on, caught my eye and came purposefully to sit down by my side. Although I had expected him to come to me, I was ill at ease. There we sat, not in the dark, not in the wild, not in disagreement, but awkward in the cold light of day. I pushed myself to the furthest corner of the seat and looked away. I couldn't meet his eyes.

We drove towards the desert. Telegraph poles paraded along the road at equal distances, one after another. 'They are like beasts.' I pointed at them.

'Yes,' he agreed. 'Do you know about the half-man, half-wolf creatures?'

'What are they?'

'They change shape at night, and eat people.' He made a face, showing his white teeth, and laughed, a handsome beast.

'I think you are like a beast,' I said.

'Do you?' He smiled, his eyes shining. 'Would you like me to be one?'

I liked and did not like the tone of his voice – I relished it yet it made me nervous. I wished I knew how I should feel. Should I lean on him? I asked myself. I wanted to, yet I sat there, back hunched, apart from him.

I woke up in semi-darkness, as if from a nightmare I could not remember, my heart sore and heavy from the sadness accumulated in my sleep. David's familiar black jacket was lying beside me but his seat was empty. Then I saw him, at the front of the coach, asleep, his arms around Renee. A little bug was eating my heart, and I sat there helpless. I should have leaned my head on his shoulder, I had wanted to, but something had stopped me. Now I had lost him.

The coach halted at the next hotel. His jacket still lay on the seat next to mine, and I wondered if I should take it to him, but decided not to. I wanted to punish him for leaving me alone. Outside the hotel, he was jumping up and down to keep warm. He saw me, but didn't stop jumping, or come over to talk to me. I wanted to wrap myself round him to warm him, but I didn't move. I could not bring myself to move closer to him because I feared rejection. I wanted him desperately, but I was proud.

Renee turned to embrace him. 'Are you cold, darling?' I envied her. I could never have done that. My eyes followed them like those of a hungry wolf intent on its prey as they walked arm in arm up the stairs before me.

They stood before room 302 and Renee turned to say good night to us. Before she could speak, I grabbed Jade's hand and pulled her straight into our room.

As Jade gossiped into the night, I stared at the ceiling. The porch light outside illuminated a crack that extended to the edge of the room. The next room must have the same crack. I wondered whether Renee and David had noticed it. The room was otherwise spotlessly clean, which made the crack seem worse.

I cursed Building the Country, who was responsible for the

sleeping arrangements: segregation of Chinese and foreigners, that was his rule. It turned out that foreigners, even if they were of the opposite sex, could share the same room if they wanted, as Renee and David did. I kept telling myself that there was nothing more between Renee and David than friendship but the snake in me conjured up pictures that I did not want to see.

'. . . Saraa wasn't ready. Virtue's Ba sent somebody around to Saraa's Ma, who lives alone, to say that if your daughter dares to seduce my son again . . .'

'But what about Virtue?' My attention was drawn by Saraa's name.

'You know Virtue, Saraa's boyfriend.'

Jade turned in bed, and I could see her limbs in the semi-darkness. I thought of other limbs, David and Renee's. 'But I thought . . . Oh, is Saraa's boyfriend Han Chinese?'

'Didn't you know?' Jade said. 'That's what all the fuss is about. His Ba does not want him to marry a Mongolian. But Virtue is in love with her, so he chucked his job and followed Saraa. It's like an elopement. Romantic, isn't it?' She sighed, scratching one of her legs, which she had raised in the air. 'These arty people.'

I thought of Saraa as a small girl playing side by side with Virtue in the school band. 'Saraa's nice,' I said, almost to myself.

'Yes,' responded Jade sleepily. 'I like her, but I'm not sure of the boy. Anyway,' she yawned, 'must sleep – oh.' She scuffled out of bed and went to the dressing-table on her side. I smelt face cream. 'Mustn't forget this.'

I did forget female things like that, I thought, and wondered if such rituals would make me feel better. Too tired even to wash my feet, I lay like a log, dipping in and out of sleep until I woke up with the sound of rain heavy on the window-pane.

When I came downstairs to breakfast with Jade, I saw the grey sky outside as I passed the window. On the second floor, the Italian actress leaned over the rails of the stairs, watching something. When she heard footsteps, she straightened up and smiled, her elegant fingers tapping on the rail. Then she glided downstairs. I leaned over to see what had attracted her and saw the receptionist, who was a young man, and a little girl, presumably his daughter, playing behind the counter with a doll.

We had breakfast in a big hall downstairs with all the other guests. The hotel manager, proud to have a troupe of distinguished foreign visitors, put on his best menu to entertain us. He sat with Building the Country and the director. I ate little. Thunder rumbled outside and made me restless.

I saw Renee, but no sign of David throughout breakfast. When it was time to move on, I caught a glimpse of him. He hurried on to the coach and sat on the front seat without glancing at me.

Chapter 6:

The Orient Express

We set off in the heavy rain. I sat alone at the rear of the coach. I longed to see David's face but his back was to me. Like me, he was sitting alone.

At last the rain stopped, and we were surrounded by desert. I felt empty. I longed to lean on him now that I no longer had the opportunity to do so. Had I lost him? For ever? Suddenly a voice broke into my thoughts. It was Saraa's, deep and slow like that of a prophet from another time. 'That is Outer Mongolia, another country.' I opened my eyes, and saw her finger pointing to the horizon where low hills rolled beyond the sand.

'And what's that?' somebody shouted. A dark shape stood menacingly in the distance, with clouds issuing from it.

Ahead of me Building the Country laughed. 'That's our train, the most expensive prop yet!'

I rubbed my eyes and looked again. What was a train doing in the middle of a desert? At first glance, it was no different from any other train I had seen, with the steam and the gigantic wheels. As we got nearer, however, I noticed that it had fewer carriages than usual and the track it sat on was just long enough for it.

Everyone was excited by the train, and I gathered that most of the Mongolian girls had rarely seen one, let alone one used for acting. I felt apprehensive; it reminded me of the inevitable return to reality, when David would leave and my dream would end.

Labourers from the nearby towns were at work, digging ditches for the tracks to be laid. We were encouraged to help and speed up the work. It was hot, people were lazy and progress was slow. The director sent me to hurry everyone along. Virtue, Saraa's boyfriend, was in the middle of the digging group. I jumped into the low ditch they had made and chatted with him. The workers, glad of any distraction, stopped to watch us.

David walked by, carrying a piece of wood on his shoulder. I did not turn to acknowledge him. Wiping sweat from his face, he put down the wood and surveyed the low ditch. 'Is that all they've done so far?' he shouted at me. I carried on talking to Virtue. David raised his voice. 'Perhaps if we tell them we're digging for gold, they'll work quicker.'

His tone and the patronising words angered me. I turned abruptly. 'Who are you to tell these people what to do? If you are so concerned, why don't you dig yourself?' I climbed out of the ditch and stormed past him.

Virtue followed me. 'What did that foreigner say?'

'That you weren't working hard enough.'

'Well . . . I suppose that's true. It was too hot. Is that all he said?'

'Yes,' I replied.

Virtue's attention was drawn to the red flag in the distance – the director's sign that shooting was about to start – followed by the cries of the Mongolian girls. They stood to attention beside the train. Saraa looked worn out, maybe due to the heat. I stole a glance at Virtue, remembering Jade's words last night. His eyes were fixed on Saraa. Feeling the heat, I pointed to the shade cast by the train and motioned Virtue to move there but he stood as if rooted in the sun, watching the girls.

It was quieter and cooler on the other side of the train, and I stood there to enjoy the breeze. My head felt clearer, and I was embarrassed by what I had said to David. Why could I only show him anger?

Absentmindedly, I climbed on to the train and sat down on the step. I heard movement in the carriage to my left. At first I couldn't see clearly, for the interior was dark and it was bright outside. I blinked, opened my eyes again and saw the Italian actress, in a blue velvet dress, sitting on a dark red velvet sofa. A tall thin man stood behind her, the hairdresser, with several pins in his mouth.

'I saw the most amazing thing this morning in the hotel.' Her voice sounded clear and cool.

The hairdresser, with all the pins in his mouth, could only mutter, 'Eh?'

'I saw that Chinese man kissing his little daughter. Very cute. I thought the Chinese never kissed.'

'Oh,' answered the hairdresser.

I blushed. I wanted both to correct her and to hide. But I could do neither. Somehow the presence of those two foreigners held me in its spell. The carriage had a forbidden air about it. I moved down a step. The breeze felt stronger here as I was more exposed to it, and I could no longer hear the Mongolian girls. Had they finished, I wondered.

The actress spoke again. 'I had such an exotic dream.' Her voice sounded different and strange: she was rehearsing her role. She coughed. 'I had such an exotic dream,' she repeated, with the emphasis on 'such'. She coughed again, and changed to her normal voice. 'I can't do it. My throat is too dry from the sand.'

I stood up abruptly and jumped down the stairs. So the foreigners came here to dream, did they? Foreigners like David. Did I feature in *his* dream or was he just part of mine?

I came round to the head of the train. There, in shining red and gold, were written the four characters *Dong Fang Kuai Che*, Orient Express, in fancy calligraphy. The train sat there like a giant monster, stranded, heaving, ready to pounce. I climbed up and sat in the empty driver's seat. It felt warm from the sun, which was sinking towards the desert horizon, colouring the whole sky before it dropped behind the low hills in Outer Mongolia. 'However beautiful the sunset is.' Once again, a Tang poem best expressed how I felt. The intense beauty of the sunset and the feeling of loss after the sun had gone down was the perfect image for my magical encounter with David, and losing him.

A hand rested on my shoulder – his. I touched it and leaned in towards David – my eyes were red so I could not look up to his face. I felt the lines in his palms.

We had been clasped to each other for a long time when I heard footsteps drawing near. Reluctantly I moved apart from him. Then I gazed up at him. He smiled and wiped away the tears from my eyes. A dark-faced man appeared at the foot of the steps and peered up. 'Hey there,' he said cheerfully. He held a tin food bowl – the trademark of engine drivers.

'Come on,' said David, 'we're in his way.' He led me off the train and we walked back towards the carriages, hand in hand.

They had been shooting the last scene, and we separated when we saw the director's red flag. I stood on a high slope and watched the Italian actress glide up the steps into the carriage. Renee and Marie followed, in long gowns and exaggerated red lipstick. I could see from the director's face that the shot was not perfect.

Virtue helped Saraa down from her horse and we packed up, subdued, in the fading, dusky light. Props littered the desert like archaeological artefacts.

In the morning, as Jade put on a pair of pale blue trousers, she said, 'Do you know that Saraa is getting married?'

I gasped in surprise. 'No, I didn't.'

'She has to, now, you know. They are . . . Anyway, it's got to be done.' She winked at me.

At the station, the Mongolian girls stood on the platform to wave us goodbye. They wore their ordinary clothes, soft-coloured shirts and floral-patterned skirts, their exotic costumes packed into neat boxes in the hotel lobby. As the train moved slowly, they waved, looking slender and vulnerable. Saraa ran a few steps beside it until it gathered speed. Then she stopped and waved, getting smaller and smaller until she had disappeared. We were on a real train, taking us away from our Mongolian dream. Their horses and camels, fast as they were, could never catch up with us now.

In the half-empty carriage, Renee and Marie sat down on each side of me. Marie took my hand. David walked past, saw us, disappeared and came back with a camera. He clicked it, none of us moved. He disappeared again. He had preserved the memory of me in the photo. Now he could walk away. Don't go, I wanted to shout but, as in a nightmare, I could not speak and was forced to watch the dream unfold.

Darkness fell quickly. I woke up and didn't know where I was. I could see nothing. Then I remembered. I thought of Saraa and the Mongolian girls, and saw in my mind's eye Saraa abandoning her horse to walk down the empty street to a bus stop.

Chapter 7:

Tiananmen: the Gate of Heavenly Peace

Beijing railway station in broad daylight. The sky had shrunk. The strong artificial colours hurt my eyes, which were used to brown hills, white sandy desert and green grassland. Last time I was here, fresh from Pleasant City, I was a wide-eyed student and the colour and noise had dazzled me. Now I found them offensive and gaudy. I felt alienated from the crowds after the wide-open spaces of Mongolia.

We booked into the Beijing Hotel. I did my job mechanically, helping everyone with their room allocations, then went up to my own room and had a bath. I put on a clean shirt, sat in front of the mirror and stared at myself. Although I had been away for just two months, it seemed like years. My eyes were like those of a caged animal. I took a deep breath.

Since I had arrived in Beijing, I had done everything at double speed. A timer in my mind counted the remaining hours I would spend near David. Somehow, on the train, I had managed to block the pain of his departure: while I was on the move myself, the thought of him leaving seemed unreal, but now we were in Beijing, the familiar scenes reminded me that I was to stay and he to leave. I could not bear to be alone with my thoughts like this, and walked out of my room. In the hall David was leaning on one of the human-sized pot plants. He did not seem surprised to see me.

I rushed up to him, took his hand and headed straight for the door. I had always tried not to be caught showing him affection in public, but I did not care now. He had to run to keep up with me. 'Steady, steady,' he said. We hailed the first taxi we saw and jumped in.

I put my arms around him. This was our last night together and I wanted it to last for ever. We sat there for a few minutes, not speaking to each other, until the taxi driver, a young man, staring at me in the rear-view mirror, asked, 'Miss, are you a guide?' There was an ironic tone in his voice and a trace of disdain in his eyes: he thought I was one of those prostitutes who slept with foreigners. I withdrew from David, feeling cold.

'What happened? Did he say something rude to you?' His eyes twinkled but he clenched his fist. 'I can teach him a lesson if he did.'

'No, no.' I loved his protectiveness but, in my happiness, I did not want any confrontation.

We got off at Tiananmen Square. As soon as the taxi left, David lifted me up from behind. He carried me through the crowds, staring straight ahead. I closed my eyes and heard the whispers: 'Look at that foreigner.' I had never felt so light, yet so heavy. 'Put me down,' I said, not meaning it.

When we came to the middle of the square, he set me down right in front of Chairman Mao's portrait. Sitting cross-legged opposite me, he leaned forward. 'Tell me about this place. Why have you brought me here?'

I was reminded once again of the distance between us. He knew nothing about the square, about me, about China. What should I tell him? Laoye? The Tang poem? How I had fallen in love with the square the first time I came here when I was seventeen? How I had sung about it in my childhood – 'I love the Heavenly Peace Gate... Chairman Mao leads us...'?

Chairman Mao gazed down at me, faded, disapproving. I leaned forward and took David's hands. Then I closed my eyes and wished. He drew me to him. I felt his lips on my cheek, my eyes, my lips. All my doubts vanished. I couldn't be closer to him. In my mind, I had kissed him thousands of times. The real kiss was sweeter.

FIVE

Beijing, 1989

Laolao's Story

There was once a scholar family in the South along the grand canal. They had an only son, called Li Sheng. His parents loved him very much and wanted him to become a scholar, so they shut him up in his study and never let him out until he had done his homework.

One festival day, Li Sheng was allowed out to go to town. He wandered like a freed bird. He came to the canal side, and saw a huge boat. He got on to it, and looked around in wonder – it was the most fabulous boat he had ever seen. People were busy, so nobody noticed he had got on and the boat left with him.

He watched the land recede and was not upset because he was young and wanted some adventure. The boat people told him it was too late to head back, and that he'd have to go along with them to their destination, much further north, along the canal. The boat belonged to the prime minister.

The minister asked his housekeeper for news of the boat's progress. It had been sent to collect rare antiques only available in the South. The housekeeper told him it had arrived, and of the person who had been accidentally caught on it. She commended him as a pleasant young man. The prime minister was interested and called for Li Sheng. He was so taken with him that he adopted him as a son. He had always wanted a son, but his wife had borne him only a daughter.

While he was interviewed, the young man admired the luxury of the grand house. He glimpsed the prime minister's only daughter through a bamboo screen – and fell in love with her shadow immediately. When the prime minister suggested that he be their son, he agreed so that he could be near the girl he loved. He began to court her secretly. It was not easy: even though they were now supposed to be brother and sister they could not meet, so he sent messages through a faithful maid. In due time he won the heart of his beloved and they saw each other in secret.

One day they met when the family had gone to the temple. Ying Niang – that was the girl's name – had feigned a headache and stayed behind. Li Sheng went to her room and they fell into each other's arms.

But the mother came back unexpectedly to fetch something and saw them. She was furious. The prime minister ordered the young man to walk out of his door and never come back. To make sure he made no more trouble, he found a boat heading for Li Sheng's home town and packed him off. As the boat was leaving, Li Sheng called Ying Niang's name in vain. Unbeknown to him, she had drowned herself in the same canal on which he travelled.

Li Sheng returned home, heartbroken, but his family were overjoyed to see him – they had thought him dead, as he had been away from home for nearly a year. They shut him up again to study. Before long they found him a wife even though Li Sheng still missed Ying Niang. But what could he do?

Another festival came, a year to the day after he had left home. Li Sheng was allowed out to wander again. He went straight to the canal and walked along the bank, thinking all the while of Ying Niang. He saw a crowd, and heard singing so he drew nearer. He was shocked to see Ying Niang dancing, semi-naked. When he looked closely, he saw that she had sprung from a huge oyster shell. When she noticed Li Sheng, she stopped singing and began to sob so pitifully that all around her wept too.

The fishermen who had caught her was annoyed. He had caught a giant oyster, he said, and had been about to cook it when this woman had sprung out from it and begged him to let her dance – 'That way, you will earn much more than you can from fishing,' she had said.

Li Sheng begged the fisherman to sell the oyster to him and gave him all his money. The fisherman thought it too little, but Ying Niang went inside the oyster shell and would not come out to dance. Reluctantly the fisherman sold the oyster to Li Sheng, who took it home and put it into a huge bowl in his study. At night he told his wife he was going to concentrate on his work and was not to be disturbed even by her, but when all was quiet, he clapped his hands, Ying Niang came out of the shell and cried on his shoulder. She told him she had drowned herself in the canal after he had left but had woken to find herself transformed into an oyster. She had followed the tide and arranged to be caught by the fisherman so that she could be near Li Sheng.

Now Li Sheng shunned all company, stayed in the study day and night with his oyster lover and was happy as heaven. All his family were delighted that he was so diligent with his studies.

One night, his wife walked past the window and heard singing and laughing. Suspicious, she peeped inside and discovered Li Sheng with his oyster lover. She ran back to tell her parents-in-law who were furious and terrified. They could do nothing while Li Sheng was there, though, so they composed a letter to him from his favourite uncle, which asked him to come to see him as he was dying. Li Sheng told Ying Niang he had to go away. She looked at him with doom in her eyes and begged him not to leave her. Li Sheng said, 'I have to go, my uncle is dying. You stay here in the bowl and don't come out until I call.'

As soon as he was out of the house, his family came and

found the giant oyster. They clapped their hands. Ying Niang would not come out. They tried to force it open, but it was tight as iron. They knocked the shell, but it was hard as a rock. At last, they put it into a giant pot and boiled it for seven days. The crying from the shell was terrifying, but they persevered until they could hear it no longer.

When Li Sheng came back, they told him they had discovered a giant oyster and had cooked it for him. Li Sheng was devastated. He couldn't eat or drink and stayed in bed all day long. On the seventh night he had a dream in which Ying Niang appeared to him and scolded him for not listening to her. 'If you really miss me,' she sobbed, 'find the oyster and open it. You will find a hard bit that is not cooked. It is my heart. You will take it and bury it just outside your study. A plant will grow from it. That will be me. When the flower ripens, you take it and boil it into a paste. Whenever you miss me, you inhale some. It will make you forget your pain.'

'It was the Opium Flower, Taotao,' Laolao said.

Chapter 1:

No. 7 Science Institute, Ministry of Defence

<hr/>

At Beijing airport I sat down to watch the westerners leave. I said goodbye to Renee and Marie, and shook the director's hand. We had shared a Mongolian dream together and now it was time to wake up. Marie was tearful and Renee hugged me. David stood beside us. He was not a man for words, and now he had even fewer to say than usual.

At last it was his turn to say goodbye, and I realised we would never meet again. I was sure of it. He hugged me. 'I must come back to see you,' he said. His cheeks were sunken, and he avoided my eyes. It was over, his dream holiday and my first love. I had learned one of life's contradictions: that the man who had first touched my heart with his kindness could do the ultimate cruelty to me.

Soon afterwards, I registered myself at the Science Institute and moved my luggage from Building the Country's house to the room I was to share with another girl. I waited for David's letter. Three days, one week, two weeks, a month went by. In my heart I had known he would not write, but I clung to the hope that he might. I refused to believe that my feelings for him were not reciprocated. I replayed his words over and over, clutching at straws rather than facing my inner conviction – the prospect of his never returning was simply too bleak to bear. He had said, 'I must come back to see you.' Surely he had meant it – he could not lie to me. How could he erase the magic of our encounter so easily from his memory? We had been soulmates in the most beautiful landscape in the world, which must have meant something. Perhaps he had written to me, but the postman had wanted the stamp, damaged the letter in trying to get it off, and been too ashamed to deliver it. Perhaps he had had a terrible accident and injured both his hands so he could no longer write. I invented numerous explanations for his silence.

As the months went by, the realisation that he would never write sank in and I became depressed. After work I hid in my dormitory reading *The Dream of the Red Mansions*. The story of Black Jade and Treasure took on a new dimension as I wove it into my own. But the moment I put down the book, I missed him. Never in my life had I longed for anybody so much. I wanted to talk to someone, but how could I admit to anyone that I had fallen in love with a foreigner?

The Institute was situated in a suburb in Beijing, a self-contained entity. Like my old university, it had its own canteen, bathhouse, barber and football team. I had two ID cards, one for the outer gate, one for the inner building, and both gates were guarded twenty-four hours a day by soldiers with guns, who checked the passes diligently with stern eyes.

The rigid regime of the Institute contrasted hugely with the carefree life I had led in Inner Mongolia. I had become used to the relaxed ways of the grassland, and now I felt like a caged bird, wings clipped. It made my longing for David all the more powerful. I became absentminded. One day in the canteen, I stood in the wrong queue, and by the time I realised my mistake, the other queue was so long that I would have no time to eat. Then the girl standing at the front called, 'Come here,' and I went to join her.

It was my room mate, Sweet Grass, tall, thin, stylish, wearing a black leather jacket. She worked in the personnel department of the Institute. She came from the suburb of Beijing and was dating a boy who lived in the eastern district, 'but not very seriously.' She was light-hearted about most things, except food.

We sat down with our meal and I asked her how long they had been dating. 'About six months.' She stuffed her stewed aubergine, the colour of mud, heartily into her mouth. 'We are thinking of getting married.'

'So soon? Do you love him?'

'Love's got nothing to do with it. We want to marry so that we can get a flat together. Our work unit will give us one if we're married. Then we'll have the privacy we need to talk about love.' She told me of the long queue for flats at the Institute. 'The problem is finding somewhere you won't be watched,' she confided. 'If you go to the Peace Park behind our Institute at night, you won't find an empty seat. We used to go there a lot. You have to be careful not to get caught.' She smiled coyly. 'We went to his parents' house once when they were not there.'

Before Mongolia, I would have been shocked to hear such talk, but now it gave me the confidence to tell her about David. Although my relationship with him had never been physical, the fact that he was a foreigner made even my affection forbidden. It felt good just to talk about him and she was warm and sympathetic. Unlike most Chinese girls, she wasn't scandalised by my love for a foreigner.

During the day I sat in the office translating documents about transport vehicles, planes, missiles, the technical details of which I didn't understand. I sometimes wondered about the consequences of my translation, those phrases that I only half grasped because nobody else, not even my supervisors, knew any better. Would I unwittingly cause an accident? Would a rocket fall from the sky because of my error? My supervisor was a middle-aged man who wore the dated blue jacket of the seventies and smiled placidly. He was kind, yet distant. There was an older man in the office, too, but I had only seen him during his rare periods of good health, when he talked obsessively about his operations and his pills.

There was no pressure at work: we translated, we had tea, then lunch, a nap, and more translation. Then it was home for Mr Tan, my supervisor, who lived just round the corner, and my dormitory for me, a minute's walk away. I had too many long evenings after work to linger and remember.

One late autumn afternoon I went to see Forever Green. I told her how suffocated I felt at the Institute. Building the Country was not there, which was just as well – I had no idea how much he knew of my infatuation with David. I had not cared on the grassland, but here . . .

Forever Green shrugged. 'Have you thought about going somewhere else?'

'But I am assigned to my Institute. There is no way I can leave.'

'You can at least try,' she insisted. 'I think you can ask to be lent to another work unit. You'd still belong to the old one, your personal file would stay with them, but you would go and work somewhere else for perhaps a year or two, provided the new company paid the old one a fee for your services. I know people who have done it. Taotao, things are not as rigid as before. I'm sure you will be able to do something about it.'

Her confidence was reassuring and I started to ask around. I did not care where I worked, so long as I would have more freedom.

Winter was long in Beijing. Soon my hot summer in Mongolia was a distant memory. Trudging through deep snow in and out of work, I sometimes wondered if it had all been a dream. On one of the rare days that I ventured into the city centre by bus, I overheard a man next to me say, 'The radio said this cold spell is the result of cold air from Siberia blowing through Inner Mongolia . . .' Wrapped in my heavy winter coat I found it hard to imagine it being cold in Mongolia. It should always be sunny and lush.

The first day back at work after the Spring Festival holiday, Building the Country rang me: 'Taotao, we are recruiting a full-time interpreter. Forever Green said you might be interested. I have recommended you to our manager.' I gasped with excitement and Mr Tan looked up from his desk. I covered my mouth and moved the phone to the window, where I saw the guards changing shift. Snowflakes danced playfully around the marching men. This was too good to be true. 'You will have to do a test – we have three other candidates,' he continued.

Despite strong competition – the other candidates were all graduates from more famous universities in Beijing – I was offered the job.

Chapter 2:

A Window to the Outside World

T he company was based in the city centre, on one of the small lanes off the Avenue of Eternal Peace in a small row of one-storeyed houses next to a Buddhist convent. There were no guards. I would be working next to the bustling traffic in the street – although I still had to sleep in the Institute's dormitory. The film company did not have living quarters for its employees. My steps were light and I felt spring in the air – the trees on both sides of the road were in bud, promising warmth and a fresh start.

When I reached the door, a short, middle-aged man limped out with a bowl of food and threw it onto the ground. A mother cat appeared out of nowhere with five kittens and devoured it. I went up to him: 'Excuse me, is this the Window to the Outside World Film Company?'

To my surprise, a very feminine voice replied, 'Yes, you must be Taotao. I am Shadow. You'd better come in and meet the manager.'

The manager was a short, plump woman of around fifty. She wore a thick pair of glasses through which her small, expressionless eyes peered at me. Her office was on the dark side of the bungalow. When I went in, I felt as if I was entering the cave of a hibernating animal: it smelt.

Building the Country greeted me and showed me to my desk. I was pleased to see I had a room of my own – at the

Institute, I had shared an office with two other colleagues. My desk was by the window and when I looked out I could see the traffic. That day I watched cyclists' backs bent like bows as they battled against the strong spring wind, and saw that trendier young people had already shed their winter coats.

I enjoyed my first day at the film company, and working with Building the Country again made me feel more connected to my Mongolian adventure. As soon as I sat down at my desk he gave me a list of foreign journalists: my first project was to assist at a press conference for a forthcoming film about an American woman teacher who had befriended a Chinese man. I spent the whole morning on the phone.

After work I pushed my bike out of the shed and into the street – I had bought a second-hand one as soon as I learned I had got the job. I went into one of the clothes shops Shadow had shown me in the lunch-break and came out wearing a new blue coat. It was expensive, but I bought it anyway. At the film company, I would earn much more than I had at the Institute so I could afford to be a little extravagant.

The bright orange street-light had come on and I joined the bicycle stream that had flowed past my window all day. When I had first arrived in Beijing, I had dreaded joining it and the work routine, fearing that I would be trapped. Now I was part of that world, and beginning to like it. I realised that routine could be good – reassuring and comforting. It represented normality.

In the next few weeks I did more work and met more new people than I had in months at the Institute. I met journalists, film directors and film stars, people I used only to see on TV. I assisted in two news conferences and translated a film script. Every day when I went home, I made Sweet Grass envious with stories of my encounters with the famous. 'At this rate, you're going to be a star yourself, and I shall have to ask for your autograph.' She rolled her eyes at me.

I smiled coyly. My busy work schedule meant I had less

time to miss David – in fact I hadn't thought of him for quite a while. Perhaps time did heal, after all.

We had little response to the phone calls I had made on my first day about the news conference – few reporters were interested. Building the Country and I organised it anticipating a small turn-out, and in the event, only four people came. One, an American who had sounded rude over the phone, turned out to be a pleasant, engaging person. He was tall, slim, attentive, and nodded encouragingly at me when I stumbled while interpreting for a renowned film director, who spoke in a heavy Shanghai dialect.

During the interval, the American strode over to me and gave me his card. 'Call me,' he said, in a brisk, efficient way. He placed it underneath a glass of wine, took the glass next to it, and smiled. 'I'd like to see you again.'

Robert was the special correspondent of an American newspaper in Beijing, and I was flattered by his attention. He said I had the best English accent he had heard in any Chinese he had met in Beijing.

That night, I kicked off my high-heeled shoes and slumped into my bed, tired but satisfied. Sweet Grass came up. 'Hey, jetsetter, there's a letter for you.' I snatched it from her and recognised the handwriting. 'It's from Steel! My friend in Pleasant City! He's coming to Beijing.'

'Who is Steel? And what did you do tonight to be home so late?'

'Oh, nothing, it was just a reception for the film company.'

Sweet Grass shook her head. 'There was more to it than that. You look different.'

I hesitated. 'Well, there was this man, an American journalist, he was very nice to me.'

'Oh, yes? What's he like?'

'Tall, slim, good-looking, brownish hair.'

'Is he old?'

'Older than we are, but I didn't ask him his age.'

'So,' she chuckled, 'are you going to date him and forget David?'

'Don't be silly. And don't mention David again.'

She stood up and walked towards the basin set up with a wooden frame by the door. 'I just want you to be happy,' she said. 'You've got to move on, you know.' She stooped to splash warm water on her face. 'Find a man, and play with him.'

Like you and your boyfriend, I thought, but I could never be her. I wasn't interested in casual affairs – I was too serious. I wanted to be involved – totally involved. It was some time before I slept that night.

Chapter 3:

'Sensual, S-E-N-S-U-A-L'

A few days after the press conference, I was reading a letter from Saraa. She had just had a baby girl and sounded happy. 'How are you, Taotao?' she asked. 'Are you still missing David? Or have you found new love?'

Did I still miss David? Not as I had a few months previously. Perhaps Renee, who had written me a lovely letter shortly after they got back, had been right: 'Life does go on, baby, and you will feel better one day, even if you do not believe me now.' I saw how right she was. There was life after first love, however passionate it had been at the time. There was the spring to look forward to, there was ... A familiar voice spoke outside the door.

'Steel!' I jumped up, rushed out of the door. Steel was asking directions from the tall nun who moved about like a haughty crane. 'Steel!' I grabbed his hand tightly, ignoring the nun's frowns, and dragged him into my office. 'Sit there ... drink this ... eat that.' There was a big grin on his face.

Finally I settled down opposite him. He looked taller and darker, somehow more mature. Was it because of his thick beard? Unconsciously, I touched my chin. He mirrored me and laughed. 'I haven't shaved,' he said.

The telephone rang. I gestured in apology to Steel and picked it up. It was Robert. Would I have dinner with him tonight at Maxim's? It was one of the best restaurants in

Beijing. I felt breathless. Why did everything always happen at once? Steel beamed and my heart jumped. 'Yes,' I said, 'I'd love to come.'

When Building the Country saw me with Steel he said I could leave work early to be with my friend so all afternoon I rushed Steel around. This was his first trip to Beijing, and I felt guilty that I couldn't be with him that evening. I dragged him through the Temple of Heaven and the Lama Temple, and then we rowed a boat on the newly thawed lake in Beihai Park.

When dusk descended, I waved goodbye to him at the park gate. I was soaking wet: Steel had splashed water over us when he rowed the boat back to the bank. He hadn't overcome his clumsiness, I thought, and smiled to myself. I hesitated a little before I boarded the bus to see Robert, but decided not to go home and change. If I did I'd be terribly late, and somewhere at the back of my mind I did not want to dress up. I had seen too many doll-like Chinese girls sitting next to self-satisfied, grinning foreigners, and did not want to be branded one of them. I was different.

The moment I stepped into the luxurious hotel next to Maxim's, where I had to meet Robert before our meal, I wanted to run away. Here, even the waitresses dressed as if they were duchesses. One, with long polished fingernails the colour of blood, peered down at me as if I was a peasant who had just got off a horse-drawn donkey cart. I wished there was a hole in the ground I could dive into. Then Robert, dressed in an impeccable dark suit, waved at me from a crowd of equally immaculate westerners. Instead of going up to him I stood rooted to the spot, paralysed by shyness. In a few seconds he was standing before me, clean, warm and attractive. I looked down at my crumpled clothes. 'Sorry, I fell into a lake,' I murmured, pursed my lips and fidgeted.

He was full of concern: 'Oh dear. I hope you weren't hurt. Come and sit down.' He steered me away from his friends and settled me on a sofa. 'Can I do anything for you?'

My wet trousers, which still clung to my legs, were hidden now and I felt better. 'I'm sorry to have turned up like this, I feel so underdressed.'

'You look lovely.' I shook my head. 'I mean it, you really do,' he went on. 'I like . . . your red shirt. Just the kind of thing I imagined a Chinese girl would wear before I came here, but you're the first girl I've seen in one.' I laughed, and relaxed. 'Can I get you something to drink?'

'Orange juice,' I said, without thinking.

'Are you sure? I can get you something more exotic.'

'I don't drink alcohol. I'm a Chinese girl.'

He laughed. 'You are funny,' he said, and walked towards the bar.

I took a deep breath. Robert was not the first westerner I had met in Beijing: through my work I knew quite a few but although some had shown interest in me I had been careful to keep my distance. Since David had gone, I had longed for him but I had also felt humiliated that he could leave me like that, and that I had been powerless to confront him. The lesson I had learned was that foreigners were not here to stay but as tourists to play, as journalists to report or as business-men to profit. The journalists were the worst and I could see why the government disliked them: they only noticed bad things, and it hurt our pride – the Chinese skin is as thin as rice paper. Also I had detected a difference in attitude between the westerners I had met in Beijing and those I had known in the wilds of Inner Mongolia. The latter had lived and worked alongside us, suffered the same inconveniences and hardships, while the former lived like princes and were detached, arrogant.

But Robert seemed different. He was warm, light-hearted and courteous, and I liked the elegant way he dressed. I watched him standing in front of the counter, while the band played a western melody. The rhythm captivated me, and I let myself drift. I had heard western music on the radio, but never live. I didn't notice when Robert came back with my glass and sat next to me. 'You look transfixed. Was it the music?' he asked.

I nodded. 'What is it?'

' "Waltz of the Flowers", Tchaikovsky . . . I think,' he said, his eyes still on me. 'It's one of my favourite pieces.'

We sat and listened in silence. The music made me want to dance, and I wished I was wearing a long dress, like the one my English teacher, Lucy, had worn at her party. When the music ended we stood up to walk next door to the restaurant. My trousers had dried and I felt more comfortable. I hummed the tune softly to myself.

'You have a good voice. Do you sing?' he asked, as he strode briskly alongside me.

'I used to, when I was a child.' I remembered the revolutionary songs Ma had taught me. 'Actually I know some English songs: "Row, row, row your boat . . ." ' I sang, and he joined in, but at the end I sang ' "Life is interesting," ' and he, ' "Life is but a dream." ' We stared at each other.

'Are you sure that's right?' he asked.

'Yes. It's in our English-language textbook. Why?'

'Oh, Christ,' he exclaimed. 'How extraordinary.'

'Our version is much more positive. Yours is too melancholic, too bourgeois,' I teased him, as he stepped aside for me to go into Maxim's.

Hors d'oeuvres, main course and dessert. The food was so rich that my cheeks went red. Eventually Robert leaned back and put his hands behind his head. His legs seemed to grow longer. 'So, why did you fall into the lake?' he asked.

'I was with a friend, rowing a boat in Beihai Park.'

'Your boyfriend?'

'Well, no, he's just a good friend.' Steel was not my boyfriend, but he was special and I regretted my hesitation.

Robert looked thoughtful, then raised his glass. 'Here's to us.'

I raised my orange juice. 'Here's to . . . friendship.' I

watched the bubbles in his glass.

My thoughts went back to the lake. Ours had been the only boat on it, and I had stirred the water with my finger. The air was cold, and so was the water. 'You haven't changed a bit,' I said to Steel.

He leaned forward and reached for his colourful, rather girlish bag. He saw me staring at it. 'It's Willow's. I left in a hurry so I took hers.'

'You are engaged now? When will I taste your wedding sweets?' I said.

He was silent. Then he looked up. 'She is engaged to someone else, by her family,' he said slowly.

'And you just let that happen?'

'It's a complicated family thing . . .' he whispered. 'We're still seeing each other. I – I actually quite like it this way.'

It had shocked me to hear Steel talk about his relationship in such a detached manner, yet somewhere in my heart I had been relieved. I couldn't explain why.

Robert stopped my train of thought. 'And here's to no more daydreaming. We don't want you falling into the lake again.' His eyes twinkled.

I thoroughly enjoyed being with Robert. I felt light-hearted and attractive for the first time since David had gone away. We talked about Beijing, western music and Peking Opera, which he hated. I learned that he had not long been in China. He had reported from other parts of Asia, but China had always fascinated him. 'It's such a vast country. I'm really looking forward to seeing more of it, not just the capital. Have you been outside Beijing?'

'My home town is in the North-east, I went to university in the South, and I spent two months with a film crew in Inner Mongolia.'

'I'd love to go to Guilin, in the South.' There was an enthusiasm in him that I had found lacking in other foreigners I had met.

Soon we were talking like old friends. I enjoyed his stories of other countries he had been to – it seemed that he had crossed more bridges than I had roads. When we drank our coffee he leaned forward, his eyes fixed on mine, and said, 'You're such a sensual girl.'

'Sensual? I don't know that word.' I blushed, suspecting it had something to do with sex.

'You don't know what sensual means? S-E-N-S-U-A-L. Well, it means your senses are acute, you like to enjoy things in life with your hands, your ears, your eyes, all of you. You like to touch, to smell and to listen.'

'And to eat,' I added, looking down at my empty plate. 'So it's a good word.'

'Of course it is. What did you think it meant?' I didn't tell him.

At the door of the restaurant, we said goodbye. Robert had offered to take me home in his car, but I refused: I did not want him to see my humble dormitory which would make such a contrast with the glamorous interior of the restaurant. He was welcome to give me a taste of the high life, but not to see how I lived. I was also nervous about being seen with a foreign journalist in my heavily guarded Institute.

As I walked towards the bus stop, I thought of David. What if he had stayed? Would our intimacy on the grassland have survived in the city? I had been lucky that my romance in Mongolia had been allowed to develop without interference – I was away from people who knew me and the atmosphere had been relaxed. But in Beijing, with its curious crowds, the Public Security Bureau Police, and my colleagues, there was just too much suspicion.

The bus did a tour around Tiananmen Square before it passed Maxim's. The ticket collector, who had neglected his duty, was dozing. I had been on this bus many times before and had admired Maxim's with its glistening lights. Tonight I had been inside, and a stylish, attentive American journalist had described me as 'sensual'.

Sensual, to do with the senses. Decadent, foreign and

bourgeois, I liked the word. I took it as a compliment. I liked men to flatter me, and foreigners were good at it. Chinese men? Steel? I laughed at the thought. So much of my upbringing and culture centred on my responsibility as a daughter to defend and increase the family honour, and it weighed heavily at times. Robert had made me feel like a woman, a desirable, attractive human being. I preferred that.

But the thought of Steel brought me sharply to earth. He had alarmed me that afternoon on the lake. At one point we had stopped rowing, and the white stupa on the little hill at the edge of the lake was reflected in the water. ' "It was difficult for us to meet and more so to depart, the east wind blows weakly and the flowers decayed". ' His murmur broke the silence.

' "The silk worms spin silk until death, and the tears of the candlewax do not cease until it melts into ashes", ' I added.

Our favourite Tang poems brought back Pleasant City days and walks along the West Lake. 'I don't know how anybody can love so passionately.' I sighed.

Then, like a cold wind blowing, I had heard him say: 'Do you know why I am really here?'

'To attend a conference on teaching English, of course.'

'Yes, but more importantly to meet up with other students in Beijing universities to publish a magazine.'

'Not an underground one?'

'Well, yes, if you want to put it that way.'

'Steel, life is too short to live dangerously.'

'Taotao, life is too precious to waste.'

I opened my eyes as the high-pitched voice of the ticket collector called, 'The zoo, last stop, everybody off.' He was wide awake and hurried us away as if we were visitors who had outstayed their welcome. One man looked bewildered as the ticket-collector shouted, 'Get off now! Do you think we'll drive you home? Off! Don't you understand Chinese? What are you staring at me for?'

I got off the bus, haunted by the disappointment in Steel's

face when I left him. His devotion to me was in vain but I knew what it was to love and be scorned, and I wanted to give him a comforting hug – but I could not. I was a proper girl, a good girl who had fallen in love with someone she shouldn't, but I had hidden my feelings, as my upbringing required. Perhaps I had hidden them too well, and that was why David had not written to me.

The zoo stop was like a deserted state border. The streetlights were still on, but the pedlars were packing up. A beggar leaned on a sign that read, 'Beijing City Zoo', and snored standing up as I walked past him. For a moment I lost my sense of direction, but a strange calm rose in me. I could live as a shadow and just wander, I thought.

A drunkard approached, looking me up and down with leering eyes, and my senses returned. I fled to the next bus stop and waited to return to the Institute.

Chapter 4:

'I Have Numerous Uncles'

I busied myself with the translation of business cards into English for the company. I had difficulty with Shadow's: his Chinese job title was *zongwu*, which in English meant general duties. The translation was misleading: his job involved arranging outings, distributing goods the company received from other organisations, and booking the manager's flight tickets. In fact, he was a secretary, but vanity stopped him calling himself one. I wrote: 'office manager.' He looked up the words in the English–Chinese dictionary on my desk and seemed surprised. 'Manager? I am a manager in English?'

'Yes,' I said encouragingly.

Steel phoned and asked me where I had been last night. I said I had gone out with a girlfriend. 'I waited for you at your dormitory until eleven o'clock. Your friend Sweet Grass fed me.'

I looked over my shoulder, Shadow was still grinning incredulously at his grand English title. 'Shall we meet tonight?' I said, feeling guilty.

'I can't, I have to see someone about this . . . business of ours.' There was a pause, and then he said, 'Actually, Taotao, why don't you come along? I'm sure my friend won't mind. I'll meet you at seven at the gate of the Northern Technology University. It's only about ten minutes' walk from your dormitory.'

After lunch, Building the Country strode into my room. He was working on a co-production project with a Japanese company and was thus nicknamed Hanjian the Traitor. 'Hello, traitor,' I said.

He whispered, 'I hear you have promoted Shadow to manager.'

I chuckled. 'Office manager. Manager of the office.'

'The poor man. He's quite sad, really. He was a brilliant Peking Opera actor once, famous for the Monkey King. Then in the Cultural Revolution his leg was broken by the Red Guards. That's why he walks the way he does. He says the manager here saved his life and he has been following her faithfully like a dog ever since. I don't care for him personally – he's too soft, and he likes to cry like a woman.' I thought of Shadow's soft feminine voice and supposed that a man like Building the Country would find it distasteful. But I could not despise him: I remembered him feeding the kittens.

Northern Technology University reminded me of my student days. Steel and I followed the streams of students banging their food bowls, arguing and laughing. They looked young, I thought, even childish. Following loud laughter, we went into a dormitory room. I coughed as Steel lifted the curtain: three boys looked up, each holding a cigarette, and a girl with long slender legs leaned against one of the beds, playing a guitar. 'Steel!' shouted a short, stout boy, and jumped up to meet us.

Steel shook his hand then turned to me. 'This is my old friend Taotao, who works in the media.'

Everyone in the room was impressed. 'The media, the media!' they shouted.

The short man smiled at me. 'I am Knowing Enlightenment. These are my friends Small Flat, Old Horse and', he pointed at the girl, 'Bell.'

I squeezed myself next to Bell, and the boys sat on low stools in the middle of the narrow room.

'How many are coming from your university, Steel?' asked Knowing Enlightenment.

'I don't know exactly, but I'll have a better idea in a few days' time. I'm sure a lot more students are coming from the Central China Technology University. Somehow they are always more dependable than us, although I hate to admit it.' This prompted laughter all round. They went on to discuss food and lodging arrangements. I gathered there would be a big influx of students to Beijing from all over China.

At work, I had another news conference to organise, this time for Building the Country's Chinese–Japanese co-production. In the course of ringing round journalists, I called Robert's number, and was disappointed when his Chinese interpreter picked up the phone. 'He is not in Beijing,' said the stern female voice.

'Can I ask when he will be back?'

'I don't know. Who are you anyway?' I felt shy and slammed down the phone.

Looking up I saw the manager standing outside my door, then quietly walking on. She had been eavesdropping. I was nervous with her, though I couldn't say why. I opened the window, and saw the back of the Guizhou carpenter sawing at a piece of wood. He was always there, part of the scene, outside the window. The weather changed, but he remained the same, his back to me, forever chipping away. After a while, Shadow walked out with his food bowl on his way to the nearby General Trade Union Office canteen for lunch, taking advantage of their cheaper meals. I had my own favourite dumpling shop just round the corner. I picked up my handbag.

The tall, elegant nun I often saw out shopping was ahead of me carrying a big basket. I followed her out of the lane. She was walking faster than usual. When she came to a small puddle, she gathered up her grey gown and jumped over it. I heard her giggle. I was puzzled by her sudden frivolous behaviour. She had headed towards the General

Trade Union Office where a small group of people had gathered around the bicycle shed. She disappeared into the throng and I followed.

A student stood in the middle of the crowd reading from a leaflet. I recognised it: there had been a pile of them in Steel's friends' room at the Northern Technology University, and I suspected they might even have printed them. I had listened closely to them, admiring Knowing Enlightenment's intelligence and humour and witnessing once more Steel's stubbornness. 'Demand more open government and the punishment of corrupt officials' – the slogan rang in my ears as I had left them to go home.

Lunchers coming in and out of the canteen soon filled the space by the gate, and the old woman with a red band around her arm who charged five *mao* to look after bicycles leaned on one, gazing around in disbelief – business had never been so good. Still more people poured in from all directions: nannies from Anhui with babies in their arms, wandering carpenters from the southern provinces, the young carpenter who worked outside my office window – even Shadow was there, listening intently. Every now and then he shovelled food into his mouth with his chopsticks. The nun stood next to him, the basket by her feet filled with food and drink. I realised she must have brought it for the student. Occasionally she glanced around her, but most of the time her eyes were fixed on the young man standing opposite her on a wooden box, whose chin barely showed signs of a beard.

I watched quietly, feeling a closeness with the crowd. Every face was so friendly, even the mean old bicycle woman who had charged me extra once for overstaying. I felt proud to have been around at the start of all this, with Steel and his friends.

Before the crowd dispersed, I went back to the office, skipping and hopping all the way, like a rabbit in a field. The quietness of the corridor met me as I reached the spot where the manager had stood to spy on me. There was a nasty smell, almost animal-like, strong and thick. I shuddered and waved my arms about to disperse it. Then, out of the corner of my eye, I saw the manager again, watching me from her office two doors away. I forced a smile at her and went to my own room. There the smell disappeared and a new one arose. It was Shadow, who shared his wife's face cream, clapping his empty food bowl as he sang, ' "I have countless uncles, and none of them ever popped by . . ." ' I clapped my hands for him, delighted by his singing. ' "But they are dearer than any of my family . . ." ' It was from the Peking Opera I had been taken to see with my mother and Laoye. The 'uncles' were Communist agents in disguise during the Nationalists' rule, and the song told of how ordinary people sheltered them pretending they were their uncles.

'Shadow!' the manager called angrily. Shadow was into the final stretch. He stopped for a second, then continued at breathtaking speed to the last note. He took a deep breath and ran like a hurricane out of my office.

I clapped and heard another clap answer mine. I turned round and saw the carpenter's head outside the window. He, too, had been spellbound by Shadow's performance and I waved. It was the first time we had acknowledged one another's existence. For a moment our worlds overlapped.

Chapter 5:

Madonna of Tiananmen

I stood in the crowd at Beijing railway station waiting for Ba. He was coming to Beijing for a business meeting. Even in the glorious late-afternoon sun, the station was a dirty, depressing place. Would I recognise my father in this crowd? A blue-uniformed ticket collector chased away the homeless sleeping by the gate.

There was a scuffle around the gate, and people pushed past me, calling relatives' names. I saw many young faces I was sure were students'. So it was happening, I thought excitedly. Ba emerged, carrying heavy bags on both his shoulders like a peasant. His eyes darted uncertainly about the sea of faces in front of him. I watched him for a few seconds before I shouted, 'Ba.' I hadn't seen him in about a year, but it had felt longer – so much had changed in my life. I waved now. 'Ba!' He didn't hear so I shouted again: 'Ba! Ba!' and gestured frantically. Finally he saw me and a smile lit his face. He nodded to the man walking next to him, also loaded with luggage, and soon they were standing in front of me.

We arrived in a small guesthouse beside a big restaurant from which emanated strong smells of beer and food. Ba always stayed here because it was close to the city centre. It was open only to employees of the factories and organisations affiliated to the Textile Department where he worked. Here he could catch up with old friends. His room was at the end of the corridor on the second floor. I checked the bags. One was full of goodies for me from Nainai and Ma, all my favourite food: wind-dried meat, dried shrimps, dried mushrooms, hawthorns, soft rice noodles, foods only available in my home town, and a big sack of rice, the fragrant north-eastern rice that tasted of fruit. I lay on Ba's bed and ate, while he leaned against me, flipping the TV channels, chatting, laughing and calling me a greedy pig. When his colleague came in, he stood up and asked me to stand as well. 'This is Uncle Yong.'

He nodded at me. 'Please, sit down, I am going out soon. I just want to fetch my bag.' He turned to Ba. 'I'll come and call you when it's dinner time.'

After dinner in the hotel canteen, Ba and I walked slowly along the Avenue of Eternal Peace. He said he had been promoted – he was now head of the factory. I had guessed as much from the respectful manner of the man travelling with him, and was pleased for him. Tiananmen Square was ahead of us, and unusually busy. Noises and crowds greeted us, and Ba looked around suspiciously. 'Is today a festival or what?'

'I don't think so,' I replied. 'But let's go and find out.'

It was the biggest open-air party you could imagine, with the happiest crowds. Eager, smiling faces and banners bearing slogans greeted us: 'Welcome, Mr Democracy', 'Down with Corruption', 'The Chinese People Have Finally Stood Up', they read. Thousands of voices assaulted our ears, in different dialects, different languages, laughing, talking, and singing. We heard the 'Internationale', and snatches of pop songs from tape-recorders around which people danced. The air was rich with the smells of noodles, bread, sweat and per-fume. In the distance, somewhere on the edge of the square, bicycles were crowded together. Leather-clad lads revved their motorbikes.

We moved between clusters of people, listening, Ba with his hands behind his back, leaning forward attentively. We stopped by a group of workers in uniforms beneath a Beijing Underground Drivers' Association banner. They were joking among themselves, and a pile of leaflets lay on the ground in front of them. I picked one up and Ba came closer to examine it. He read it quickly, laughed nervously, pointed at a printing error, then motioned to me: 'Put it back.'

'Why?' I laughed, and put a copy into my pocket.

He snatched it from me, threw it on the pile and dragged me away. 'Do you think the government will let this sort of thing carry on? These people will have to pay for their actions. I don't want you to get involved with them, do you hear?' He saw my pursed lips and added, 'There will always be movements, and people like these will suffer. The Party never forgets – you must believe me. You haven't seen anything of life, but I've been through so many movements. Don't say anything out of the ordinary. You may think you're all right, but somebody always remembers and reports it.'

Ba never lectured and this was the longest speech on politics he had ever uttered in my presence. I nodded. There was no point in arguing with him: his obsession with and fear of movements had made him a coward. 'Be small,' he seemed to be saying, 'and have a safe life.' Yet I had never encountered any real danger, and the whisper of 'Caution' that I had heard since my childhood made me crave a more carefree life. And there were always more frivolous people about to tempt me. A young worker whistled at us. Ba saw him. 'You see? Such impertinent behaviour,' he said.

I became impatient with him. His comment had sectioned us off from the people in the square. I longed to feel at one with them.

Soon we approached another circle, of bespectacled scholarly-looking people arguing about the difference between socialism and capitalism, watched by eager-looking students. Ba agreed to stop and listen to the conversation, making a concession for what he thought looked like a respectable debate. I moved a few steps further in. 'Steel!' I exclaimed. He turned round.

Almost simultaneously, a voice called, 'Taotao,' from

behind me. I turned, and Robert waved a notebook at me. A petite, serious-looking, middle-aged Chinese woman was standing next to him.

'This is—' I was too excited for words.

'We've met!' laughed Robert. 'I've been interviewing him for the last half-hour. I didn't know you two knew each other, though.'

'Steel is—'

I was interrupted by two students who were impatient to continue their philosophical debate. 'So you said, Steel, that we should be more realistic about socialism?' one asked. The middle-aged Chinese woman – Robert's interpreter, I guessed – immediately started to translate with efficiency but no enthusiasm, as if she were a robot.

'Yes.' Steel threw me a quick, welcoming glance and went on, 'We have always been told that socialism was the first stage of Communism, and Communism the ideal society that would follow from it. But the reality is that we are perhaps not ready for socialism, even. If you think of what has happened in China in the past thirty years . . .'

I watched Steel and, for the first time, admired his physical beauty: that long thin figure, with the cloth shoes that looked stylish on him, the shy smile on his bespectacled face. The man who had recited Tang poems with such passion was now debating Marxist theories. I was proud of my friend. Still I was shocked to hear his daring statement on socialism and capitalism. I glanced around to make sure that people were not alarmed, but I could see only eager, fascinated faces, and Robert leaned forward to follow his interpreter's translation, his tall figure bent towards her.

Ba tugged at my sleeve, almost timidly. 'Let's go,' he pleaded. 'We have stayed long enough.'

We had to fight our way out. It was like swimming against a strong tide. I fought reluctantly, and as the struggle became more and more difficult, my anger rose. I did not want to leave the square, and neither Steel nor Robert had noticed I had gone. Like magnets they had been drawn back into the conversation.

At last, breathless, we were outside the tide. Ba drew a deep breath. 'Phew, what a crowd! Your mother would have hated it. Who is that foreigner?'

'Oh, he's a journalist. I met him through work.'

'Journalist? Be careful of them, the government doesn't like them.'

'Ba,' I said irritably, 'he's just an acquaintance. I have nothing to do with him.'

'Good. You have a career now, and I don't want you to spoil it. Oh, I forgot these,' he said, changing the subject. He felt in his pocket and drew out some photographs – some shots of Ma, one of Nainai making dumplings and another of her posing in front of a flower-bed outside her new building. Nainai looked younger and Ma older. In one Ma leaned on the new sofa, and I was surprised to see that she was wearing makeup. My skeleton dolly stood conspicuously on the table before her, wearing a set of new clothes. I was touched and handed the photos back to him. 'How is Ma?'

'She's well, she'll be retiring next year so she is a bit anxious about what to do. Don't give them back to me. They're for you to keep.' I clutched the envelope and walked on.

'How old do you think that foreigner is?' he asked.

'I don't know – forty-ish, a bit younger than you. Why?'

'Well, I'm just curious. You know, with foreigners it's difficult to tell. I wonder what your Nainai would say if she saw him. She'd probably call him a ghost and run away!' he laughed.

He insisted on walking me back to the bus stop to wave me goodbye, but I wished he would just leave me to find my own way. There was such a distance between us now. As we walked away from the square, my heart sank and I realised I despised his small, safe, provincial world with its promotions and family ties.

Then I thought of Tainainai, her naughty winks and fantastic fairy stories, and of Laoye, his elegant voice reciting Tang poems and his calligrapher's hands. Although they had been through so many movements, they had shown me a different world, a world to which I could escape and from which I could draw strength, a world of my own.

I felt a pang of pity as I saw Ba walk away. The bus began to move and I waved at him. But I was determined to head back to the square. I decided to get off at the next stop and walk back. 'Ticket for one stop,' I said.

'No tickets necessary,' everyone around me shouted in unison.

'Why?'

'You are a student, aren't you?' Before I was able to say anything, they shouted, 'Yes, she is.'

'And I am a professor!' giggled a fat middle-aged woman, standing next to me clutching her shopping-bag.

'Well, anyone who is a student, or a professor, who is going to the square or who has just come back from the square is exempt from buying a ticket,' the ticket collector said gallantly, to universal cheers.

I ran from the bus stop, and struggled through thronging crowds flowing from underground station entrances and bus stops, or pushing bicycles. Now I was swimming with the tide, rather than against it. At the edge of the square I encountered the bikers again, parading up and down the wide space in front of Chairman Mao's portrait. I had a sense of *déjà vu*. I had been here, I had longed to be here. I had been here once before, in Inner Mongolia: that sense of space, of liberation, of generosity of spirit that I had found on the grassland, in the absence of any human presence, I found again now in the square. There had always been something special about Tiananmen Square, but today it was the grassland restored to me. It was heaven. The bikers were the eagles swooping across the wide empty space of the plains. I stretched my arms wide.

I looked for Steel and Robert, but felt drawn to each circle I walked past. I lingered and listened, sometimes even talked. By the time I saw Robert again, I was intoxicated with new ideas and the atmosphere. He took my hands in his. 'Taotao, I am so pleased to see you here.' He turned to the people around him. 'This is my good friend Taotao.' Then he whispered into my ear, 'Isn't it wonderful to be here? Will you help me? My interpreter has gone home, she has a baby to look after. Will you translate for me? I need to write so much down and ask so many questions.'

His enthusiasm was infectious. The atmosphere in the square was infectious. There was a fever to communicate. We all caught it.

An old wrinkled peasant woman tugged at my sleeve. 'Is he an important foreign cadre?' she asked timidly, in a heavy accent, and pointed at Robert. Before I had time to reply, Robert beamed at her and the old woman grasped his hands. 'Can you tell them to punish those who bullied my daughter in my county?' she said. 'I want justice, and my local cadres won't give it to me. I have come to Beijing to see the big cadres, but they have refused me. I sat down in front of their houses and was taken away. I wanted to see the Chairman. This is a socialist country, isn't it? We are the masters, aren't we? We must have justice.'

I translated. Robert nodded and held her hands tightly. 'Yes, you should have justice.'

The old woman was in tears. Some young men near us laughed. 'Look, Granny, he's a journalist, not a cadre. He can't do anything.'

'But he seems so important. He looks like a big cadre,' she insisted.

The young men turned to Robert. 'We know Madonna. We like her songs,' they chanted.

The old woman let go of Robert's hands reluctantly and we moved on – into a group of middle-aged women. 'What are they talking about?' Robert asked.

'They're complaining about rising food prices.'

'Don't we all?' He laughed light-heartedly. 'Ladies,' he gestured to me to translate, 'would you prefer to go back to the old days when food was cheaper but there wasn't much around?'

The women paused, and looked at us curiously. Then one, wearing a yellow scarf, smiled at Robert. 'You're right. We have more choice now. The peasants are allowed to bring their produce into town and there is a market just below our flat so I can buy fresh vegetables every week.'

A tall thin woman said quietly, 'We used to be poor, but then everybody was the same. Now some are so much richer, like the cadres. They don't need to spend money to buy things because people give them things for free – they want favours. It's not fair on the rest of us.'

'No, that's corruption,' Robert agreed. He whispered to me, 'I've never seen Chinese people speaking their minds so openly in all the time I've been in China. Isn't it wonderful? Don't you feel proud?' His eyes twinkled with excitement.

We moved from crowd to crowd and were received as if we were heroes. 'America!'

'VOA!'

'BBC.'

'Join us, join us.' It was difficult to keep up with the talk as the noise and the crowds increased.

Encouraged by the warm reception we were given wherever we went, my initial anxiety at being seen with a foreign journalist was gone. I smiled to the cameras raised ahead of us, and I stood next to Robert as if we were comrades-in-arms. The camera flashes made me feel like a film star, and I looked, with secret pride, at the envious faces of the girls around me.

In the small hours, I picked up a bicycle, one of many unlocked ones, and cycled around the vast space of Tiananmen Square. Robert had dashed off to catch up on some sleep and to prepare and file his stories. There were fewer people about now, but those who remained had got together in small circles, some lying down, some sitting, still talking. I had got to know some of them well through our intense discussions. I saw myself in the square with David, on our first night back from Inner Mongolia, and felt now that the past had connected with my present life. There was a purpose.

Chapter 6:

The Temple of Heaven

After work we met by the South Gate of the Tian Tan, the Temple of Heaven. Robert had asked me to choose a place for our meeting: 'Wherever you want to take me. You are the local, you know best.'

'Tian Tan, then,' I said.

'Why Tian Tan? What's the story behind it?' I didn't know, I just loved it. I knew vaguely that it was where the Emperor had worshipped and prayed for rain.

I asked in the office. Building the Country shook his head, the manager looked uninterested. It was Shadow who knew the story of Tian Tan. I had been brought up to believe that all things of the past were negative: oppressive, decadent religion had been the opium of the people, a feudal superstition. I had been shaped to look towards the future, whatever that future might be, even though now the picture of Communism was blurred. A well-informed foreigner like Robert was probably more aware of my heritage than I was.

But I was a native. The buildings and the landscape reflected the vision and genius of my ancestors, and Robert could only look on in silence: he could appreciate the architecture of the different dynasties with the eyes and heart of a man who had seen much of the world. I glided down the long avenue of trees leading to the temple with memories of my outings with Sweet Grass, with my friends at the Institute, memories still fresh, undimmed by the passing of time. For me the trees, the modern benches, the ancient building, the blue sky and my feelings all blended into one experience from which I drew pleasure. I felt as if I were a tempestuous artist and Robert a studious historian.

Everyone we encountered was heading home as dusk was near. Robert wore an old army hat and a traditional Chinese jacket, which made him less conspicuous, and we wandered along the long corridor of trees towards the round structure in the distance. A sense of the vastness of time, of history, came over me as I looked at the dark blue dome of the main temple. I felt that an era was passing.

Robert asked me again about the history of Tian Tan, and I repeated what Shadow had told me. Tian Tan had been built in 1420, for the Emperors to worship heaven and pray for good harvests. It was the most important of the four temples surrounding the Imperial Palace: the Temple of Earth, the Temple of Sun, the Temples of Moon and of Heaven. He listened, and watched me intently as I spoke. When I had finished, he nodded. 'Fascinating. I have some books in English about Tian Tan. I can lend them to you, if you're interested.'

Then I told him the story of the scholar and the oyster. As I knew it so well, I told it fluently, but I was not sure he was listening.

We reached the round circus called the Echoing Gallery. No one was around, and I started to run which I always did when I came here with friends. I ran right round the circus, then stopped exactly opposite where Robert stood and waved at him. 'Bend down, and listen,' I shouted. Then I whispered to the wall. Robert took off his hat, bent down and listened. A light breeze blew his brown hair as he looked up to the sky and the new moon. He straightened up.

I stayed where I was; something in the air made me apprehensive about approaching him. Then I walked slowly from the other side. My steps echoed. 'Did you hear what I said?' I murmured, in the unique quietness of evening. 'Yes, I did,' he said, and waited for me to come closer. 'Touch me, you said. Touch me and kiss me.' He kissed my forehead.

I trembled. Perhaps I had said that. I read desire in his eyes, before a bird disturbed us; it cried, flew swiftly past us and out of the round enclosure, startling the moon.

The oddly-dressed westerner drove like a drunkard along the Avenue of Eternal Peace. I sat beside him. When I touched his shoulder tentatively, he shot a glance at me. Eyes – what language they spoke. We had no need to talk. We were soon at the gate of the Foreigners' Compound. The silent guard stared into the car under the street-lights. Robert beamed at him and sped past. I glanced back, fearing that the guard had wanted to stop me going in. Suddenly I was scared. 'Should I have—'

Robert put his hand on mine reassuringly. 'You don't have to do anything, you are with me.'

His room was surprisingly bare, a clean, tidy bachelor's room. I went straight to the bathroom and sat there. I did not know what to do. Things were happening so fast. The bathroom was bare too, except for a dressing-gown. I went up to sniff at it and liked the smell. I studied myself in the mirror. Surely I should look different, I certainly felt different. I opened the door.

As I came out, he drew me to him and we embraced. The oyster and her scholar. Stolen, snatched pleasure, how they must have indulged. I tasted his saliva. I chewed the inside of his lips. All I wanted was to melt into him. My clothes came off as if they were an old skin I needed to shed, and the fragrance of our bodies made me drunk. There was something in that smell I could not have enough of.

He lifted me up, walked through his office to the bedroom. My eyes glanced at his desk, the fax machine, the small table lamp with its weak light. I saw our reflection in a big mirror. I had never seen myself naked like this before, I had never seen a male body naked before. The nakedness made my eyes burn.

He didn't know it was my first time. I behaved as if it was not. I felt ashamed of my ignorance and acted as if I had been there and done it all before. Desire also gave me confidence, too much confidence – he took me for an experienced woman. Each time the flame went up, I extinguished it. I made him hot, then cold again like the most experienced seductress. He cursed me, and accused me of being a conceited woman. I was hurt, kissed him for forgiveness, and made him hot again. As the night went on, I was torn between my physical desire and my equally powerful instinct to protect myself. He grew impatient. He turned his back on me and refused to let me touch him.

I lay awake, staring at the ceiling. What would people say? What if my parents ever found out? Stories came to me of women who were secretly filmed as they made love to foreigners. Sweet Grass had told me a story of a girl who had slept with a foreign expert in her factory where she worked as an interpreter. Somehow the propaganda cadre of the factory had managed to film their lovemaking and the girl was shown the result. She committed suicide. Robert was certain his telephone was bugged. I looked for a crack in the ceiling that might conceal a secret camera. I could hear the cars driving past the Avenue of Eternal Peace outside the window. Inside the flat the humidifier hummed permanently, mingling with Robert's gentle breathing next to me.

I was angered by his indifference. What was this body to do? I did not trust myself to touch him, but my eyes smoothed his skin. His body was marked, explored, like his person. Mine was unblemished, unclaimed. I wanted to touch him again. I had never touched a body so intimately before. Why was the closeness so intoxicating?

Some time after midnight there was a knock at the door. I

sat up, wide-eyed, my heart racing. The police? They had
come to get me. There was a name for what I was doing: *feifa
tongju*, illegally cohabiting, and with a foreigner, worse, an
American, worse still, a journalist – I could hear the snigger-
ing of a policewoman, who assumed the face of my university
political teacher. At the age of twenty-one, I was responsible
for my own actions and could be imprisoned for 'prostituting
with a foreigner' or 'passing on state secrets'. Love was not
something they understood.

I waited, but no more sounds came from the door. Perhaps
I had been dreaming. I sighed and lay down again. At dawn, I
got up quickly and quietly. Feeling my way down the cold
wall of the corridor, I suppressed my tears. I felt a failure: all I
had gained was an appetite I could not satisfy. I cursed myself,
and Robert for bringing it out in me. I walked past the guard
with a smile, behaving as if I had just passed a normal night
and was a legitimate resident of this forbidden cluster of
buildings.

I struggled home, shaking like a leaf with a fever I didn't
know I had.

'Well?' Sweet Grass enquired. 'Did you do it?'

'Don't ask me, I don't know,' I answered as tears overcame
me.

Chapter 7:

Rationed Passion

I should have known. I should have been warned. An eruption shook me. I experienced a burning desire for fulfilment, for this itchy body to be touched.

I was a different woman. I discovered my breasts and my lips – and started to plaster my mouth with lipstick, applying it in public as if I was merely doing up a shoelace. I now outdid those girls whose painted fingernails I had sneered at.

I started looking carefully at men. I noticed what big bones Building the Country had, and my eyes followed his hips as he walked to the photocopier. My own steps were different – unhurried, languid, like a cat. I smiled slowly, as if the person I was talking to shared a secret with me. I spoke slowly, paused between sentences, listened to the echo of my voice. The men exchanged glances, and Shadow whispered to me, 'Have you found a boyfriend?'

'No.'

'Oh. Would you like me to introduce you to one?'

'No,' I said firmly. 'Who needs a boyfriend?'

Building the Country, who had been watching us, handed me a videotape. 'Illegal copy of a foreign comedy, it's in English.

'Would you like me to translate it and write the words down?' I was puzzled.

He laughed. 'There's no need. It's not for work, it's for fun.'

As I left, he shouted after me, 'Enjoy it.'

Sweet Grass was cooking a noodle soup and soon the room smelt of it. We ate it and then we had tea. As she drew the curtains, I remembered the tape. 'Want to see a foreign comedy?'

'Only if you can translate it into Chinese for me.' She was not enthusiastic.

During the film we yawned a lot. It was not very funny and the quality was poor. I started wondering why Building the Country had given me the tape. Mercifully it was not long and when the screen went blank, I got up to turn it off. Sweet Grass was already in bed.

Before I could push the button, something else appeared on the screen.

'What was that?' Sweet Grass shouted from her bed.

The quality was still poor, and the screen was full of white patches, as if the tape had been watched many times. At first we could not figure out what it was. After a few seconds, a clear picture of a woman's huge breasts appeared. We didn't look at each other during the whole hour of the sexual orgy on the screen. Raw sex was presented graphically as if it was a dinner served in front of us. Our room smelt so familiarly of our own girlish things, our face creams, the noodle soup: on the calendar was the picture of the demure, traditionally dressed woman, whose face had grown so familiar to me. Yet here on film was the act Robert and I had started but did not finish. I was not disgusted but took it in greedily. This woman, moaning with the relentless pushing of the man, had no dignity – but she had satisfaction. Dignity was all I had wanted to keep then, but desire was all I cared about now. I remembered how, years ago, I had stolen into the kitchen and finished the smoked pork Nainai had saved specially for Spring Festival. I had told myself I was only going to have one mouthful, but that one mouthful became two or three, until I had eaten it all. I just hadn't been able to help myself. I felt sick afterwards. Food had been rationed then, and good food was even more scarce – as sex was even now. The restrictions increased one's appetite.

I wondered why Building the Country had lent me the tape. I suspected that Forever Green was behind it. I thought of their marriage, and their youth. 'We did everything in our youth,' she had said, in Beihai Park. I smiled to imagine them devouring such videos in their middle age.

That night I dreamed of David, of his naked body wrapped around mine. On the grassland, his body had never really existed for me, except for his hands. I saw him as the embodiment of some animal, the spirit of a soulmate, not a physical human being. He was as fantastic as Robert was real.

Later in the dream David lifted up Renee, took her to the edge of the grassland and glanced back at me. It was windy and his hair was blown across his face; the tall grass waved at his feet. 'Put her down,' I shouted. 'You must come to me.' I stripped off my skirt and walked towards him. I felt the long grass caress my body and started running, chasing him. Suddenly he dropped Renee and turned back. He was no longer a human but a wolf – the wolf I recognised from my childhood dreams, the wolf that had appeared in my parents' residential block. Now, years later, I knew why the wolf had come.

The next morning, I slept until I felt the sunshine on my back through the curtain. There was no sound from Sweet Grass's bed. I was impatient for her to rise and stretched and yawned noisily, determined to wake her. Eventually I heard a moan: 'Taotao, are you awake?'

'Yes.' I sat up in my bed, suddenly apprehensive. Was she going to mention last night?

'Have you ever wondered,' she paused, then poked her head out of the mosquito net, 'why you always fall for foreigners?'

This caught me off my guard. 'It wasn't like that, it just happened.'

'Nothing "just happens",' she replied mockingly.

'But David and I just clicked, and the setting was perfect – anyone would have fallen in love there.' I remembered our conversation on the truck, how magical it had felt.

'Perhaps, but not with a foreigner.'

'I wasn't thinking of that when I fell in love!' I protested. But her words had struck home. Could this really have something to do with it?

'Is he good-looking?'

'Yes, very – and so is Robert.'

'Vain,' she giggled. I shrugged my shoulders. No, I decided, it was because David was different. I had never met anyone so spontaneous.

'I suppose they both seemed so carefree; something in me was freed when I was with David, and that's how I feel with Robert, too. I love that feeling.'

'But what about Steel?' She shot me a look from across the net.

'You are joking, he's the shyest person I know!'

'In his mind he is a free spirit.' She glanced at me again. She was right, but I simply did not desire Steel the way I did Robert. This was more than I could admit.

'Maybe I am just too curious,' I said.

The students still gathered around my office block to read aloud from their leaflets. The nun still carried food to them. I took to following her – she always seemed to know where they were. But she would not talk to anyone.

The carpenter who worked outside my window warmed to me and I struck up conversations with him. He came from Guizhou, in the deep South. His girlfriend was a shopkeeper in Guiyang. He had come to Beijing to make enough money to marry her.

'And have you?'

'Well, yes, but I want to stay longer. Beijing is so big and there are so many interesting things here.'

'But your home town must be lovely too.'

'Yes, there is nothing like it on earth – you must go and see.' He hesitated and added, 'But it is so poor.'

The weather did not help. The flowers blossomed, birds sang and cats called. I recalled the scenes in *The Dream of the Red Mansions*. I now knew what 'making clouds and rain' meant. Robert had lit a fire in me, and I bombarded him with telephone calls, but he sounded distant. 'We should stop this. I am too old for you, and I don't want to take the responsibility.'

His being older had never bothered me. Now that I thought about it, both Sweet Grass and Ba had commented on Robert's age. I added, 'What has age got to do with it?'

'It has a lot to do with it. How old are you?'

'Twenty-one.'

'I'm forty-three, old enough to be your father. You don't want a father for a boyfriend.'

'Come on, you know it's not to do with age. You are my equal.'

But Robert did make me think of my father – he made me think of every man as Ba. They all made love to women, as my father had to my mother. I could not imagine my parents making love. I had never even seen them hold hands. Ma was Ma and Ba was Ba, and together they were my parents. But I was overwhelmed by a new fondness, imagining them being close. It made them vulnerable, human.

Robert and I were at the Friendship Hotel swimming-pool. I sat beside it, dangling my feet, and he emerged from the water and sat down next to me. I wanted to put my arms around him. I wanted to kick him in the water and have a water fight. But I could not: the Chinese cleaning lady was looking, and there was a trendy-looking Chinese couple nearby. The Friendship Hotel was relaxed enough for us to swim together, but there it ended. It was painful to watch the young couple hold hands, to hear them argue openly. They talked as if nobody else existed.

Beneath the water my feet found his. Our eyes met. His were red. Did he not sleep well? Was he working late again, rushing from the square in the small hours and back to his office to write? Or had he been tortured by desire, like me? I dared not ask. Words failed me in his presence. His experience, not his age, towered above me like Mount Tai. All those countries he had visited, all the wars he had been through – women must fall in front of him like fallen leaves. Why should he want me?

He looked around the pool and sighed. 'I don't think we should meet again.'

'No, please. We can meet like friends. Just like this.'

'I can't be your friend.'

And no more could I be his.

He said he had never desired a Chinese woman before. We were not his type; we were small-breasted, modest and hid our sexuality. Our smiles were polite and clean but 'tasteless like the boiled hot water which is the national drink of your country', he said, launching insults at me. He preferred the Tibetan and Mongolian women he had met in his travel to remote areas: he had found their open gaze refreshing.

But I embraced the insults, believing they were thinly disguised sour grapes. I watched the Chinese girl bobbing up and down in the water. That was me, small but compact, with stored energy.

Robert spoke again. Apart from the age difference, there were other hurdles ahead of us: my sense of dignity, my upbringing, my idea of love, his reluctance to bear the burden of being my first lover. Stories of other foreign colleagues who had slept with Chinese women and been filmed by the Public Security Bureau Police worried him too. The more he tried to persuade me not to sleep with him, the more I convinced myself that here was a caring man who was worth it. The further he pushed me away, the nearer I wanted to be. I was mad for him and, in my desperation, flaunted my youthful body as the only weapon I had. I squeezed myself closer to him and cocked my head. I acted childishly and shamelessly.

He loved me, I decided, and I loved him. That meant I could get away with anything.

'Marry me.'

'What did you say?'

'Marry me,' I repeated. Marriage – that was what many people, like Sweet Grass and her boyfriend, planned. 'Marry first, then talk love. Then we would be official, we would have the privacy, we wouldn't be filmed,' I said breathlessly.

His feet let go of mine and he paddled them in the water. 'Are you proposing to me?' He looked at me oddly. 'So you want to marry me.'

'Yes.'

'So you can have an American passport?'

'What?'

'Isn't that what all you Chinese girls want? For us foreigners to marry you and give you a passport to America?'

My first impulse was to push him down in the water and drown him. How dare he doubt me? 'You Chinese girls' – was that how he saw me? One of those dolled-up women in the hotel bars? I hoisted myself up abruptly and dived into the pool. In the water I sobbed. What a rat! What a brute! How could he? I splashed and kicked furiously. I swam a full circle of the pool and he was still where I had left him. He pulled me to him beneath the water and whispered, 'I'm sorry, I shouldn't have said that. It's just something a colleague said.' I shook my hand free of his and sat next to him without a word.

After a long while he said, 'I would marry you, if that was what you wanted.'

That did not make me feel any better, I did not want a proposal like that. How wrong and confusing it had all been! Why wouldn't he conform to my culture and upbringing, make me happy and willingly marry me? Why should I be the one to succumb to him? To sleep with him illegally, in sin and in fear.

It was then that I suspected he did not love me, and that I did not really love him – or not enough. If he loved me he would marry me, and if I loved him, I would sleep with him whatever the world thought. He had never said, 'I love you,' and I suspected that that was why, that night, I had not given in to him. I needed that reassurance, not a half-hearted marriage proposal. I needed to know that he loved me spiritually and emotionally as well as desiring me physically. I wanted him to be head over heels in love with me, like in a novel, like a perfect love story.

Then I saw his hunched back, and realised it was a fantasy. He had an older man's knack of separating desire and affection from love. It came from having fallen in love many times. Life was a book he had read, a hill he had climbed. But it was all new to me.

I was determined to be a friend to him, to work my way slowly to him, to win his heart and then his body, but he wouldn't let me. I had either to be his lover or out of his life. He would not come to me on my terms: for him our relationship was about desire, not love.

The bell rang. 'Last five minutes. Everybody out,' shouted the pool attendant.

I walked beside the pool to the deep end. A spiral staircase led to a diving-board that stuck out over the water. The Chinese boy had perched on it like a bird and swooped off it several times. His girlfriend had cheered him on. My mind had been set on jumping off it since I came in.

I climbed up the spiral staircase. I was on the top. I stared down into the water and felt dizzy. The other couple had left and only Robert was there. He stood, half-submerged, in the shallow end, watching me. The cleaning woman stopped work and leaned on her long broom. From where I stood they both seemed small.

I stared at the water. Hair had taught me to swim on our last night together in Pleasant City in the moist, warm South. She had pushed me, the girl from the dry cold North, into the lake. That swim had liberated and transformed me. Since then I had loved swimming, had cherished this new skill. I remembered gazing down at the West Lake and how, that night, I had jumped in and drawn strength from the darkness surrounding me.

Fear of water, fear of the unknown.

I feared losing control. I feared that once I made love to him, I would be vulnerable. All my life I had kept myself under control, even in Inner Mongolia. I had lost my heart there, but not my head – and I could not afford to lose my head. If I was exposed for sleeping with a foreigner, I would be paraded in the streets like Lotus Blossom or that girl in Sweet Grass's story. To be branded a loose woman, to be seduced and then deserted by a man – worse still, a foreigner – would be the biggest disgrace I could bring upon my family. A high price to pay for love – or lust.

I retreated from the edge of the board and climbed down the steps. Robert met me at the foot. The cleaning lady was gone and he put his arm around my shoulder. 'Do you love me?' I asked.

Instead of answering, he pushed me in the direction of the female changing room. 'Go and get dressed. I'll meet you outside.'

'Do you love me?' I repeated.

He turned and left me.

Outside the swimming-pool we stood silently. I watched his red eyes, redder still now from the swim. The dying sun beamed on his face, he blinked. The wrinkles around his eyes deepened, and I spotted a strand of grey hair I hadn't noticed before. Suddenly he looked vulnerable. Had I pushed him too hard? It had never occurred to me to worry for him, but what if he were found out? Would he lose his job? Would he be deported from China? Did any of this matter if we loved one another?

He bent down to me: 'I do love you, in my own way. But . . . you are too impatient, my little one. Love grows over time. You have to grow with it.'

We parted, and did not meet for several days.

In broad daylight, I could sometimes see his point and the world seemed sorted out: barren, depressing but in order. Things could perhaps carry on as they had. But at night my world was turned upside down: desire for him would haunt me relentlessly.

The weather started to get hot. Sweet Grass and I went to the square every evening, and the atmosphere of excitement echoed my own awakening. I felt in tune. I felt accepted. People talked about anything and everything. A stranger would stop me and begin a debate. I mingled with workers, students, rubbish-collectors and university professors. It was as if for the first time in our lives we had all found our mouths and all we wanted to do was talk.

Robert was there almost all the time. He was always more affectionate with me in the square, and somehow it felt right to be close to him, even to hug him openly. We were surrounded by a halo of warmth, a feeling that we could break all convention. Groups of excited young men sur- rounded us, chanting, 'Free love, free love,' in English, while making victory signs, their girlfriends leaning demurely on their shoulders. In these nightly casual rendezvous, which we never arranged formally, our love and desire for each other grew. I felt sure that things would work out in the end. Interpreting for Robert as he spoke with people in the square, watching him laughing and joking with them, made me realise why I had fallen for him. He was spontaneous, the opposite of my father.

I saw less of Steel. The students began to set up tents and sleep overnight in the square. Some nights, if I stayed late enough, I caught sight of figures cuddling inside candlelit tents. Steel and his new friends, Small Flat and Big Enlight- enment, were busy liaising with the citizens of Beijing and intellectuals from all over the country to form a bigger alliance for the democracy movement. We did not have time for lengthy talks, but he gave me brief reports as he rushed here and there, always in demand. There was a spring in his step and a glow on his face. Once, as we stood beside a tent where Bell was playing her guitar to two other students, I told him to be careful. He had looked at me oddly: 'What is there to fear? The people are on our side.'

The spontaneity was spreading. Everyone in the square caught it. Shadow caught it. Steel caught it, and it made him attractive. But what about me? All my life things had been planned for me, by my parents, teachers, and who-ever was in control. My parents had chosen my school carefully, the food ration in my childhood had been decided by the neighbourhood committee; our work units were assigned to us by the government; the marital flats were assigned to us by our work units. I was comfortable in the system and I had resigned myself to it. Until now I had seen no reason to rebel. Like a frog in a well, I had looked up to a small patch of the sky and thought myself queen in that land.

Then I leaped out and saw the world outside the well. And I needed to love the man I wanted to love.

I had been to Robert's flat only once since the night I had spent with him. Now he had asked me to help him sort out some notes of interviews he had done in the square. His flat doubled as an office and I was introduced briefly, formally, to his Chinese interpreter, the serious-looking middle-aged woman. She stared at me hard from behind her glasses, then ignored me.

It felt different from the last time I had been there. The window was open and sunshine streamed in with the noise of the traffic. Robert maintained a professional air throughout the morning, and it was sweet torture to sit so close to him without touching him. Once in a while we were interrupted by the interpreter, who asked him some questions. She talked to him in a very direct way, rude and intimate, as if they were close.

The telephone rang constantly. Robert dashed about the flat, and kept apologising to me for his absence. Once when he was called to the phone I wandered near the bedroom. The bed was unmade. I remembered the smell of our bodies – smells always stayed with me. I closed my eyes and imagined us entwined. When I opened my eyes, I saw the female interpreter staring at me. Did she know? I knew that they all had to be screened to work for foreigners: they had to be politically trustworthy and made regular reports to the Foreign Affairs Department. Would she report me? What about the secret camera? Perhaps she controlled it. Perhaps that was why she looked at me in that strange, knowing way. She could legitimately work alongside Robert and spent all day in his flat. I wondered about the evenings. Did she stay late sometimes? Did she and Robert . . .

I stopped myself before I was carried away with jealousy. As I said goodbye to Robert, I asked casually, 'Your interpreter, how old is she?'

'I don't know, I never asked. She must be in her late thirties – she has a young son. That's why she can't come to the square or stay too late with me.'

'She seems quite young to me. Do you like her?'

He laughed. 'Do snap out of it! I told you I had never desired a Chinese woman except you, my little one.'

He walked me to the big gate with its stern-faced guards. 'She is very professional, my interpreter,' he said, 'but I could never get close to her. I don't have a clue what she likes or dislikes. She wears a mask in front of me because I am a foreigner and a journalist.' His eyes were on a family of Africans playing in the yard, two girls walking hand in hand, their long-robed parents looking on benignly. 'But you are different. You treat me as if I am just another human being.' He turned to gaze at me.

The sun shone on the happy family and I felt weepy. Just another human being? But he was the world to me. 'I hate these guards and these walls,' I said, looking away.

He touched my shoulder tentatively. 'Sometimes I wish we were not in China . . . But you know you are too young.'

The weather was becoming hotter and I felt as if I was in a limbo. Every few days the strain became too much: I would ring him and say mad things to him. Something had to happen. Why was the world still going round? Then one day Building the Country came to say we were going to Yunnan, the southern most province, the following week to make a film with an English botanist. 'You look too thin, Taotao.' He paused before he went out. 'And if I were you, I wouldn't spend too long on the phone. These walls have ears.' He nodded slowly at me.

I stared at him. Did he mean the manager? I remembered when she had eavesdropped outside my door. I had grown careless lately: in my infatuation I had forgotten the need for caution. I shuddered. 'Yes, I know.'

He came closer. 'I have wanted to say this to you for a long time, as a friend of your parents. Remember who you are, remember that however attractive a foreigner is, you cannot alter the fact that he is not here to stay. Don't fall for him unless he can marry you.' Then he left the room.

How had he known? Perhaps he knew about David too. I blushed and paced around the room in agitation. *Don't fall for him unless he can marry you.* Well, your warning was too late, Building the Country, friend of my parents. I had already fallen and there was no looking back. I remembered what he had said about the manager. Only yesterday she had called a meeting to discuss 'how to defeat bourgeois liberalism' and warned us to resist 'bad influences from the West'. She reminded me of my political teacher at university, who had criticised me for staying a night in my foreign teacher's flat. I had been only a student then, but the incident would have been written in my personal file, which followed me wherever I went, and the manager would have read it. That would explain the knowing look on her face whenever she saw me.

I turned to the window. Lunchtime again, and the nun was

291

on her daily pilgrimage to the students. There was a determination about her that made me feel ashamed. She walked past my window, and nodded at me, the first time she had done so. I read a message in the nod: live your life. It seemed to be a sign of recognition, of encouragement.

I stood impatiently at the door of the Orchard Tea House, waiting for Robert. The bright red lantern illuminated the Tea House sign in the darkness. I had persuaded him to meet me to say goodbye. I had had to push him hard, partly because he tried to avoid seeing me in private, partly because he was so busy. A revolution was happening in Beijing – even the ice-cream seller had gone up to the square to participate in the debates – and all I cared about was my longing for him. I must have been mad. The tea house had been renovated in the old style to attract tourists, and coachloads of foreigners were transported here to have a taste of the traditional culture, comedy acts, Peking Opera, acrobatic and magic shows. I had suggested meeting here because I could pretend to be his tour guide.

I watched a group of noisy Americans following a pretty mini-skirted Chinese girl into the tea house, followed by a young Chinese couple. I waited anxiously. Beside me the Chinese couple, waiting to be let in after the Americans, complained, 'Why do you give foreigners the better seats?'

The woman at the door sneered, 'Because they pay double.'

I heard the squeal of brakes and turned around to see that Robert's car had pulled up inches from where I stood. He jumped out. I held out a hand to him, wanting to preserve the impression that ours was a purely professional relationship. He winked at me to show he understood and shook my hand. 'I just came back from the square.' He looked at me appreciatively. 'What an exciting time this is.' He grinned, like a little boy who had been given a new toy. 'Have you been up there today?'

The performance started, a traditional comedy routine. All the Chinese laughed. The American tourists turned to the mini-skirted girl, who translated. Some laughed, others shrugged their shoulders and picked up their cameras. I turned to Robert: with his casual shirt and jeans, he might easily have been a tourist. I acknowledged the distance between us. I was one of the objects he studied; he went to the square, soaked up the excitement, reported it and was gone. Meeting a woman like me was part of the attraction of working abroad. Yet for me this was all too real; to accompany him to the square and his flat, I risked my work, reputation and freedom. I could not afford to flirt with him. There was no future for me with this foreigner.

We applauded the comedy talk. Robert clapped and yawned. 'Going to the square is not all of my life,' I snapped. I turned to watch the next performance – Peking Opera. He had said he hated it.

The mini-skirted girl leaned towards the man on her left and started talking fast. He nodded earnestly. I remembered going to see *The Tale of the Red Lantern*, one of the eight revolutionary operas, with Ma, Laolao and Laoye. I had been bored – but how could anyone not be if the story was all they were interested in? I had sympathy with the puzzled foreigner. I wondered if he was asking questions as I had – why did the hero not have a wife, his mother no husband and the daughter no boyfriend? All the heroes in these eight revolutionary operas were spouseless. Was the whole of China a monastery?

I peered at Robert beside me. He was concentrating hard on the play. He didn't like the Peking Opera, he had said, but he would like to learn, to understand why Chinese people liked it, or at any rate the older people. 'Shall I tell you the story?' I said, acting professionally. 'No, don't bother, just enjoy it yourself.' My hands were grabbed under the table. He leaned forward and whispered, 'I missed you.'

My defences blew away like autumn leaves in the wind. The attraction was real, my feeling was real. I could not deny it. I wanted him. I could not think ahead. I could think only of the present.

'Let's go to your flat,' I said.

He shook his head.

'Why not?'

'I told you. I think what we did was unwise. I am sorry I started it, it's all my fault. But it can't continue. I just don't want you to get hurt. Listen to me, you're playing with fire, do you know that?'

I supposed I was. I couldn't help it, though. The spark I had felt on our chance meeting in the square had become an engulfing fire that lit up my life and, like a moth, I flew to it. I would get burned, but I couldn't be without it.

'I don't care,' I said miserably. 'I want to live.'

Later, as we waited for the traffic lights to change, I argued with him, but despite my pleas and tears, he would not relent. He had insisted on taking me home in his car. I watched the traffic jam on the Avenue of Eternal Peace. Tiananmen Square was on our right, lit up and full of crowds and tents. I longed to jump out of the queue of traffic and be mobile. In the middle, on the traffic island, a uniformed policeman wearing white gloves surveyed us. Once, he glanced at us. The lights still did not change.

I stared at the bicycle masses opposite, and realised that I had come a long way. I used to be one of them, but now I had found my own stream and my own path. Ever since I had returned from the grassland I had been a different person. The cyclists were ready to pedal as soon as the signal came. I bit my lip. My world and his, would they ever make peace? Could my world ever approve of us?

I lifted up my skirt, reached out for Robert's hand, and put it on my thigh. He chuckled, and stroked it. 'I think that policeman's looking at us.'

'Let him, I don't care. I don't care if the world collapses. Just touch me,' I said between my teeth.

The lights changed, the bicycles splayed across the wide road like a heavy cloud. Robert pressed the accelerator lightly, his hand still pressed by mine on to my thigh. In this pose of defiance, we drove past the open-mouthed policeman, who stared down at us incredulously. There was chaos on the Avenue of Eternal Peace that day, as the traffic policeman confused his hand signals, staring blankly at a scene he thought he had dreamed.

Chapter 8:

Glow-worms Light the Path

⋯◆⋯

The bungalows were scattered among tropical flowers and bushes. I opened a window in mine and breathed in the fresh air. Building the Country talked loudly in the corridor to our local guide. Professor Yang, the Chinese botanist, a middle-aged woman, slept behind me, snoring gently. After a four-hour flight, a long delay and a bumpy bus journey, she was tired.

A knock on the door, then Building the Country's voice: 'Taotao, Professor Yang, it's dinner-time.' She woke and sprang to her feet, a small woman, but full of quiet energy.

We had dinner in a canteen – very meaty, but delicious. I met the English professor for the first time. He was pale, wore thick glasses and seemed distant. He and Professor Yang had met once before at an international conference. I interpreted for them as they reminisced. Building the Country listened politely. It was going to be a low-budget movie, he had confided in me. Not much was asked of our company, except to organise local workers and access to places. 'Treat it as a holiday,' he had said.

Professor Yang was from Beijing. In the 1960s she had been sent to the countryside near here for re-education and worked as a labourer at the tropical reserve, internationally renowned for its collection of rare flowers. This was her first trip here since she had left in the early 1980s. Professor

Hutchinson, the Englishman, spoke some Chinese he had learned from a Taiwanese in London, so he and Professor Yang sometimes talked without me.

The fans whirled above our head. Through the open window, I could smell flowers mixed with hot night air, which was sweet, heavy, pungent with tropical spices. I felt drunk.

In the morning we interviewed Professor Yang's former colleagues in the city of Kumming in one of the town's biggest hotels. I stole out to telephone Robert. I begged him to come down – I wanted to see him, I missed him, I said. He said he missed me too, but . . . 'Do you know what's happening in Beijing?' he asked. 'One of the most exciting times in your history and my most important assignment in China. All your compatriots are out in the square, asking for democracy, doing all the things Chinese people never do and shouldn't do. The government has declared martial law, but everybody has ignored them. You should be here yourself to see this. I can't leave Beijing now.'

'Come for a couple of days. I really want to see you. There are demonstrations here too. You can add this to your coverage. None of your colleagues will get this news – there are no foreign journalists here.' I was not lying: on the way to the hotel this morning, the car had snailed along behind hundreds of students and we had resorted to walking, the two professors and I. Building the Country had sat lazily in the car: he said he had seen bigger crowds in his Red Guard days. The crowds here were a small dish compared with the big banquet they had had then.

I asked Robert how he had managed the translation of his interviews in the square, and he said he had found many willing volunteers. 'How about your interpreter? Can't you persuade her to come out? Surely it's her duty,' I said bitterly.

'I told you, Taotao, she has a young son. Besides, I don't want her there. I have more freedom without her.' There was a pause. Then he laughed. 'Taotao, you're not still jealous of her, are you?'

I felt better. 'Do come down – I miss you.'

'Do you know how busy I am? I've had about three hours' sleep per night for the last week.' He was quiet for a moment. 'Mind you, things have quietened down a bit, so perhaps . . . There are demonstrations there, you say? Give me your address in Kumming, but I can't promise anything.'

For a week we lived in the tropical garden, making short excursions to the nearby countryside. Apart from the demonstrating students, there was nothing to remind me of life in Beijing. We ventured to the minority areas, full of wooden buildings, with animals sleeping on the lower level and families in the upper storeys, which were reached by creaky wooden steps. Wherever we went we were invited into spotlessly clean houses for drinks. Life here was pleasant, like a slow-moving river, knowing its course, never changing, following the path marked out for it over thousands of years.

I began to miss Beijing and my friends there: Steel and Sweet Grass as well as Robert. I thought of the crowds in the square, the leather-clad biker lads. I missed my bicycle and looked forward to cycling in the warm summer night, as I had before I left Beijing.

We met hunters, who described to us encounters with tigers, leopards and snakes, tales that were wild and unbelievable until they showed us their trophies: a tiger skin, a withered monkey's paw. We sheltered in monasteries, where giggling teenage Buddhist monks played in puddles, scolded by their masters who worried that they might spoil their glowing golden robes. The two professors sank deeper into their discussions of plants and their habitats, followed by periods of reflection, punctuated by sudden exclamations, unfinished sentences and shared smiles.

I changed into summer wear. It was only late May, but it was hot and everything was ripening. The flowers gave out their fragrance and beauty, and blossomed as if they would not live another day. At night their pungent scent was overwhelming, as if the whole world of nature was trying to conquer our own. We had to fasten the windows shut to keep out the mosquitoes, but the night air still crept in. Professor Yang always slept well, and I lay awake enviously.

I had never been so aware of my own body. In my childhood, it was something that was trained and shaped for a great purpose: we ran round the playground ten times each day, in honour of the 'Long March' made by the Red Army so many years ago, hardening ourselves for the revolutionary future. There was the almost impossible 'Annual Physical Training Target' which assessed our high-jumping, long-distance running and other physical skills, again to ensure our suitability for a future revolutionary role, as 'the children of the motherland, who will carry forward the hopes of the older generation of revolutionaries'. I had not really thought of my body in any other way, until Robert had touched me.

I breathed in the hot night air, and remembered his smell. I did not feel complete without him. It was as if I had left a limb in his flat. I missed his smell: I had stored it up and at night I released a little to comfort myself, as if I was an addict smoking the forbidden opium.

He was a breath of fresh air. All around me were people who lived cautiously. My parents, terrified by movements and punishments, had brought me up in their shadow, with whispers of caution. Allowing myself to fall for Robert was a way of rebelling, but why wasn't he paying for his spontaneity? He had no fear because he had no need to fear: he was in no danger because he was free.

And I was not. I feared, and my fears were well founded: the Public Security Bureau Police and the public humiliation.

I turned in my bed. Some night bugs buzzed. The smell of the flowers was overpowering. Life was short. I was as awake and alert as the moon outside. I listened to the beating of my heart.

Why was I blaming Robert for this? Why was I using the police as an excuse not to sleep with the man I wanted? Was my brain cheating my heart? Was the head a better judge than the heart? Why couldn't I just be true to my feelings and do it?

One night we came back with a local man who worked at the weather station on top of a hill in Kumming City. Professor Hutchinson wanted to talk to him about the climate changes in the area. He told more tales of the wild – how a tiger had been discovered not so long ago, on a foggy night, up where he and his colleagues worked. Professor Hutchinson drank beer with him, urging him on, and Professor Yang listened indulgently. The fans at the canteen where the interview was conducted turned lazily above our heads. I glimpsed the darkness outside. The air was close and humid. 'So were there wolves, there?' asked Professor Hutchinson, a twinkle in his eyes.

Then we heard soft footsteps, a gentle knock. We looked up. Who could it be? We were the only residents at the tropical garden. The door was pushed open and Robert came in.

Then he disappeared as the lights went out. 'What the hell . . .' Professor Hutchinson shouted.

The weather man giggled. 'Oh, no, a power-cut. This happens about once a week, didn't they tell you?'

'How long will it last?'

'Sometimes it comes back on immediately, but it could be the whole night.'

I floated towards the door. I reached out and grabbed Robert's nose. Despite myself, I giggled. He smelt of Beijing – dust, office and sweat. I heard chairs moving. 'This way,' I whispered, took his hand and led him to the path. I walked fast. I felt the wooden rail and remembered a small turning on the left towards the well where some bushes grew. 'Follow me,' I whispered. I was sweating and my heart beat fast.

I found the steps of the well and heard the frogs at the bottom. I stopped, blinking: thousands of lights twinkled around me, wandering, drawing patterns in the air.

I had to be in heaven. 'Stars,' I murmured, as he rained kisses on me, and I felt myself fall. 'Stars,' I insisted. And I was a rose, the petals opening, waiting for the rain after a long drought. When it came, my body danced, shuddering with a newfound joy. I wanted never to come back to earth again.

The radio crackled into life, and simultaneously the light at the end of the path lit up. The electricity was back. The glow-worms faded. I opened my eyes. Robert was in front of me wiping sweat from his face.

Suddenly I heard heavy steps coming towards us down the path, and Professor Yang's voice: 'Taotao, is that you?'

I stood up quickly. 'Where on earth have you been?' she asked. 'I searched for you everywhere. Who is this?' She shone the torch at Robert, who blinked and raised his hand to shield his eyes from the bright light.

'I am a friend of Taotao's, from Beijing,' he said, in broken Chinese.

Professor Yang moved the torch beam away from his face and stood demurely in the path. I tried to sound normal. 'Have Building the Country and Professor Hutchinson gone to bed?' I asked.

'Yes. They were snoring when I walked past their room. Are you coming to bed?'

'Yes,' I said hesitantly, looking at Robert. I could not touch him in front of Professor Yang. 'I'll see you tomorrow, then,' I said, and reached out my hands. But Robert stepped up to me, took me in his arms, and kissed my cheek. Then he walked briskly away and disappeared at the end of the path.

Professor Yang's eyes followed him. 'I once knew an American, nearly twenty years ago . . . It's late, let's get in.'

I lagged behind, looking back up the path. Robert had gone, but his smell hung in the air. Professor Yang switched off the light in the porch, and the glow-worms returned.

That night the weather changed. There was thunder, lightning, and raindrops hammered at the window. My bed shook.

After the heavenly experience earlier that evening I was now being given a glimpse of hell. In the darkness neither seemed real but I fell asleep with a deep sense of premonition.

When I woke the sun was streaming in through the window. The corridor was quiet, nobody was up. What a night it had been. I stretched like a cat, my eyes closed, and went over the scene by the well. I had tasted the forbidden fruit, but now I wanted more.

I jumped out of bed, found my shoes and went outside. The ground was muddy, the air sweet, the flowers refreshed, the colours vivid. The morning dew was still on the petals, I touched them and wondered why Robert hadn't rung me from his hotel. I had looked forward to spending the next few days, the weekend, with him. We wouldn't have much to do workwise as the person we wanted to interview was away.

I felt as if I had only now started to live. I had discovered a secret that had been kept from me. The world was wonderful, everything in its place, and I was part of it.

The weekend passed with no news of Robert, and there was nothing I could do, because I did not know which hotel he was staying in. On Monday morning we resumed our interview with the weather man. We sat in the canteen where Professor Hutchinson fed him more beer, and more incredible stories poured from his mouth. Towards noon Building the Country came up to me: 'A call for you, Taotao, from Beijing.'

I ran out of the canteen, down the wet path, glimpsing the well where I had been with Robert; a big clump of Canna lily lay where we had been, struck down by the wind, its long spike of orange flowers withered in the mud. In the corridor, I picked up the phone. 'Hello?'

'It's me, Taotao, I'm back in Beijing. I had to take a flight early on Saturday morning. Are you OK? Nothing happened there?'

'No, what do you mean? Of course I'm OK. Why are you in Beijing?'

Liu Hong

'Didn't you hear about the massacre?'

'What massacre?'

'Oh, Christ, the army opened fire and killed many, many people. Beijing is in chaos. If you don't believe me, listen to VOA.'

'Oh, VOA, it's propaganda, I don't believe it.'

'For God's sake, listen to me! China is on the brink of civil war. The army is everywhere, and your people are being killed. I can still hear shots. There are bullet holes by my wall, the one facing the Avenue of Eternal Peace. I'll show you when you get back.'

Chapter 9:

Oyster Love

We were bound for Beijing, about which we had heard conflicting news. There had been a massacre, thousands of people killed, Robert had said. According to the TV news there had been scuffles with a handful of trouble-makers but the heroic People's Liberation Army had now restored order. Forever Green and Professor Yang's husband both told us that they heard gunshots at night, but they were all right.

The air hostess looked sulky as she acted out her emergency landing routine before her audience in the half-filled aeroplane. Building the Country sighed and reached out for another beer. Professor Yang leaned on me, her eyes closed. My premonition on the thundery night had been correct. Where was Steel? Was he safe? I was gripped by guilt. The faces I had seen in the square, familiar and unfamiliar, rose up to haunt me. Those who had dreamed of and worked for a better future had died while I, selfish coward, lived.

Our first priority had been to pack Professor Hutchinson off on an aeroplane. He was called to the phone during the late afternoon, and the news was broken to him. He came back looking nervous. 'Taotao, I must leave as soon as possible. I have been told by the British Embassy to get out of China on the first available flight. There has been unrest in Beijing and they fear it will spread to the rest of China.'

After that the weather man was the only one of us in a good mood. Building the Country went out to phone airlines, and came back with the news that all flights were full. Professor Hutchinson's face dropped, and he watched the weather man, who was still drinking, with distaste.

When the man had finished, he wiped his mouth. 'What's the matter? Why do you all look so serious?'

Building the Country said briefly, 'We can't find a plane to take Professor Hutchinson to Hong Kong. All the flights are booked.'

The weather man slapped his thigh. 'Why didn't you say so earlier?' He told us that his brother's wife's friend was a pilot and usually had some seats reserved for 'family contacts'.

'No harm in trying,' Building the Country said. The weather man's friend indeed had a spare seat, so Professor Hutchinson gave him a big hug and called him 'my good friend'. Professor Yang was in tears as she and Professor Hutchinson shook hands.

We stayed for three more nights in the tropical garden – there were no flights to Beijing. Everyone was subdued; the team spirit and party atmosphere had disappeared with Professor Hutchinson. Building the Country phoned our company. 'We all have to go back to report to the manager what we were doing before, during and after June the fourth.'

None of us spoke during the drive into Beijing. It was not the city we had left; it was not the city I knew. Troops with guns lined the route from the airport to the centre, soldier after soldier. Their guns pointed towards pedestrians, cyclists, cars and us. We saw jeeps and tanks. The company driver told us we could not go via the Avenue of Eternal Peace, that route was sealed off, so we did a long detour and it was nearly dark before I got home to my dormitory with Sweet Grass.

Opening the door I saw a familiar bag on my bed – Willow's. Relief engulfed me. Steel was all right. He must have been staying here.

I switched on the small black and white television that Sweet Grass's boyfriend had given her. The news: a student with his head held down by the police – neighbours had exposed him as one of the 'trouble-makers who threw bottles at the PLA men' – and another 'arrested at the southern border as he was trying to escape overseas'. There were some shots of the crowds in Tiananmen Square. The screen froze on a young man's eager face while the presenter's stern voice spoke: 'An evil-doer trying to stir up trouble.'

I remembered these cameras flashing at me while I translated for Robert. A cold sweat broke out on my back.

Where was Sweet Grass? I looked around anxiously. The room smelt of her things. Some men's trousers were on her bed. Careless Steel. I went to pick them up. Behind me the door opened and I turned to see Sweet Grass with a bowl. She looked startled. 'You – I thought you were away.'

'Yes, but . . . Tiananmen – I am back.' I went up to her. 'I see Steel has been here.'

'He *is* here. He has been since Sunday.' She put down the bowl, took from it some wet shirts – large ones – and began to hang them around the room. She seemed very familiar with his clothes. 'He has been ill since he came back from the square and I have nursed him. He's OK now – he's just gone out for a walk.'

Her proprietary air annoyed me. I sat on my bed. 'You . . . Steel, you and Steel?' I stuttered.

'Yes, me and Steel. You might as well know that we are lovers now,' she said calmly. She tried to pick up the trousers from my bed – I had been sitting on them.

I stood up. 'You stole my friend behind my back, and all the time I thought you were my best friend.'

'I didn't steal him, you deserted him.' She folded the

trousers carefully and put them on her own bed. 'What kind of friend are you? He came to Beijing to see you and what did you do? Went to see your foreign lover, leaving him all alone. I fed him, we became friends, he came here to look for you when he was chased from the square, ill and weak. Where were you then? You don't care about him, you don't care about anyone but yourself and that foreign man!'

Her words stung me. 'I do care for Steel!' I shouted. 'I have been missing him – and you.' But my voice was weak and unconvincing. Looking for an outlet for my anger, I threw Steel's bag at her. The contents flew out – the pamphlets he had been carrying when he first came to Beijing.

She picked one up. Now she raised her voice: 'What are you making a fuss about? You never loved him! You are too selfish to love a man like that! He is on the wanted list now and will be arrested if the police find out where he is. There! Are you scared now? He told me you were afraid of getting involved. You didn't dare have sex with that foreigner even though you wanted him, did you? All you can do is make everybody want you while you play safe. I despise you! You don't even dare to love the men you love.'

Me, a coward? How dare she accuse me like this? Play safe indeed! How could Sweet Grass, who had sat and listened enviously to accounts of my glamorous work, and accepted my gifts, say such things to me? I felt dizzy, my hand was raised and I was about to slap her when two hands caught mine from behind. I struggled and saw Steel's face. 'It's not true, don't listen to her. Look, I am back, I'm here. I have come to see you.' Tears streamed down my face.

Steel held my hands silently for a few seconds, then let them go and walked to the window. The room was quiet and I noticed, with a guilty pain in my heart, how thin he was. When he spoke, his voice had a hardness that I had not heard before. 'I have decided that I can't stay here any longer. Any minute the police will be after me. If I am arrested you will both be in trouble. I am going South to stay with some relatives. I will be safer there.'

'No!' we cried.

Sweet Grass jumped off her bed. 'I am coming with you.' She was quick and decisive.

Steel squatted down in front of me. 'Don't be hard on yourself, Taotao. You have never loved me.' He put a hand to my mouth to suppress my protest. 'I fell for you the first time I saw you and I thought I loved you all these years. But something happened these last few months and . . . It's not because you've neglected me, or because you are in love with someone else, it is my own feelings that have changed. Now I know I can love differently, and just as powerfully.' He glanced at Sweet Grass, who threw him a conspiratorial smile.

They left. I got up and walked about the room absentmindedly. Slowly I unpacked my luggage and picked out the souvenirs I had brought for Sweet Grass and forgotten to give her. I laid them on her bed.

The dinner bell rang downstairs. I imagined Sweet Grass and Steel in Pleasant City, among the crowd. What would Sweet Grass think of the South? As far as I was aware, she had never before left Beijing. I thought of my own first journey from the North to Pleasant City. It would be very hot now in the South. On the lower level of the block someone was splashing and singing in the washroom. I went up to the window, and leaned outside. The guards were changing shifts; they walked stiffly. Sweet Grass and I had leaned outside like this to laugh at them. The sun was setting, Fragrant Hill beckoned in the distance; it was a beautiful evening. The world spread itself beneath me, with endless opportunities and promises. 'Life is too precious to waste.' Steel had been true to his words.

I did not have much time before the curfew.

Clutching my suitcase, I walked slowly down the stairs and past the guard, who smiled at me for the first time. I hailed a taxi. 'Beijing Hotel.'

The streets were empty, people rushing to get home before dark, their heads low as they pedalled hard on their bikes. Nobody lingered to enjoy the sunset, and soldiers dispersed groups of more than three people. That was the order.

Sweat poured down my face, and the driver switched on the air-conditioning. The heat was suffocating and I longed to breathe fresh air. Driving through the city, I remembered the nun I had seen near my office. 'Live your life,' she had said.

How had I lived? I had lived comfortably, been fed, clothed and educated. I had what people thought I needed, and I had always been content until I started needing the simplest thing: to love.

I had to live. I had to be free to make a choice, even if it was a wrong one. Let me dive into the water and trust it. Let me choke a little, and I will learn to swim.

Beijing Hotel reminded me of an airport. I rang Robert. He must be there, I prayed. Let him be there – I might not have courage like this again.

I pressed my face to the glass door as his car pulled up – I admired the reckless way he drove. He was here, there was no time to change my mind. In your noble pursuit, Steel, wish me luck for this small selfish gesture of bravery. In the grand scheme of things, my revolution will never compare with yours, and I have done it purely for myself.

Hair, watch me dive.

Robert saw my luggage, and paused. Despite our brief yet intense physical closeness, we were still strangers in a way. Would he be my conspirator? I held my breath. He picked up my luggage without a word and started towards his car. I followed.

Before the Foreigners' Compound he braked. 'You'd better lie down in the back seat when we drive past the compound gate. They are not letting Chinese in now.'

I did not move. He waited. The engine was running. I

watched his face in the dark. 'I don't want to hide, I haven't done anything wrong,' I said.

We drove past the gate and the soldier with his gun. The bayonet pointed to a clear blue sky where a bright moon had appeared, witness to all, yet saying nothing.

In his room I unpacked slowly. I was calm, and felt the peace of having resolved a dilemma. He watched me. Then he looked at his watch. 'I've got to go out for a while, but I'll be back about nine.'

'OK.' I smiled at him.

Before he left, he said, 'Don't open the door for anyone other than me.'

At ten he was still not back. I found a fish wrapped in foil, and a bottle of wine. I cooked the fish, remembering Laoye's skilful hands. Soon the fragrant smell spread through the kitchen. I leaned over the pot and breathed in deeply. Delicious. I sat down and ate it.

Then I poured myself some wine, and lay down on the floor. I smiled blankly towards a hidden camera somewhere in the ceiling, and raised my glass to the silent onlookers.